PRAISE FOR THE EMPTY

The Empty Room is an entirely accurate portrait of alcoholism... real... believable. Davis is without a doubt an exceptionally talented writer.
Globe & Mail

Raw and disturbing, yet we keep reading, spurred by the clarity of the writing and intensity of the description. Davis offers a completely believable picture of one woman's decline and helplessness. She makes us feel we are inside Colleen's skin, guaranteeing our empathy. As a writer, Davis has the rare ability to mine her own experience and create fiction from what she palpably understands. It is an enviable talent and her novel allows those of us who have never been there to grasp the hell of being an addict, of how sorry things can get when we waste our lives. *The Empty Room* is scary in places, touching, and often sad. It is a great psychological portrait of a woman under the influence.
The Toronto Star

Davis brilliantly tackles alcoholism. . . A serious, sorrowful book, The Empty Room, is a masterful portrayal of an addiction.
The Telegraph Journal "Here Magazine"

Davis portrays the frustrating doggedness of an alcoholic unable to recognize her problem with such insight ... Her alcoholism has a narrative; it explains why she's become the woman she's become. Davis skillfully juggles Colleen's past and present.... vivid ... heart-wrenching scenes of tenderness.
National Post

The Empty Room, excellent itself, joins an impressive list of literary novels devoted to the evils of booze. She captures all the mannerisms, rationalizations and cover-ups of the classic alcoholic in a remarkable novel that proves to be a real page-turner. Davis moves seamlessly in and out of Colleen's mind as she convinces herself she either needs the next drink or must prepare for when she needs one later. Davis shows her mastery of dialogue and also her versatility. Davis succeeds in giving us a character we continue to hope for even as Colleen's situation grows more and more grim; and she skillfully shows the funny side of horrific and degrading scenes while never causing us to laugh at her protagonist, always retaining our sympathy.
Winnipeg Free Press

The Empty Room is an unflinching depiction of a woman's descent into alcoholism ... tells the truth about the lives of everyday folk.
Montreal Gazette

Davis puts readers deep into Colleen's mind so they can see her fight the bottle to get her life back.
Halifax Chronicle Herald

THE
EMPTY
ROOM

Also by Lauren B. Davis:

AGAINST A DARKENING SKY
OUR DAILY BREAD
AN UNREHEARSED DESIRE
THE RADIANT CITY
THE STUBBORN SEASON
RAT MEDICINE & OTHER UNLIKELY CURATIVES.

THE EMPTY ROOM

By Lauren B. Davis

Library Window Press

The Empty Room
Copyright @2013 by Lauren B. Davis

Published by Library Window Press

Library Window Press
94 Gallup Road
Princeton, Ontario
08540

ISBN: 978-0-9998134-0-9

For R.E.D. – if it weren't for you, this wouldn't be fiction.

"And the dreams that you have, alone in an empty room, waiting for the door that will open, the thing that is bound to happen . . ."

—Jean Rhys, *Good Morning, Midnight*

Good Morning, World

It was Monday morning, and Colleen Kerrigan woke up wondering why she was chewing on a dirty old sock. She tried to pull her tongue from the roof of her mouth; it peeled away, dry and swollen. Her fingers told her she didn't actually have a sock in there, which was something of a relief. She must have been sleeping with her mouth open, probably snoring like a wildebeest. The late-October sun butting up against the window barely made a dent in the murk. She rarely shut the curtains because her eighth-floor window looked out onto the parking lot and the old Dominion Coal and Wood silo. Besides, who wanted to peek into the windows of a nearly-fifty-year-old woman?

The man's voice on the radio said the high today would be seven degrees Celsius, with a brisk wind and the possibility of showers. His voice was sharp and irritatingly upbeat. She shut off the clock radio with a slap of her hand and dragged her legs over the side of the bed, her head fuzzy, her stomach churning. She had slept in her T-shirt and sweatpants, which she hadn't intended. In fact, she didn't exactly remember going to bed. She hadn't even bothered to take off her bra and the wire must have dug into her left breast as she slept. It hurt. Or maybe it was cancer.

Good morning, world.

Her eyes settled on the framed postcard of Dylan Thomas's writing shed at Laugharne, which she kept on the bedside table. The tiny room, the whitewashed walls, the simple desk and chair, the photos on the walls, the crumpled bits of paper, the bottle, the astonishing work Thomas created there . . . this was Colleen's idea of perfection. If she concentrated on the image hard enough, it would manifest itself in her own life. She hadn't written anything in a long time, but she would again, of this she was sure. Beside the photo lay the Bible. Many of the Psalms she knew by heart. They felt like a doorway—one of many, but one which suited her—into the world of Spirit she was sure lived just beyond her fingertips, just out of reach, but which nonetheless beckoned to her. The Bible was open now to Psalm 38. *My wounds are loathsome and corrupt, Because of my foolishness.*

Sometimes the Divine had a wicked sense of humour.

As she sat up, her head, and the room, spun. She held onto the bed for a moment until it righted. Was she coming down with something? Her sinuses were painful and her throat a bit sore. An ear infection, perhaps. That would account for the dizziness. Her tongue still felt woollen. Maybe she should just go back to bed and call in sick. But no, she'd taken too many sick days these past few months. She'd need a doctor's note for any more. Her head ached and her bladder felt about to burst. She limped into the bathroom—her knee was bothering her again—and as she sat on the toilet she noticed new bruises on her legs and arms. Where had they come from? She must fight off the hounds of hell in her sleep. Maybe she sleepwalked? She reached for the toilet paper and her left elbow pinged sharply. She cupped it with her right hand. It was tender, just at the joint. When had she banged that? She was going to have to start taking better care of herself.

When finished she made her way down the hall to the kitchen, where dishes crowded the sink and the yellow linoleum floor stuck to the soles of her feet. She drank club soda from the bottle in great gulps, hoping it would do its work and settle her stomach. The clock on the stove said it was nearly 7:30, which meant she had to rush or she'd never get to work on time. On the counter, next to the hideous green cookie jar with the painted cherries—this had once been her mother's—stood a vodka bottle. Colleen froze, the club soda bottle still pressed to her lips. Some of it dribbled down her chin and she wiped it away with the back of her hand. She stared at the vodka bottle. She picked it up and jiggled it, hoping it was merely an illusion, some trick of the light making it look nearly empty. It should be at least half full. But no, a mere inch or so sloshed about in the bottom. This simply wasn't possible. She didn't drink that much yesterday, surely. She must be losing her mind. She wondered if she'd miss it very much.

She put down the bottle. Yes, she thought, I've rather enjoyed my mind. I will not drink today, she vowed.

She remembered the bottle had been nearly full when she poured the first glass and added cranberry juice,

3

sometime just past noon yesterday. She had munched some potato chips with that first drink, and had meant to pop a frozen macaroni and cheese into the microwave for dinner, but she never did. Vodka, chips, some peanuts . . . she had started watching *Law & Order.* Such a reliable show. No matter what time you turned on the television it seemed there was a *Law & Order,* in one of its many variations, on some channel or another. That Latino actor, so handsome; she could look at him all day. She remembered that, and something afterwards, some stupid confusing movie, and then she remembered picking up her guitar and singing . . . Joni Mitchell, soundtrack of her youth. And Tom Waits. Music filled up the space, drove away the silence of the empty rooms.

She could not possibly have drunk all that vodka. But there it was, the near-neon accusation of it. She couldn't go on like this, and she wouldn't. She felt hollow inside, as scooped out as an old Halloween pumpkin. Hollow and jangled.

A muffled buzzing came from somewhere in the vicinity of her living room. She put down the club soda. The telephone. Where had she left it? She had disconnected her land line six months ago, seeing no reason to pay for two phones. More economical, certainly, but the problem with a cell phone was that one was constantly misplacing it. Yes, there on the sofa. She picked it up and opened it. The readout said, "Spring Lake Place."

Oh, for God's sake, not *now,* she thought. She could just let it go, ignore it. But what if it was *the* call? "Hello?"

4

"Is this Colleen Kerrigan?"

Colleen walked back into the kitchen. She recognized Carol's voice. Carol was the nice nurse and from her tone this was just one of those calls, not *the* call. "Hi, Carol."

"Your mother is here, Ms. Kerrigan, and she'd like to talk to you if you have a minute."

"Trouble?"

"Well, she just wants to talk to you."

And Colleen knew what that meant. She picked up the club soda bottle and took another swig. "Put her on."

Pause, and her mother's voice in the background, the words unintelligible, only that awful, curt irritation.

"Colleen?"

"Hi, Mum. I don't have much time. I have to go to work. How are you?"

"Terrible."

Of course. Colleen couldn't remember the last time her mother had given a positive answer to that question. Even before the mini-strokes she suffered last spring, which destroyed whatever remained of her impulse control and most of her memory and forced her move into Spring Lake Place, Colleen's mother had to have been the most negative person on the planet.

"What's the matter?" It was an unwavering script.

"It's horrible here. This woman, she comes in and takes the . . . candles . . . potatoes . . . *things* and I've told her not to. I don't want anyone in my room."

"I know, Mum, but she's only taking your laundry." The recurring laundry issue. Last week her mother had threatened to kill an aide over it—a threat that, with Mother, one couldn't completely discount.

"I don't want them to take my things . . . my cake . . . the trolley . . ." The aphasia worsened when she was irritated. "Oh, I don't know, I'm too tired. I don't sleep."

If Colleen were to believe her mother, the woman hadn't slept in thirty years. "Just let them take your dirty clothes. Isn't it nice not to have to do your own washing anymore?"

"I want to do my own cleaning. There's nothing to do here. I hate it. I wish I was dead."

Don't we all, thought Colleen, and she hated herself for it. "I know, Mum. I know it's tough, but I'll try to get you moved out of there soon."

"I'll be dead by then."

Or I will be. "I have to go, Mum. I'm late for work. But I'll talk to them, okay?"

"That would be good, dear."

"I'll talk to you later."

"It doesn't matter; I don't care," her mother said, and hung up.

Colleen flipped the phone closed and rubbed her temples, as though trying to rub the whole conversation away. Before her mother went into the nursing home she hadn't called Colleen in twenty years. Colleen always called her, dutifully, every two weeks, taking forty-five minutes to listen to her mother's chatter, her complaints and the latest gossip from the seniors' centre. It seemed much like the behaviour of high school girls, full of petty grudges and little betrayals. Grating as it was to listen to this, week in and week out, it was one of the few things Colleen could do for her mother, who was, after all, pretty much alone in the world. Husband dead, no siblings, and friends who didn't seem to stick. Deirdre Kerrigan had long ago alienated most of her living acquaintances. Colleen had once thought her mother, like other mothers, might want to see more of her as she got older, but this was not the case. Her mother, after all, was not like other mothers. Deirdre rarely wanted to see her, and had claimed illness or fatigue or a dirty house as an excuse any time Colleen suggested they get together, which was, Colleen admitted, a relief to both of them. Christmases were a hell they had agreed to give up ten years ago, and which, after her mother's last suicide attempt on Christmas Eve of that year, they never discussed. Last year Colleen sent her mother a large gift basket of expensive treats—chocolate, wine, biscuits, cheeses—picked specially to suit her palate. When Colleen called to wish her mother a Merry Christmas, nothing was said about the basket and so Colleen asked her if she'd received it.

"I got it," said Deirdre.

A long pause followed. Colleen didn't want to ask, knew she shouldn't ask, but nonetheless asked, "Did you like it?"

"It wasn't what I wanted."

"What did you want?" Colleen asked, taken aback. Just when she thought she'd built fortifications against all her mother's weapons, Deirdre pulled something new and sharp from her bag of tricks.

"What does that matter now? This is what you sent, so thanks for that. Thanks a lot."

Her mother had sent her nothing. Deirdre Kerrigan's mental state worsened when she was around her daughter for some reason—the depression, the suicide attempts, the obsessive thinking. It was hard to love a mother who fought so hard to keep her at arm's length, but it was harder still to give up the idea that one day it might be different.

Colleen put the cold club soda against her temple. God, it was so sad. What a non-life her mother had had, and this was the way it ended? Without even a little peace? *Please God, don't let that be me. O keep my soul, and deliver me: let me not be ashamed; for I put my trust in thee.* She put the bottle back in the fridge, noting something fuzzy in the crisper that she was not up to dealing with at the moment. A stab of icy dread streaked along her spine. She could *very well* end up that way, couldn't she? Or worse.

Don't think about it now. Only this: you will not drink today. Not today.

Soggy Crows

It was early evening, a time when she and her mother usually went downstairs with a bowl of barbecue potato chips to the TV room of the split-level house and watched *The Man from U.N.C.L.E.* or *Daniel Boone,* or sometimes *Bewitched,* which nine-year-old Colleen liked best. On that night, however, her mother watched *Bonanza* with steely indifference. She wasn't sewing either, as she usually did, her hands busy hemming or putting on buttons or sometimes crocheting an afghan or a sweater. Instead, she clutched a tissue and held a glass of scotch, cradling it between her palms as though she were cold and it warmed her. Periodically she sipped from the glass and then snuffled loudly into the tissue. Now and then she seemed to stifle a moan. Tiny and dark haired, with a black sweater wrapped around her shoulders, she looked like one of the soggy crows perched on the branches of the oak tree outside their home in Burlington when it rained, glaring at Colleen's window, as though she had no right to be warm and dry while they suffered so.

Colleen sat at the far end of the couch and tried to concentrate on the television show, but need radiated off her mother in waves. Already in her pyjamas and pink terry-cloth robe, Colleen rolled the robe's belt up tightly, let it out and then rolled it up again. She couldn't leave, because then her mother would say she was deserting her.

"So, that's how it is," her mother had said once, when Colleen, her throat thickening with shame even as she spoke, suggested her mother should be more easygoing, like her dad. Her mother's eyes were hard with resolve, and pitiless. "Well, now I know where we stand," she said, "and don't think I'll forget it." She didn't speak to Colleen for a week, and then only because Colleen broke down and cried so much she threw up.

Colleen vowed she wouldn't ever let her mother punish her that way again, which meant she had to keep her as happy as it was possible for the woman to be (which, even at nine, Colleen didn't think was very happy at all), and right now that meant staying, watching her mother drink and cry and drink. Colleen felt herself drowning, her mother a dead weight dragging her under.

Minutes ticked by, and then her mother finally said, "Your father is a shit, you know that?"

Colleen pulled Pixie onto her lap from where she had been sleeping on the couch between them. She stroked the cocker spaniel's long, silky ears and the dog sighed.

"Of course, you've always liked your father better than me, haven't you."

"No. I love you both."

Her mother sniggered. "Well, he's drinking us into the poorhouse, how about that for your wonderful father? And he's got other women, too, did you know that? Little whore of a secretary."

"Mum, please . . ."

Her mother blew her nose and threw the soiled tissue into a half-full basket by the end table. "What do you care? I might just as well turn drunk myself. Bottoms up!"

As the pitch of her mother's voice rose, Pixie's head popped up. She hopped off the couch and moved to an armchair at the end of the room, Colleen's father's chair. Putting her chin on the armrest, she eyed them.

"Even the damn dog!" said her mother. "Even the damn dog."

"It'll be okay, Mum. You don't have to be mad."

"If it wasn't for you, I could have left long ago." She blew her nose and pushed the wadded tissue into her pocket. She turned her gaze to Colleen. "Get away from me," she said.

And there it was. Now Colleen was expected to beg, to plead with her mother to love her: *please don't make me go away.* Colleen recognized the look on her mother's face—part defiance, part despair and part regret—although she was too young to have words for what she saw. She only knew her mother wanted her to play a familiar, terrible, hurtful game that Colleen never won, no matter how hard she tried.

Not tonight. She got up and headed for the stairs. Pixie jumped down from the chair and followed.

Her mother gasped. "Pixie! Get back there. *Sit.*"

The dog obeyed, but looked so longingly at Colleen that she felt guilty for leaving her behind. She started up the stairs.

"I see it now, Colleen Kerrigan. You're your father's daughter, aren't you."

At the top of the stairs, Colleen stopped and tightened her belt, her stomach roiling. Her father sat in the dark in the living room, right in the middle of the good sofa where no one ever sat unless there was company. Colleen couldn't make out his features in the dark. He was smoking and the blue-grey smoke was thick. Colleen walked toward him.

"No, Colleen. Not now," he said.

She stood there on the carpet and felt something in the middle of her chest crink, like a sudden running-stitch in your side. Where was she supposed to go? Who was she supposed to go to?

"Nobody wants me," she wailed, although she hadn't meant to.

"Ah, Jesus," her father said. "Come here, pet, come here."

She ran to her father, who smelled of cigarettes and scotch, and buried her face in his chest, letting out great wrenching sobs. "Everybody's so mad all the time," she said.

"I'm sorry, pet. This isn't your fault. It's my fault. Mummy's right about that. I won't drink any more, I won't. I promise."

She didn't believe him, of course, but it felt good to have his arms around her, and so she said, "I believe you, Daddy. I believe you."

It's a Knock-off!

In the shower, the water felt good and Colleen wanted to stand there for hours, but there was no time. She didn't bother to shave her legs either. Thank God for pants. Yuck, there was mildew on the pink shower curtain. She had to buy a new one. That pink was the colour of Pepto-Bismol, or Pepto-*Dismal* as she called it. Why had she ever bought it? It was vomit-inducing. She'd buy a new one—something in a cool pale watery blue. Clean and fresh.

When she stepped out of the shower, the towel she rubbed over her face smelled of mildew too. Disgusting. Her stomach cramped. When was the last time she did laundry? She patted herself down, since she'd read in a magazine that rubbing too hard could stretch the skin. Red dots had appeared on her torso over the past few years. Her doctor said they were nothing, just cherry angiomas, whatever the hell that meant. Colleen noted the scatter of them across her chest and stomach. Maybe her liver was giving out.

"That's it, kid," she said out loud, "your drinking days are over."

A quick look in the mirror. This was always a dangerous moment in the day. So much depended on not hating oneself completely at such an early hour. Mirrors were treacherous objects. As a little girl, she read Hans Christian Andersen's story about the Snow Queen. A wicked sprite fashioned a mirror with the power to make everything good and beautiful look ugly and mean, and all

15

that was ugly and horrible look even more atrocious. The mirror was smashed into a hundred million and more pieces, some no larger than a grain of sand, and these flew about in the world, and when they got into people's eyes, there they stayed, and then people saw everything perverted, or only liked looking at that which was evil. Splinters even found their way into the hearts of some people and that was the worst of all, for their hearts became like lumps of ice. Colleen was not convinced this was merely a fairy tale for children, and even entertained the possibility she had such a speck of tainted mirror in her eye, for she thought the world a pretty shabby, violent and decaying place and couldn't understand why some people seemed so happy all the time, so impervious to the grief and sorrow of humanity. It was hard to believe perceptions could be so different, and impossible to tell who was right.

She considered her reflection now, and there was no sugar-coating what she saw. She grimaced at the haggard woman she saw before her, bared her teeth and shook her head. Men had once told her she was a pretty girl, they had desired her. Everyone told her she had such good bones, that she was lucky to have inherited her mother's cheekbones. She did not see good bones. She saw a neck no longer firm, a softened jawline, a nest of lines around her eyes. A crease ran up her cheek. Her eyes were puffy and bloodshot, and a pimple reddened her chin. How the hell could she be almost fifty and still getting pimples?

She had an urge to smash the mirror. People did such things. She could do it. She could ram her fist into the mirror. But she'd probably break her hand. She could throw something. The canister of bath salts. She could throw that. She pictured a shard of glass actually flying into her eye. Blood and pain. She hung her head and swallowed back unexpected, and inconvenient, tears. She pressed the heels of her hands into her eyes. *Stop it. Stop feeling sorry for yourself.*

She took her hands from her eyes and got to work. A quick swipe of mascara. But she dropped the wand in the sink, leaving a black smear against the flesh-coloured porcelain. Her hands, she realized, were trembling just a little. She towel-dried her hair, which was good hair, fine, but lots of it and with a slight wave. She plugged in the hair dryer and used her brush to lift the hair from the roots. Ordinarily she'd bend over and dry her hair upside down but this morning such an acrobatic manoeuvre would invite disaster. When it was dry enough she piled it on top of her head in a messy but, she thought, charmingly bohemian twist, and secured it with a silver clip.

On a little plastic shelf over the towel rack miniature perfume bottles were arranged in a circle: Dior, Trésor, Chloé, Oscar de la Renta, Angel, Perry Ellis 360, Intuition, Ysatis, Opium, L'Air du Temps. Looking at the two tiny doves in etched glass on the last bottle brought to mind Ali, the beautiful young man from the Canary Islands, who once gave her a bottle, which she spilled down the back of her dresser the very night he gave it to her. The whole room smelled of gardenia and jasmine for a week. Ali turned out to be married to a woman (possibly two, he was Muslim) back home. Goodbye, Ali.

Colleen loved these tiny bottles. She bought them years ago at Christmas when the department stores sold them as gifts. She felt she deserved a gift. They were so pretty and light and held all the promise of a lovely dress and a sparkling night, one filled with possibility. She imagined they contained magic potions. Sometimes she took them off the shelf and carried them to the living room, lined them up on the coffee table and lit candles round them, creating a sort of altar. She picked up the squat inverted triangle of the Trésor bottle. Dust filmed the glass. She cleaned it with her thumb. She really should give the whole place a polishing.

She glanced at her watch. 8:10. She'd never make it. Lipstick, but forget the foundation. No, just a dab of foundation on the broken blood vessels along her nose, and powder, to take the sweat-shine away. Jesus, but her stomach was a mess. She ran naked to the kitchen, smeared a couple of salted crackers thickly with butter and stuffed them in her mouth. Good and greasy. For some reason that always helped. She shouldn't have anything else. Certainly not now. There were rules about these things. But . . . there was so little left in the bottle, and a quick swig would settle things down, she was sure it would.

Drinking before breakfast, however, was against these rules. She often woke up at around 4 a.m., heart pounding with anxiety, legs twitching and restless, as though they'd gone to sleep and were about to burst into pins and needles. This morning had been no exception, and before she managed to fall back to sleep, she vowed she wouldn't drink today. A detox day, as she called them.

Sundays were *supposed* to be detox days, but Sunday had been such a lonely day. There was only so much reading she could do, only so much napping. A wee drink made everything prettier, and far more tolerable. And so today, Monday, would be her detox day.

Back in the bedroom, with the recriminating unmade bed and the not-terribly-clean sheets, she slipped into underwear, the same bra she had slept in, black pants and blue turtleneck. She crammed her swollen feet (she had spider veins on her ankles now, her *ankles* for Christ's sake, when did that happen?) into knee-high stockings and black pumps. Tonight, when she absolutely would not be drinking, she'd do laundry. For now, this would have to do.

She hunched into her red wool coat. The red was flattering against her pale colouring, she knew, and the A-line shape hid a variety of flaws. It had cost too much, and she shouldn't have bought it two years ago when her credit cards were already burdened. It was rather cutting-edge then, though, and she couldn't resist. Now, even if it was a little out of fashion, she preferred to think of it as classic. She tried to channel Audrey Hepburn, her chin's insouciant and slightly defiant thrust.

Colleen squared her shoulders. "Nothing is impossible," she said aloud, quoting Hepburn. "The word itself says, 'I'm possible'!" It was a sort of morning incantation. Some people strapped on St. Patrick's Breastplate; Colleen preferred Hepburn.

Colleen grabbed her keys from the bowl on the end table and then remembered her phone. She picked it up from the counter and popped it in her purse. Just then she had a sort of muscle memory. *The phone.* Did she call someone last night? She did. Oh Christ. Whom did she call? She spoke to Lori around eight-thirty or so. Yes, that was it, because *The Sopranos* was on. But they hadn't talked long. Lori had kids, after all, and a life.

Colleen was in the hallway now and just about to press the elevator button when it occurred to her she might have called a man. Yes, it was a man's voice she recalled, but whose? She prayed it wasn't *him.* Jake. She groaned and felt a rush of panic. It probably was Jake, but she wouldn't think about that, not now.

Oh, lovely. Now she was channelling Scarlett O'Hara.

Last year she got a phone bill with a long list of calls she didn't remember making. When she called the phone company to complain, a woman explained they were from a charge-by-the-minute service. All at once it had come back to her. The late-night commercials with a handsome man saying, "Call now, ladies, I'm waiting to talk with you." It had sounded sexy and forbidden and she'd thought, *just this once, why not?* Who knew what might happen? But she had to keep paying for more minutes, going deeper and deeper into some mysterious telephone labyrinth where the man on the other end *almost* said something naughty but never really did. Apparently, she'd been on the phone for some time. Apparently, she'd made a number of calls. "My damn roommate," she said, and assured the woman at the phone company that she'd handle the matter.

The elevator pinged and the doors opened. It was packed, as it always was at this hour, but she squeezed in. Most of the people in the car were young women who worked in the gleaming offices and fancy clothing boutiques downtown. The one with the fancy suede coat, the classic, not-a-hair-out-of-place blond French twist and diamond studs in her ears, worked at Holt Renfrew. Colleen pictured her there, tall and graceful and utterly self-absorbed behind one of the cosmetics counters. She went into the store one lunchtime, wanting to buy some new blush, but when she approached the girl, emboldened by the fact they were neighbours, the girl's gaze skimmed over her as though she were a cleaning lady or something, and she turned to assist a decked-out matron. Colleen had nearly burst into tears, although she didn't really know why, not even now. What did she care if some club-bunny, some little tart like that, acknowledged her or not? She'd never been back to Holt's, not once.

Now, she smiled in a general sort of way at the crisply dressed young things with their polished hair and nails and perfect skin and tiny waists. The smile was meant to be self-assured, as though she could float through any trial in life with the serenity of a Buddha. She hoped it didn't look stiff. She couldn't bear it if anyone suspected how she longed for an empty elevator.

"Morning," said a blond girl in a black coat.

"Good morning." Lovely girl, thought Colleen. She noticed a rhinestone pin in the form of a dragon on the girl's lapel, which was approximately at the level of Colleen's nose. "What a pretty brooch."

The girl merely smiled. Colleen felt short. When did everyone get so tall?

A couple of the young women talked to each other about someone named Danny who was apparently hot, *hot,* and everyone ignored Colleen. A young man in the back, shorter than most of the women but still taller than Colleen, wore sunglasses, which was *such* an absurd effort at coolness Colleen might have chuckled if she weren't feeling so queasy.

It seemed such a short time ago when she was one of these young girls, her waist an impossibly slender twenty-three inches, her hair long, swinging freely down her back, her delicate ankles shown off to full advantage by a pair of four-inch heels. How many young men had asked her out, on this very elevator, for a drink or a meal, or something else?

The elevator air was thick with the combined fug of seven or eight different perfumes and Colleen held her thumb and forefinger beneath her nose so as to block some of it. Her poor stomach. Did these girls have no thought for anyone but themselves? Didn't they take into consideration the fact so many people were now allergic to perfume? Of course they didn't. They were self-centred in the way of the young.

They stopped on the sixth floor to let in more people, a couple this time, holding hands, dressed in head-to-toe black, he with a silver buckle on his belt in the shape of a death's head. Colleen had to step back and practically press up against the girl from Holt's, who, of course, wouldn't step back herself. The girl in black had pink hair this morning. It wasn't always pink. It had previously been green and blue and several shades of red and a black so deep it was indigo. Colleen knew this pair. In the summer, the girl wore dresses of astonishing skimpiness, revealing tattoos so extensive they covered her arms like a blouse. Where could such a creature possibly work? What demimonde existed where such a thing was permissible? Like those waiters and waitresses in the Queen Street restaurants with piercings in their eyebrows and lips and noses and great plugs in their earlobes, creating enormous loops of flesh. They called it neo-tribal, for God's sake. Colleen considered it an insult to regular old tribals. What happened when they took the plugs out? The flesh-hoops must dangle and flap. A sheen of sweat broke out on Colleen's forehead. *For the sake of your stomach, don't think of that now.*

At last they reached the ground floor. Everyone bustled out, but most turned left, heading for the exit to the parking lot. Colleen and two girls walked to the front exit. Colleen had never owned a car and couldn't imagine how most people afforded one—the gas, the insurance, the parking, the maintenance. The girl who worked at Holt's, the *cosmetic girl,* for God's sake, had a car. How was that possible? Maybe she earned a little extra on the side. When Colleen first moved to Toronto from Burlington she knew girls like that—leggy, buxom things who worked as receptionists and hostesses, but who lived in apartments Colleen certainly couldn't afford and who never paid for a meal or a drink. Professional girlfriends. Not her, no way, thank you very much. She was no one's plaything. She had been propositioned—in nightclubs as well as offices where she'd temped—by men she was sure could afford mistresses, but she didn't like them, with their loud voices and scotch breath and arrogance.

She pushed open the glass door and, once outside in the cutting October wind, had a choice to make. The stop for the bus that would take her to the subway was right across the street, but no one was waiting at the shelter, and if she'd just missed the bus there might not be another for fifteen minutes. She looked at her watch. 8:25. If she walked, it would take ten minutes, but that extra five minutes might make all the difference. A gust whipped a leaf into her face and it stung like a slap. She looked down the street but there was no sign of the bus. Looking the other way, toward Yonge Street and the subway, she thought she saw it.

"Shit," she said, and started walking.

She crossed to the other side of the street, just in case the bus did appear and she could make it to one of the two stops between here and the subway. She already felt a burning sort of pain right on the balls of her feet, and these weren't even high heels. She tried to ignore it. The wind buffeted her face, making her dizzy. She sucked in air too quickly, and that made her stomach even dodgier. She had never thrown up in the mornings, the way she'd heard some people did, but there was always a first time.

When she was thirteen and learning how to smoke (something she worked very hard at, since all the cool kids smoked), she used to get appallingly nauseated. Once, while riding the bus to the shopping mall, she smoked a Matinee cigarette pilfered from her mother's purse. *Imagine being able to smoke on buses, or in movie theatres, the way we used to!* By the time she arrived at the Burlington Mall, she was sure she was going to throw up. The only question was, would she make it to the bathroom in time, or would she throw up on the floor outside the pet store? She reached the toilet stalls and stood there, trembling, sweaty and pale, her mouth filling with saliva, wanting only to heave and get it over with. Then the waves passed and off she went, to smoke again another day, to repeat the same madness over and over until, finally, she smoked like a pro.

Now, Colleen was so busy trying not to wobble in her dizziness that she forgot to look behind her and *whoosh* the bus sped by.

"Shit!"

She walked faster, afraid she might actually start crying. She should have gotten up earlier. She shouldn't have bothered with a shower. She mustn't cry; her mascara would run. There was nothing to be done but walk and hope she made her connections. When she reached the subway station she hurried down the stairs with a hundred other rushing people. They reminded her of those biology

25

films showing white blood cells swooshing through veins. She caught a whiff of urine. Heard a thousand pairs of shoes tapping on the tiles, the shriek of brakes as the subway approached the station. She was propelled forward by the force of the bodies around her and into their midst, away from the handrails. She wondered what would happen if she stumbled and fell; pictured her body, in her pretty red coat, trampled underfoot. What if there were an emergency, with all these people crammed together? If there were a bomb, or a fire? They'd never get out.

A train pulled in and people exiting the car swam in two directions like salmon swirling in a spawning pool, some trying to get up the stairs, Colleen and others trying to get down. She reached the platform and shouldered forward. As she neared the doors she looked down at the gap, which she hated. It would be so easy to get pinned between the platform and the subway car, mangled and crushed . . . *Don't think about that.* Then she was inside, just barely inside, with bodies a solid wall in front of her and even more perfume smells and coffee-and-orange-juice breath, which was one of the worst smells in the world. Someone pushed in behind her and she lurched forward into the back of an older black man.

"For heaven's sake," she said, "there'll be another train in a minute. No need to crush us all."

The man turned to look at her. His eyes were yellowish and the pores on his shiny skin large and open. You could, as her mother used to say, drive a Buick into one of those pores. "Sorry. Not you," she said.

"No problem," the man said. "Sardines have better lives." He turned away.

Colleen manoeuvred so she could at least grab hold of a tiny portion of pole. A woman who had pushed in after her stood facing the doors, so her absurdly poofed-up blond hair was in Colleen's face. Colleen tucked her purse under her arm—this scenario was a pickpocket's dream—and brushed the woman's hair out of her face.

The woman glanced over her shoulder and glared at Colleen with one heavily made-up bright green eye (contact lenses, no doubt). "Excuse *me*," she said, and then turned back to the window. "Jesus. Really."

Colleen thought it would almost be fair justice if she vomited right into that rat's nest of bottle blond.

At Bloor Station she had to transfer to the westbound trains and over to St. George Station. If it had been a nice day, if she weren't so hungover (yes, might as well just admit that), and if she weren't so late, she might walk over to the Geography Department where she worked, but today there wasn't much choice. When the doors opened, she exited the train, edged her way past the hundreds of people waiting to get in and inched down more stairs to the east–west train platform. It was chockablock, bodies pressing, people being pushed to the edge. Colleen could not help but think of Nazi cattle-cars. She checked her watch. It was just gone nine. She was officially late, but then again maybe so were all these other people and surely there must have been a problem on the line. That's what she'd tell them at work. Perhaps there was a jumper. No, that was an awful thing to say, but on the other hand, there might have been a jumper.

She snorted. The Hepburn-insouciance didn't seem to be working.

She pressed ahead, shoulder to shoulder with the others. A train came, regurgitating an astonishing number of riders, all of whom pushed to get up the stairs, while behind her more people tried to get down. Colleen's breathing became shallow and her palms sweaty. Her stomach growled. She'd have to pick up something to eat. It would help settle her tummy. She could hardly breathe with all these bodies around her. Somehow she managed to get near the front now, *too* near in fact. She hated being this close to the edge. All it would take was some maniac at the back of the crowd to push forward and they'd all topple into the path of the oncoming train. Saliva rushed into her mouth. She was sure she'd vomit. She was thirteen again and about to humiliate herself utterly, irrevocably. Everyone was surely looking at her; they could see she was sick and hungover—

"Are you okay?" asked a woman about her age.

"I'm fine. Stomach flu maybe."

The woman held out a bottle of water. "Would you like this?"

The bottle was half empty. "No, thanks."

The sound of the approaching train deafened her. She felt as though it might jump the track, mangle all of them on the platform. She must get out of here. She swivelled and met a wall of faces, some irritated, some bored and bland as paste.

"Excuse me," she said, "excuse me . . ." and tried to elbow through, but no one moved.

Then the train was in front of her and the door opened and people pushed past her. All right, she had to get to work. Soldier on. She lifted her head, took a gulp of air into her lungs and lunged forward. There was a seat, oh God, a seat on the other side of the aisle. She snagged it, plopped down and wiped the damp from her upper lip. The woman with the water bottle stood nearby. She smiled and Colleen smiled back. The man in the seat next to her moved his leg away, as if afraid she might be contagious. She must look horrible. If she could just sit here for a moment with her eyes closed and breathe, she'd be all right. She'd be all right.

People stood next to her so closely, so packed in; a woman's handbag dangled next to Colleen's ear. She put her hand up so it didn't smack her and the woman tugged the bag away and glared at Colleen as though she were about to snatch it. Nobody wants your bag, thought Colleen; everyone can see it's a knock-off.

Colleen's stomach was settling at last, and she was quite sure now that she would neither vomit nor pass out. At the Bay Street Station many people got out, but only a few got on. There was a little breathing room at last. 9:10. Well, it couldn't be helped. She'd stay later tonight, that's what she'd do. She'd walk right into David's office and say there had been a problem on the line and she was very sorry, and she'd be happy to stay late tonight to make it up. He wouldn't mind that, surely.

The man next to her wore headphones. Given the audible thumping bass and squealing voices, the volume must be up to maximum. He looked like a Bay Street guy, but one never knew what sort of lives people really lived. She'd worked at a brokerage on Bay Street for a while between jobs at the university. It had been the early '80s when everyone was rich and fat and lunches consisted of three or four martinis. She remembered Bruce, a trader, who had crawled out of the elevator on all fours one afternoon around three o'clock. She'd felt nothing but contempt for him. After all, he was responsible for other people's money, and look at the state of him. The other traders had thought it hilarious, but then, they were three sheets to the wind themselves. How could anyone get to that point? Even then she'd had her standards, which was why things hadn't worked out for her in the stock market world. She was probably the only secretary not sleeping with someone. Well, there was that one time, but that didn't count; Isaac had been too drunk to get it up and she'd sent him home to his live-in girlfriend. But she'd loved to go out after work with the boys. Loved to show them some of the bars they didn't know—the soul bars, the jazz bars way off the Bay Street beat. She could drink them under the table, too, and did on many a night.

Then, there was that night when Brian, her boss, made a pass and she called him a sleaze and he got mad and she could see then she wasn't cut out for Bay Street.

She flushed to think of that now. He *was* a sleaze. Colleen
had met his wife, for God's sake, and yet he thought
nothing of telling her about how this girl or that girl was
going down on him behind his desk and not to put any calls
through to his office. And those girls who thought those
guys would leave their wives because they did things the
missus wouldn't. What fools. She knew better. After all, her
father had always, in the end, come home to her mother,
hadn't he? For what that was worth.

You're a Smart Girl

His name was Thomas—he was never called Tom—and he drove a silver Bentley, although Colleen had no idea how he paid for it, since he did little more than hang around the office, drinking scotch with Brian, or holding court at Three Small Rooms in the Windsor Arms Hotel with the rest of the *glitterati*. He was an investor, he said, and had persuaded her boss, Brian Stack, to put a good deal of money into some film deal, something starring Donald Sutherland. Thomas was an Englishman who wore his thinning hair in a greying ponytail, and lifted weights so his biceps bulged rock hard under his crisp white shirt.

One day Brian suggested Colleen join him for lunch with Thomas at Winston's, a nearby power-lunch spot. Very art nouveau—all red velvet chairs and Tiffany lamps—a diner over which the owner, Joe Arena, presided like a Mafia don.

She wore a black pencil skirt, a cobalt blue blouse and very high black heels. Thomas looked her up and down as she approached the table and patted the banquette next to him. "Sit here, baby." When the waiter appeared he ordered sixteen-year-old Lagavulin for the three of them. "And make it a Winston's," he said, meaning the obscenely generous pours that had helped cement the restaurant's popularity.

"Ice?" the waiter asked, looking at her but not the men.

"And ruin a good scotch?" she said. "I think not."

"Exactly so," said Thomas.

The drinks arrived.

"What do you think?" Thomas asked as she sipped the dark liquid.

"Wonderful," she sighed, and it was.

"What do you taste?"

She considered. Brian, his newly installed hair plugs as evident as cornrows, looked on with amusement, but also with something like proprietary pride. She understood she was expected to be more than purely decorative. For that he could have brought any one of the several secretaries with whom he was having sex. She sipped again, flared her nostrils and breathed. It was like inhaling the Highlands, all moody and alive with dark magic that coursed down her throat and into her veins.

"Richness. Peat. Smoke." She closed her eyes and rolled her tongue, then chuckled. "Fruitcake . . . something else, seaweed. Sweet seaweed." She opened her eyes to find Thomas smiling at her. "You should drink this late at night," she said.

"While reading poetry, don't you think?" He winked. "We should try that sometime."

He called her later that week and said he was going out to dinner with his friend, Mohammed, who was the Saudi protocol adviser to the Ontario government. She should come. It would be fun. Mohammed was a wonderful guy. She and Jake had had a terrible fight involving one of his many girl "friends." She thought it would serve him right if she had a few friends of her own.

"Why not," she said.

Mohammed's apartment was a surprise—sleekly modern, with expensive carpets, but filled with all sorts of trinkets including a number of glow-in-the-dark necklaces Mohammed said were terribly popular among the Bedouin. "I bring them back by the boatload," he said. They went to dinner, the three of them, at a Middle-Eastern restaurant Mohammed had purchased up the street from his apartment so he could cook baklava whenever he wished without messing up his own kitchen. He ordered for them, wonderful dishes of red lentil soup with cardamom, spiced chicken and rice, cauliflower with cilantro, and for dessert, baklava he assured them he had made himself. She was surprised when he ordered wine with the meal, since clearly he was Muslim.

"We are not in Saudi now," he said, catching the expression on her face. "To be a chameleon is a harmless yet most useful talent, no?"

Throughout the meal he told funny stories about the excesses of the Saudi royal family, such as having to ask the London department store, Harrods, to close down because one of the Saudi princes wished to buy everything in all the windows, right now, and pay for it with stacks of cash he kept in the boot of his Rolls-Royce.

"And did they do it?" she asked, laughing, unable to imagine that much money.

Mohammed, his black eyes flashing with good humour, said, "Of course, my dear. That's what money is for."

It was a pleasant evening, but when Thomas said he had to call it a night and Mohammed suggested she might, perhaps, like to stay for a drink, she declined. While he was an interesting and clearly powerful man, he was also at least forty-five, and besides, although the evening had been amusing, there was Jake, wasn't there?

Mohammed, ever the perfect gentleman, hailed a taxi for her and kissed her hand, telling her how charming she was.

The next day, Thomas arrived and asked Brian if he could take her out for lunch.

"Don't you think you should ask *me*?" she said, a trifle miffed.

He took her not to Winston's but to a restaurant near the office, and when they were settled with a glass of wine he said, "You made a good impression on Mohammed last night."

"He's a nice man," she said, noncommittally.

"We have a proposal for you."

She perked up at that. Working for Brian was fine, but she was always on the lookout for a new opportunity,

35

something with better pay, which seemed assured given Mohammed's stories and his restaurant and his apartment. Travel, perhaps? Something for the government?

"I'm listening." She sipped her wine. It tasted of violets.

"Perhaps once, twice a month, certain dignitaries from Saudi come to Toronto, or Montreal, or New York. Often, they travel with their wives and it is important the wives are treated with the utmost respect but that their seclusion is maintained. They wear the *abaya,* the black cloak, and must be segregated from men who are not family members, but they are women"—he smiled in a condescending way—"and like all women, they love to shop. You would be entrusted to make the appropriate arrangements and to accompany them, acting as a liaison and ensuring all is as it should be."

Babysit a bunch of segregated women? That wasn't something she wanted to do, even if getting a glimpse into the world of a harem would be fascinating. It seemed odd that Thomas, film-producing Thomas, would be involved in this sort of thing. Something shadowy was taking shape, something about where Thomas's money actually came from.

"I'm flattered, but I don't think it's really for me."

"That's not all, of course. In the evenings, once the women are safely in their beds for the night, you would have the opportunity to entertain the gentlemen. They are well-educated, well-travelled, sophisticated men who, of course, would like to experience the world in ways that would not be appropriate for their wives." He sipped his wine. He licked his lips. "Mohammed took quite a shine to you. Well done."

Colleen took a large drink from her wine, which now tasted not so much of violets but of vinegar. "I don't think I understand you."

"Of course you do. You're a smart girl." He reached over and took her hand. "You would be extremely well compensated for very little work. These are generous people; they like to give gifts."

"Gifts?"

"Indeed. Cars. Jewellery. Property. Works of art."

She pulled her hand away and put down her glass. Her cheeks flamed. "You're out of your mind, and I don't know why you'd think I'd get involved in something like this. You're nothing but a pimp."

She picked up her purse and went to stand up, but Thomas grabbed her by the wrist and pulled her down again.

"Who the fuck do you think you are?" he said.

His fingers bit into her arm, and later, when she was safely home with a large glass of scotch that might not be as good as his fancy single-malt but suited her just fine, she would find five distinct bruises there.

"Let go of me!"

"Oh, don't kid yourself. I know exactly who you are, Colleen."

She pulled her arm away and stomped back to the office, full of righteous fury. She stormed into Brian's office and told her what had happened, demanding he do something, take action, get rid of that guy.

Brian folded his hands and said, "I don't know what you're getting so bent out of shape for. Sounds like a compliment to me. And nobody made you go out with Thomas's friend."

"Are you kidding me?"

"Thomas is a valued client. Perhaps you'd better get back to work." By way of dismissal, Brian picked up the phone and began punching buttons.

A week later, Brian asked her out for a drink after work and she thought perhaps it was his way of apologizing. They sat next to each other in a black leather booth at the back of Trader Joe's. Halfway through his second martini Brian leaned over and tried to kiss her. She pushed him back.

"Brian, for Christ's sake. You're acting like a sleaze. I know your wife!"

"Leave my wife out of it," he said as he slid out of the booth. "And if you want to play the good little girl, you might stop going out for drinks with married men. Remember that at your *next* job."

And so she was fired. The next day, officially so. She'd never been fired before. She wanted to believe it was simply a matter of badly behaved men, but a bony little finger of doubt kept tapping her on the proverbial shoulder. Perhaps she did give off the wrong signals, but she didn't mean to. She liked the teasing and the play and the attention. They were colleagues. It was networking. She never intended it would lead to anything. People got the wrong impression. She didn't mean anything. It was just drinks, after all.

A Luverly Bunch of Coconuts

The subway arrived at the St. George stop. Hers. She zipped into the coffee shop on the corner and bought a breakfast sandwich with cheese and bacon, which she ate as she walked the long blocks to her office. It wouldn't do to let anyone know she had stopped to get food, late as she was. Cheese and bacon, she thought as she chewed, pulling a bit of paper wrapper from between her teeth. Not exactly the fare they once served at Winston's.

The grease and carbohydrates soaked up some of the acid in her belly, and by the time she reached the building in which the Geography Department was housed, she felt half human again. She stopped at the elevator, which was notoriously slow. All three cars were at the top floor, so she headed for the stairwell. She popped a mint in her mouth as she climbed. Four sets of stairs, and frankly, by the time she reached the top she was a bit shaky again.

When she first came to work at the university, she was only eighteen, and she'd planned to work during the day and take classes at night so she could get her degree in English Literature with a minor in Comparative Religion, since her parents hadn't put any money aside for her education. She took courses in the short story, Canadian literature, Shakespeare, John Donne, Victorian Realist Novels, world religions, Celtic saints. Each semester she swore she'd buckle down this time, do all the reading, never miss a lecture, write the papers, hand them in on time, but a few weeks in she found herself slipping, making excuses to miss one class and then another. She was so young then, younger than many of the students, in fact. There was always an invitation to a party, or to go out for drinks or a bite to eat. She'd get home late, have a glass of wine, start to read and fall asleep. She'd fall behind. Eventually she'd withdraw from class, vowing to do better next semester. She never got the degree.

She worked over in the Transcripts Department for a year at first, and ran up and down the stairs like an athlete. She remembered some woman saying that must be how she stayed so slim. And really, she was still slender now, although things seemed to have shifted around a bit. Her waist, her tiny twenty-three-inch waist. That was gone. From the Transcripts Department to the English Department (where she'd been so sure she'd take courses and begin writing *seriously,* maybe even do an MA in Creative Writing), then off to Bay Street for *that* little interlude, followed by a wild foray into the music business, back to the university and the Medical Research Department, then to the Registrar's Office, the History Department, the Faculty of Theology at St. Michael's College, and now . . . here.

She had met *him* at the university in 1978 when she was twenty and working in the English Department. Jake. Beautiful Jake, who boxed in the Golden Gloves, light heavyweight, and won a silver medal; Jake of the amber eyes and the *café au lait* skin. He smelled of cinnamon and his chest was hairless. He studied finance. For four years she and Jake tangled round each other. She was the only girl his boxing coach, the gnarled little French Canadian

Michel Lucien, would let come to the matches, because she was a lady and never freaked out if Jake got hit, if the blood flowed. Jake moved into her apartment for a while, and then he went to New York to be a big-deal stockbroker and she was supposed to go with him and get married but she didn't, not when she found out he'd been sleeping with that stewardess. Flight attendant. *Whatever.* Her name was Jane Smith. *Jane Smith,* for the love of God. How unoriginal. She'd told him if she ever caught him cheating, it was over, and so it had to be over, whether she liked it or not. You couldn't make an ultimatum like that and not keep it; if you did, the rest of your life would be hell, wouldn't it? And so she'd let him go and then things had gone bad for him—too much cocaine and booze—and he lost his job and came back to Toronto. He worked at a small brokerage now, but like her, he didn't keep jobs more than a few years. They stayed in touch, couldn't seem to break away completely. A now-and-again thing, always with the possibility that someday, somewhere . . . They talked, and sometimes he called and didn't say anything, but she knew it was him. She knew he was probably high, or drunk. He came close to getting married once, but nothing worked out. Now there was nobody again, not for either of them, and well, you never knew, right?

Roughly once a month she dreamed about Jake. They were strange dreams in which she didn't know she was dreaming, but thought she was awake and aware she had recurring dreams about him, and in the dream they understand each other, finally. They *know* each other and will be reunited, as they were always meant to be. They're holding onto each other, and she can smell that spicy-woodsy scent of his and feel his muscles and she's just on the verge of telling him about how she's always dreamed of him, that they've always been tied in some mystical way, and then she either realizes she's dreaming, or she just plain realizes she can't stay with him, and all this loss and grief pours down on her and her heart breaks all over again, and she wakes up in tears, longing for him.

It was ridiculous.

Did she call him last night? Probably. Heat ran up her neck and over her ears. She had to stop calling him. It did no good. She couldn't remember what she said. Jake might be the love of her life, but he wasn't safe and the better part of her knew that. After they broke up but while he was living in New York, he would come back to Toronto now and then—his family was still here—and show up at her office, drunk and crying, or at her apartment in the middle of the night. He scared her. She wouldn't let him in. He banged on her door until she threatened to call the cops. Then he went back to New York and the nobody-there calls started. She wanted him to stop, but then again, she didn't.

Colleen realized she was frowning and must look sour. That was no way to walk into the office, especially at . . . oh God . . . 9:27. She smoothed her hair and put a pleasant expression on her face. Maybe Moore was in his office at the back. Maybe the profs were all in class. Maybe Sylvia was off sick. She opened the door to the department office and there, ever so professorial in his khaki pants and tweed jacket, loomed Dr. David Moore, the Chair, talking with Sylvia, his assistant.

"Good morning," Colleen said.

"Did you all have trouble getting in today? I don't know what was happening on the Bloor line, but my God, the number of people! I waited for three or four trains to go by before I managed to get on one."

Dr. Moore merely crossed his arms. Sylvia stood next to her tidy desk, with her tight little sweater, unbuttoned just so, and her shiny black bob and oh-so-hip retro nerd glasses, her deep plum lipstick and those appalling furry boots. She smiled, tapping a file folder and said, "I'm glad I live close enough to walk to work."

"Aren't you lucky?" Colleen hung her coat on the rack, stuffed her purse in her drawer and sat down in front of the alarmingly high pile of papers and folders on her desk. Things had been so much better when Eppie Goldman was David's assistant; she had been a lovely old thing, even if she did have that unfortunate gum-chewing habit, and besides, when she retired *Colleen* should have been promoted to Assistant to the Chair. They shouldn't have hired from outside.

Why didn't David say anything? What had he and Sylvia been talking about? Sylvia looked at her and widened her eyes in the oddest way, and then glanced down to the file she'd been tapping a moment before.

Old Harry Barnes wandered in just then from the back hallway where the professors had their offices. Colleen liked Harry a great deal. He reminded her of an aged heron, or a stork. He made her think of an elderly Jimmy Stewart, especially in how kind he was, and gentle. His field was Historical Geography, the study of human, physical, fictional, theoretical and "real" geographies of the past. He always used those little air quotes around the word *real,* which Colleen found endearing.

"Colleen, dear, I have been waiting for you. We've so much to do today. Class at ten, you know, and I need the handouts I gave you Friday."

Handouts? What was he talking about? "I'm sorry, Harry, which . . .?"

Sylvia and David, who still hadn't said anything, watched her. Sylvia pressed her lips together as though trying not to say something. She inched the file on her desk toward Colleen. David's face had gone a little red and his mouth was set in that way it did when he was annoyed.

"I don't quite remember, but I'm sure they're here." Colleen just needed a few minutes to settle in, just a couple of minutes to catch her breath.

"Growth and Urbanization, 1860–1920," said Harry, as he riffled through one of the piles on Colleen's desk.

"Are you sure you gave them to me?" She picked up a pile of papers from her to-do basket, which was admittedly a bit fuller than it should be. A paper to be typed for

45

Professor Rose, the Medical Geographer, on dengue fever; something on the Olorgesailie prehistoric site in the Kenyan Rift Valley for Michael Banville; expense accounts to be tallied . . .

"Quite sure, I'm afraid. And I do need them rather urgently."

Sylvia coughed. "Colleen?"

Colleen looked at her. She was staring down at that thick file on her desk. Was that *the* file? *What the hell?*

David Moore and Harry Barnes looked at Sylvia now as well. Sylvia's skin was mottled.

"This might be it," Sylvia said, picking up the file. "It just got misplaced, I'm sure."

Colleen stared at the folder. She didn't trust this. She had no recollection of making the copies. Misplaced my ass, she thought. Sylvia was holding out the folder and she had no choice but to take it. She opened it and sure enough: *Growth and Urbanization, 1860–1920.*

"Did you make those copies, Colleen?" asked Moore.

It was very hard to know what to say. If only she could remember, but nothing was clear and everything was happening so fast, she couldn't think. "It's just copies, right, and here they are . . ."

She held them out to Harry, who grabbed them. "No matter, no matter. No harm done. All's well and all that," he said as he scurried out of the office.

46

David Moore asked, "Did you or did you not make those copies, Colleen?"

There was a trap here, she knew there was, but she couldn't see it. She couldn't see where to step. What if Sylvia had taken the file purposefully, to try to make her look bad? The idea of sabotage swelled thickly in her chest.

"I didn't give her anything. If she has them, she took them on purpose. It's all on her."

"Oh, Colleen," said Sylvia softly. "That's not what happened."

And from the hurt, puzzled look on Sylvia's face, who couldn't possibly be that good an actor, Colleen knew she had blown it. She felt the same flush she saw on Sylvia's face appear on her own. The blood rushing to the surface of her skin felt like hot needles. Maybe she could still back out.

"Maybe I forgot. We were so busy."

Moore ran his hand over his head. "I can't believe I'm having this conversation about bloody photocopies. Fine. Sylvia, did you make the copies or not? I want a straight answer."

"I just did them, that's all," she said as she fiddled with the pens and papers on her desk. She glanced at Colleen. "I was going to give them to you . . . I was only trying to help. I didn't mean . . . I mean, I thought I'd see you before . . ." She flicked her eyes toward David.

"I was going to do it," said Colleen.

"Were you?" David Moore looked unconvinced.

Her ears were so hot she was afraid they might ignite and the space under her desk looked remarkably inviting. "Of course I was." But was she? She didn't even remember Harry giving them to her. What had she been doing on Friday? It seemed so long ago. She went out for lunch with Pam, the department's librarian. They'd gone to Le Select Bistro for a bit of a Friday afternoon treat.

Colleen turned to face Sylvia and David. She was trembling and the only thought in her mind was to get the hell out of there. How could she have messed up such a simple task? She tried so hard and wanted so much to be a good employee. She was always five minutes away from being the person she wanted to be. She would be better. She would do better.

But there was Sylvia, the Cheshire Bitch. "I'd appreciate it if you would let me do my own work, Sylvia. Taking the papers only confused matters. I don't understand what your agenda is."

"My agenda?" said Sylvia. "Honestly, Colleen, I just wanted to help. I didn't mean to make anything worse."

"Let's just get on with it, shall we?" David said. "Colleen, I wonder if you'd mind coming with me for a few minutes?"

He walked out of the main office and down the hallway without even looking at her. Colleen felt as though she'd swallowed a large chunk of ice.

"It'll be okay," said Sylvia. "I'm really sorry."

Go to hell, thought Colleen, as she followed Dr. Moore.

When did this hall get so long? Her heels echoed on the tile floor and bounced off the glass-fronted doors. The fluorescent lighting made the walls look like those of a mortuary and for an instant Colleen imagined her own skin under those lights, how much like the walking dead she must look. David Moore had never liked her, not since she'd been so sick just before her mother had the strokes. She'd had walking pneumonia, she was sure of it, and she took time off to get better. She coughed so much she threw up. The spasms were so violent she wondered if she'd cracked a rib. Just as she got back on her feet, her mother's crisis dictated more time off to deal with the hospitals and social workers and all that. David had called three times a week, demanding to know when she was coming back to work and asking for a medical certificate. She got him the damn certificate. She'd been offended then and it still rankled. No one had ever asked her for a medical certificate before. Moore was a little bean-counting bureaucrat. He never reprimanded Sylvia the way he did her, even though Sylvia spent as much time on the phone with her boyfriend as she did working.

Colleen stepped into the office. David Moore was already on the phone. How rude, Colleen thought. Hadn't he just asked her to come in?

"Five minutes? Fine. Right. Thanks," he said into the receiver and then replaced it in the cradle. "Come in, Colleen. Close the door, please."

His big oak desk was in front of a window, which was the only wall not covered in book shelves, one of which, to the right, included a locked cabinet containing his prize collection of antique metrological equipment: several brass barometers, a rotating vane anemometer, a brass hair hygrometer and mercury thermometer, several pocket forecasters, and a number of other metal objects for which Colleen had no name. His desk was tidy—three stacks of papers arranged with scientific precision, his fountain pen and matching pencil resting like surgical instruments in a silver tray. The photos of his wife and daughter in matching silver frames. He drummed his fingers on the spotless leather-edged blotter and then with a wave of his hand indicated she should sit down.

Colleen sat in one of the two leather chairs facing him. Moore was silhouetted against the light, making his features indistinct, shadowy. The sun had come out and the brightness made Colleen squint and want to shield her eyes. She couldn't help but wonder if he knew how this backlighting made him look like some great inquisitor, and if he liked that. She folded her hands in her lap and sat ramrod straight. She was tempted to look down to see if the thumping of her heart was actually visible beneath her turtleneck. It was absurd. She was only a year or two younger than Moore. To be made to feel like a child called to the principal's office was offensive. The way he looked so stern, so authoritative. He'd only been Chair for a year, Colleen thought, and yet you'd think he'd been crowned King.

Two years ago, when she first came to the department from her previous job in the History Department, when Michael Banville was Chair, the whole place was more fun. They went for lunch together, had drinks together. Michael even hosted them all at his farm for a weekend. Moore would never do anything like that. He kept his distance from the rest of the department. He probably didn't think he was up to the job any more than she did and that's why he threw his weight around.

"Colleen," he said, his hands clasped, index fingers resting on the top of his nose, thumbs under his chin. "I wonder how you think you've been performing on the job the last while. I'd like your thoughts."

I'll bet he wouldn't, not if he really knew what was going on in my head. "I've been late a few times, I realize that. And if I hadn't been hijacked by this photocopying business I'd planned to tell you I was very sorry and that I'd be happy to stay late tonight to make it up."

"That won't be necessary," he said.

"I really don't mind."

"It's more than you just being late, Colleen."

"Is it?" The big toe on her right foot began to bother her, the way it sometimes did, as though the bone itself were itchy. She wriggled it around in her shoe. It didn't help.

"I think you know that."

"Let's say I don't." God, all she wanted to do was take her shoe off and scratch the little bastard. She couldn't help it; she reached down and rubbed the spot through her shoe.

"Are you all right? You look a little pale."

"I'm fine." *Stop, toe. Stop!* The sensation disappeared for a moment and then returned with a vengeance. Fuck it. She slipped her shoe off and scratched her toe violently. It hurt but that was the only way to make it stop. "Sorry. I've got an itch."

"Right, well—"

Someone knocked lightly and then, without waiting for an answer, opened the door. The woman who appeared wore a grey tweed suit with gold buttons that gave a military impression, and had a head of improbably red hair. Her hands, one of which now held the side of the door as her head poked round, were manly, even with the large sparkly rings on her fingers.

"Here I am, here I am. How is everyone?"

"Come in, Pat. Colleen, I don't know whether you know Pat Minot from Human Resources?"

Colleen fumbled with her shoe and got it back on. "Ah, no, I don't think so." She blinked several times and felt the blood that had rushed to her face and ears a few minutes before cascade to her abdomen.

"Hello, Colleen."

The woman held out her hand so Colleen had no choice but to shake it. She wanted to wipe her hands on her pants, since they'd become moist in the past half-second, but she couldn't do that; she couldn't look like she was panicking.

"Nice to meet you," Colleen said, and shook hands. She noticed that after the woman pulled back her hand, she folded her arms for a moment to discreetly wipe her own palm on her jacket sleeve.

Pat Minot took the seat next to Colleen's and turned her attention to David Moore. "Where are we?" she asked.

"I was just asking Colleen how she felt she'd been performing recently."

"Very good." Minot turned to her and smiled. She had a square, potato-y sort of face. If she'd been a man, Colleen could have imagined her as an Irish priest, about to have a heart-to-heart with a juvenile delinquent. "And how *do* you feel you've been performing, Colleen?"

Colleen suspected, in a wave of icy hopelessness, that it didn't matter much what she felt. The scene must be played out. "I've been late a few times, and perhaps a bit distracted. My mother, you see, she's had a series of mini-strokes, and it's resulted in brain damage. I'm her only living relative and it's been very difficult, getting her into nursing care, dealing with the doctors, cleaning out her condo. She'd been hoarding, I'm sorry to say, and I can't tell you the things I found in there. The shower stall was packed, floor to ceiling, with laxatives and toilet paper—and yes, I do see the irony in that—and bags of raisins, for some reason, and tooth paste . . ." Moore and Minot exchanged glances. "I'm rambling, I suppose, but I can't tell you how difficult it's been. If I've forgotten a thing or two at work, well, I would hope my co-workers would understand."

"I see," said Pat Minot. "What a stressful situation. Caregiving for a parent is awfully hard. And I wonder if that hasn't contributed to what we suspect is the real problem."

"The real problem?" And here it comes, she thought.

"Dr. Moore, perhaps, since you're Colleen's supervisor, and you work with her on a daily basis, you'd like to continue?"

"Oh. Right. Yes." He took off his glasses and polished them with a little cloth he pulled from his inside jacket pocket. "It's quite sensitive, I suppose, but the complaints have been frequent."

"What complaints? From whom?" Colleen sat up a little straighter. The best defence might demand she bristle.

"If I might suggest, Dr. Moore, it's best to simply be direct here. As direct as possible."

"Right. Yes. The thing is, Colleen, we believe you have a problem that's affecting your performance here in the office."

"Do you?" Colleen stuck out her chin and pursed her lips.

"Let me be, as Ms. Minot says, *direct.* Colleen, do you have a drinking problem?"

Oh, Christ. "What are you talking about?" *As though Moore hadn't been tight as a violin string at the last start-of-the-semester party.*

"We believe you do." He held his hand up to stop her from speaking. "You're not really hiding it as well as you think you are."

If ever there was a moment to bristle, this was it. "I find your tone pretty insulting."

Moore sighed and replaced his glasses on his nose. "I am not here to judge you, Colleen, but the situation must be dealt with. We can't go on like this."

"It sounds very much like judgment to me. I resent this, David, I really do." It was important to sound confident and insulted. It was important to give the impression of shock. "You're making it sound as though I'm some sort of lush or something, and I don't know who's put these ideas into your head, although I suppose I can guess."

"There's no need to get excited, Colleen," said Pat Minot. "We'd like to help you."

"I don't *need* any help. I need to get back to my desk and do my work."

"Must we do this?" David looked at her as though he were a disappointed father.

Colleen realized it would be unwise, at this point, to say *fuck you,* but she reserved it for later. "David, come on. This is ridiculous; you're questioning my integrity here, and I don't like it one bit."

He sighed. "Fine. We'll do it this way, then, although I'm surprised we have to, since this is the third time we've had this sort of discussion about your performance—"

"You've never said anything about an alcohol problem!"

"Perhaps not, specifically, the drinking, but certainly your performance."

Colleen said nothing. What *could* she say?

"Right, then." He began to count off her failings on his fingers. "You are late virtually every day, and when you do arrive you're hungover and you smell of liquor. You do very little work until late morning, and then off you go to lunch, which is usually two hours, and sometimes, like last Friday, considerably longer, and when you come back it's clear you've been drinking. You are often inappropriate with co-workers as well as students, you lose things, forget to do what's asked of you, and, often as not, what you do has to be done over. It used to be that your work only suffered Mondays and perhaps Fridays, and we all knew about it and let it pass because, believe it or not, we really do care about you, Colleen. However, over the past six months or so things have gone from bad to much worse. I've spoken to you about your performance on several occasions, and I've given you written warning—haven't I done that?"

"Well, yes, but given what I've been going through . . ." Her mind raced like a demented greyhound. "I didn't think it was serious enough to warrant all this and I don't know what you mean by *inappropriate*. What does that mean?"

"Did you, or did you not . . . how do I put this delicately? . . . *fondle* Max Sinclair on Friday?"

"I did no such thing!" And she thought: if I had he would have liked it.

"You did, I'm afraid. I saw it myself. You grabbed Dr. Sinclair's buttocks and made a remark about coconuts—a song, in fact."

Pat Minot coughed into her hand. "Excuse me," she said.

I've got a luverly bunch of coconuts, sung in a Cockney accent. Colleen squirmed. She *might* have done that. It was possible there had been some teasing, but Max was young and handsome and funny as hell in that fabulous British way.

57

"I was joking. He didn't mind."

"I'm afraid he did, Colleen, especially since there were students present at the time, students who were also less than impressed." Moore cleared his throat. "And this isn't the first time this sort of thing has happened, now is it? Do we have to go over what happened at the start-of-term party?"

Ain't Nobody Worried

The main dining room in the Faculty Club was a cool sea of Wedgwood blue and white. Fairy lights hung in the potted weeping fig trees. The gold chandeliers gleamed. Faculty and grad students mingled and chatted over hors d'oeuvres—shrimp wrapped in bacon, little egg rolls, mini-quiches, smoked salmon. The bar was fully stocked and a DJ played jazz standards near a small dance floor.

Colleen had a Manhattan, and then another. They were delicious. She'd had a couple of glasses of wine at home, and was just starting to feel that happy cloud of confidence and goodwill toward men, and women too, for that matter. She wore a slinky black dress with a high collar and long sleeves. It hugged her curves. She might have put on just a pound or two since her skinny-malinks days, but that didn't mean she'd lost her sense of style. She hadn't lost her *allure,* that lovely word. *Allure . . .* it rolled around the tongue like a pearl.

She talked with Max Sinclair. He was so charming, even with those acne scars. They made his face interesting. She suspected he was gay, since he never had a woman with him and surely a man that handsome would have oodles of women. Besides he dressed so well. And he was funny. He gossiped about the other professors, especially Ron Porter, who he said had a tendency to dress in his wife's clothing. "Such a shame," he remarked, "since the poor old thing dresses like a vicar's mother." He told her how Mike Banville and Porter loathed each other. Mike was the sort of corduroy-and-khaki geographer most at home punting up the Orinoco. Ron was an urban planner with a model train set in his basement.

Colleen plucked the cherry out of her drink and sucked its potent juices. The liquor gave her such a lovely floating feeling. She arched her back. She imagined she was a ballet dancer.

"Did you know," said Max, "when Mike visited Alcatraz a few years back he sent Ron a postcard saying, 'Having a wonderful time. Wish you were here.' You have to love a man like that."

The second Manhattan pirouetted through her veins. She couldn't believe that glass, too, was nearly empty. She looked around at the groups of chatting academics, bottles of beer or glasses of white wine spritzers in their hands.

She drained her glass. "God, this party needs some spicing up, don't you think?"

"Well, it certainly calls for another drink," said Max. "Do you want one?"

"Absolutely. Go on." She winked at him.

He went to get the drinks and it occurred to her that what the party needed was some dancing. To hell with all this jazz stuff; the DJ must have something with a little R and B to it. She'd get them going.

The DJ smiled as she approached. He was too old to be a really hip DJ. He had to be at least forty-five, but then again, she wasn't exactly a twenty-year-old, was she. Still, she knew her music.

"Want to hear something?" he asked.

"Got any Motown, any Stax Records? Something with some life?"

"Stax, huh? You like that Southern soul?"

"The Staple Singers maybe?"

He grinned. "I might have a little Mavis here. Might have a little Albert King."

"Some Otis? Al Green?"

"I'd rather not get fired though, you know."

"I'll take full responsibility," Colleen said.

"You're on, Mama."

When the song that was playing finished, on came Mavis Staples' big voice, her deep, chesty *uh* of delight. She asked for the listener's help, so she could take them there . . . A couple of people looked around, but it was a brilliant choice, just jazzy enough to seem like part of the program. Colleen grinned and swayed to the beat. Yes indeed. People watched her. She didn't mind. She looked good, didn't she, in this slinky black dress, her hips swaying, a bit of belly-dancing roll here and there. She glanced around, looking for Max. He'd dance with her, get this thing off the ground.

She spotted him off by the bar but he didn't meet her eye. He was talking to the Dean. She kept dancing. Then the song stopped, too soon.

"Don't stop!" she called to the DJ.

He threw his hands up and shrugged.

"One more." She folded her hands as if in prayer.

The DJ glanced around a little nervously and then put on "The Best of My Love," by The Emotions. Perfect. That was it, a party song. A fun song. She motioned with her hands for some of the grad students to join her. A trio stood nearby. One was a bearded boy wearing a grey pullover. He tapped his foot in time to the song. She danced over and tried to pull him onto the floor. His friends laughed and he did, too, for a minute. And then he looked embarrassed.

"Thanks, but no. No thanks."

He tried to pull away, but she tightened her grip. "Come on, don't be a party pooper!"

"No, really! No *thanks*." He jerked away from her and walked away, past his laughing friends, leaving her standing there.

"Party pooper!" she called after him.

She finished out the song, although she had lost the limber, loose feeling of a few minutes before. She felt awkward and suddenly aware of disapproving eyes. She needed that drink Max had promised her. When the DJ played "Body and Soul," she glared at him, but threw in the towel and went off to get another Manhattan.

"Make it a good one," she told the bartender.

Half an hour later, she cornered David Moore behind a potted palm near the men's room and spent quite a bit of time telling him what was wrong with his department, zeroing in on the lack of women in influential positions.

"Universities are run by patriarchs," she said. "There's a lack of intuitive balance."

The smile on his face was brittle. He put his hand on her shoulder and said, "I don't think you want to have this conversation."

He was right, she didn't want to, but she couldn't stop herself; the words tumbled out of their own accord. She knew she was making perfect sense, if only he'd see. Eventually he simply walked away.

She felt close to tears, in part because of her frustration. He wouldn't *listen,* but then, too, as often happened when she'd had a little bit too much, a part of her mind stepped off to the left and watched the rest of her— watched and laughed. Practically brayed. She was not in control and knew herself not to be in control. She was at that point in the evening when she saw quite clearly things were happening that she did not want to happen. She was blurting out every little thing, and no one was more interested than she to hear what they might be. She feared she was making a fool of herself, but the train was hurtling down the track, the brakes completely blown. She tasted the whisky and orange of her drink. How many was this? Fuck it. Damn the torpedoes. She drained it.

That was a mistake. Within moments her stomach rebelled. There was no way she would make it all the way through the crowd to the ladies' room. No, it was the men's room or the potted palm. She lurched to the men's room, praying no one was inside. Vacant, thank the gods. Burst into a stall. Kicked the door shut behind her. Retched and heaved. *Up it came. Not so bad.* Some smeared mascara, and a need for mouthwash, but she would live. She might even get out of the men's room with nothing more than a giggle. *Sorry, wrong door!* She stepped out of the stall, only slightly stained, and who should be entering but the Dean of Arts and Science, Dr. John J. Stachell, a man with the face of an irritated rooster, a man with no sense of humour or compassion. He took one look at her and turned tail.

She became teary then, and the rest of the night was clouded in Manhattan mists. Someone, possibly Gloria from the Dean's Office, put her in a taxi.

The Centre of It All

Even if Colleen didn't remember precisely what happened that evening, she didn't see the necessity of going over it all again now.

But David Moore persisted. "I'm afraid we found the bottle of vodka in your desk. Or should I say *bottles*?"

There was a fifth of vodka in her bottom drawer, as well as a variety of small "nips," most of them empty. She'd been meaning to get rid of them, but lately someone always seemed to be hovering about. Colleen opened her mouth to say something, but nothing came out. All her clever words dried up and her throat felt as though someone had stuffed it with gas-soaked rags.

"That is quite against university policy," said Pat Minot. "I'm sure you're aware of that."

"Yes, of course, they were just things I meant to take home. I don't drink on the job."

"But you do, Colleen," said Moore, leaning forward, his elbows on his spotless blotter. "I've seen you myself, grabbing a little sip or two in the kitchen when you think no one's looking. You go into the bathroom and come out stinking. You think no one can smell it, but of course we can. You're reeking of it now."

She felt like crying, and she mustn't. She just had to get out of this office. If she could just have a few minutes to herself. She swallowed and took a breath. "I haven't had anything to drink today. It's nine o'clock in the morning, for God's sake."

"Colleen." Minot inched her chair closer. "Even I can smell it, dear, which means, if you haven't had anything to drink today, and I believe you on that front, I do, that you were drinking heavily last night and it's coming out of your pores. It's your body's way of trying to cleanse itself." She tried to take one of her hands, but Colleen pulled away. "All right. All right. But this is a crucial moment, for you, Colleen, and you have to make a decision. You are at a crossroads."

"I don't know what you mean." Colleen sniffed and her eyes stung. Her head was pounding.

Pat Minot reached into her pocket and pulled out a plastic package of tissues. She handed it to Colleen, who took it but did not pull one out; she wouldn't give them that.

"You have been issued warnings, both verbal and written, and yet your performance continues to deteriorate. We believe you are an alcoholic and we want you to get help with your problem. Indeed, the university is willing to assist you. Our benefits will provide for time at a treatment centre and you can use the little sick leave you have left, as well as long-term leave, for the thirty days you'll be away."

Alcoholic. Away. Treatment centre. Colleen began to shake in earnest, the tremors starting in her thighs and moving into her belly and arms. She clenched her muscles, trying to control them, but that only made it worse. She shifted in her seat, rocking a little in an attempt to disguise the shudders.

"But here's the bottom line, Colleen. You will agree to go home today, right now, since we don't feel you're in fit condition to work, and go into treatment tomorrow—I have arranged a bed for you at the Jane Ward Centre—or else we will be forced to terminate your employment, effective immediately. If you choose the first option, your job will be waiting for you upon successful completion of the thirty-day program, provided there are no further such incidents. You will also be tested for drug use, randomly, and for so long as we deem necessary." Minot held her hand up, seeing Colleen was about to protest. "Let me finish, Colleen. If, however, you choose the second option—the termination— you will receive the severance and vacation pay owing to you, but that is all. The decision is entirely yours, Colleen, but Dr. Moore and I hope you will take the help we're offering you. If you get, and stay, sober you can have a wonderful, healthy and productive life, Colleen, of that I have no doubt, but if you continue in this manner, your future is very dim indeed."

Colleen wondered what gave this woman, whom she had never met before today, the right to tell her what her future would be like. If Colleen had Minot's life, maybe she wouldn't drink either. But she had *her* life, a fucking mess of a beat-down existence and who the hell wouldn't have a drink? The idea of living without a drink at the end of each soul-numbing day to soften the wretched loneliness of it all was impossible to imagine. The truth was, she was dying for a drink right now.

She rubbed her temples, willing the jackhammers over her eyes to quit it. "I've worked at the university for years."

"We are aware of that," the woman said, "but it doesn't change anything."

Colleen looked from Moore to Minot, back and forth, and everything became still. It was interesting: the direr the situation, the calmer Colleen typically became. She knew this about herself. She was one of those people who seemed made for crisis. Doubtless this skill was the better part of the legacy of growing up in a house with a madwoman.

It occurred to her that everything happening now might just be a trick of the light, some hallucination into which she'd fallen, like Alice down the rabbit hole. She might still be safe in her bed, dreaming a foul, cruel-hearted dream. She blinked, and then held her hands up to her eyes, pressing until black and white geometric patterns appeared on the inside of her lids. Take it back, God, she prayed, please take all of this morning back and I promise I'll be better. She'd promised she wasn't going to drink today and, so far, she hadn't. This was some perverse joke of the universe, of some malevolent God focused entirely on her. Pound, pound, pound went the blood in the vessels across her forehead.

With any luck, she was having a stroke.

"We need your answer now, I'm afraid," said Moore.

Colleen opened her eyes and was disappointed but not surprised to find everything just as it had been. Was she never to get a break? Never to have a chance? The faces of her accusers were stern, implacable, and just a little hungry. Oh, yes, how everyone loved to stick the knife in, to wiggle it. They were untouchable on their moral high-ground, where the air was so very fucking rarified and a thick shiny gate, made of money and privilege, and the kind of education Colleen deserved but didn't get, protected them from having anyone do to them what they were doing to her.

"Do you," she said. "You need an answer this very minute?"

They nodded, like bobble-heads.

She knew what the right answer was. She understood she should take their help in her trembling, grateful palms; she should break down in girlish tears and thank them for their concern and consideration and tell them how long she'd been drinking against her own will (which might be true but was none of their fucking business) and she understood this was probably the moment when her life could be saved. She looked down at her hands, clutching the cheap package of tissues. There was a stain of some sort on the hem of her turtleneck. She hadn't noticed it when she dressed this morning. It was something yellowish and crusty. Colleen imagined Moore and Minot—their names sounded like some snotty law firm—congratulating themselves as the taxi took her off to a rehab centre. She imagined Moore talking to his skinny, buck-toothed wife over a wine-and-candlelight dinner about poor Colleen Kerrigan and what an awful mess she was. She imagined the narrow cot in the shared rehab room, the linoleum floor, the shoddy dresser, the communal showers, and group therapy with droopy losers whining about finding a higher power and turning their lives over to God and heaven help her she'd slit her wrists with a fork.

"I'm very sorry my work hasn't been up to snuff. I promise you'll have no further cause for complaint, for any reason," Colleen said.

"So you'll take the help we're offering?" asked Minot.

The woman must watch those reality shows on television with the snot-flying, tearful interventions for hopeless addicts, thought Colleen. She had the vocabulary down. Colleen had seen a few of them herself, enough to know that if you watched to the very end, the drunks and dopers all got thrown out of rehab, or left early, and ended up back on the bottle or the needle within months. What was the point, except to make the snivelling family members feel better, if only briefly?

"I've told you my work won't be a problem. I think that's all I should have to say."

Moore blew out his cheeks and said, "So, you're telling us you won't go into treatment."

"I'm telling you you'll never have to worry about me and alcohol."

"That's not good enough at this point, Colleen. Your choice is rehab or having your employment here immediately terminated."

"So, you're telling *me* you care about me so much you'd fire me, leave me without a paycheque or references, with my mother in extreme difficulty and me her only caregiver, with no one to help me. That's what you're telling me and you think that's right, that it's moral?" She heard the steely control in her voice, and she knew herself well enough to recognize the fury saddling up and getting ready to ride.

"Will you go to rehab, Colleen?" said Moore. "Say yes now, or I'm afraid this interview is over and you will be escorted from the building. Am I right, Ms. Minot?"

Minot's expression of concern was like that of a bad soap-opera actress. So much care in it. So much practiced compassion. It felt as though something very heavy, like stones or bags of wet sand, lay over Colleen's shoulders and chest. The weight held her down, made it hard to breathe. Screaming was an option. Baring her teeth and snarling like a cornered leopard was an option. Spontaneous combustion was an option. And for one swift second it occurred to her there was another option: she might merely toss the bags and the sand and the stones right off her shoulders and let them hit the floor with the sound of thunder and earthquake and the very heavens splitting asunder. The floor would open and swallow up all the terrible crushing mass, and bury it in the ground, dust to dust. It was possible. She had a fleeting sense of how light she would feel, how she'd float up to the ceiling a hope-filled thing, and it wouldn't matter if she needed help or if these people pitied her or felt they were better than she was because just letting it all go would be such an enormous relief.

And then Pat Minot said, "That would be a great shame, but yes, I'm afraid that's the way it is."

The way it is. Yes, that's just the way it is and nothing would ever change and people are who they are and so they ever will be. Colleen knew then that she was never going to get out from under the load of her own life. We play our parts. It is inevitable. She was not the sort of woman who would go to rehab, who would hand over her power to a bunch of strangers who were paid to pretend to care about her. She would not, *could* not show them who she really was. Her skin crawled. The very concept filled her with self-loathing. Whatever weight had shifted now lurched and settled itself again, right over Colleen's heart.

Colleen stood up and smoothed the front of her pants. "Well, then. Fuck you very much," she said.

The room was silent for a moment, and even though Colleen's head felt as though it might pop like the mercury in an overheated thermometer, she got considerable satisfaction from the looks of true astonishment on Moore's and Minot's faces. They really hadn't seen that coming, had they? She was able to arrange a small, self-contained smile on her lips, and for the first time since she woke up that morning, she felt a kind of dignity and control. Thus, she chose to think of it this way: things hadn't been good at this job for ages, and though she'd miss Harry, Max (well, maybe not Max, not after he'd said whatever it was he said about her) and Michael, she'd find somewhere else, somewhere better. And who knew, Harry might very well go to bat for her and protest her firing. Yes, that was a real possibility. Even Michael. He liked her. The possibilities spooled out in front of her like a yellow brick road.

"How sad," said Minot. She stood and faced Colleen for a moment, then turned and opened the door. A security guard stood in the hall, waiting. "We'll just walk you out then, shall we?"

The smile slipped from Colleen's face. What did they think she was going to do, go berserk, pull a gun out of her bra and shoot them all? Dignity and control, my ass, she thought. Humiliation like a riptide threatened to knock her legs out from under her. Maybe it wasn't too late? She glanced at Dr. Moore, but his face was aubergine. She felt a little weak.

So, that was that. She tossed the packet of tissues on Moore's desk. "I want my things from my desk."

"Of course," said Minot. She gestured that Colleen should precede her through the door. Then she changed her mind. "Actually, would you just wait here a moment, please. Derek, stay with Ms. Kerrigan, will you?"

The security guard nodded and Minot disappeared.

The moments ticked by. Colleen kept her eyes on the antique instruments in the locked cabinet. The mysterious devices of weather divination. They looked medieval, and she imagined torture chambers and trials by fire. A scene from a film she had once seen flashed through her mind, set in Elizabethan England, in which a man was dangled above a huge cauldron of boiling oil. The executioner asked him which he preferred, head first or feet first. It would make no difference, of course; death would come either way, horribly and in shrieking agony. Would she want to get it over quickly, head first, skin peeling off her face, eyes bursting, lips and tongue and throat searing and . . . or feet first, hoping to pass out from the pain before the oil reached . . . Why was she thinking of that now? Derek the security guard stood with his thumbs tucked into his belt. Executioner. Pitiless. Unreachable.

"Ms. Kerrigan?" Minot was back. "You can come through now."

Colleen refused to turn and look at Moore before leaving. Followed by Minot and Derek-the-Executioner, she walked stiff-legged and jerky, the trembles in her gut making any effort at grace impossible. She made her way to the office that was no longer her office. Sylvia wasn't there and Colleen supposed Minot had arranged that to prevent a scene. Colleen thought now she might well want to make a scene. It would be lovely to finally tell Sylvia what she thought of those boots, and those ridiculous turquoise glasses.

Two cloth shopping bags lay on her desk.

"You can put your things in there," said Minot.

At least we're being eco-friendly, thought Colleen, if not people-friendly.

There was surprisingly little to take. A small carved turtle one of the First Nations students had given her last Christmas, a framed photo of a winter landscape with late-afternoon light slanting through the trees that Colleen had clipped from a magazine because it looked so peaceful, a little leather notebook in which she had meant to write down her thoughts, two paperbacks, one of Celtic fairy tales, the other called *New Paths Toward the Sacred,* an old address book, a pretty fountain pen she'd bought herself and a glass paperweight in the shape of a star. On the bulletin board above her computer was an old Bloom County cartoon in which three little boys and a penguin contemplated the vastness of the universe and their place in it. One boy held up his thumb and index finger, measuring a minuscule space, and said, "That's the portion of the night sky at which they pointed the Hubble telescope for a week, the equivalent of a single grain of sand, and inside they found galaxies, thousands of galaxies with billions and trillions of stars and more beyond that." "And so what," one of the other boys asked, "is the centre of it all?" "Me," said one boy, and "Me," said the other.

Colleen left it where it was.

"Do you have everything?" asked Minot. She held out Colleen's red coat.

"I have a mug in the kitchen. I want that." She grabbed the coat and put it on, and was about to leave the office when Derek stepped in front of her. "Really?" she said.

Minot shrugged. "What does it look like? I'll get it."

The mug had a saying on it: *Peace is not the absence of chaos or conflict, but rather finding yourself in the midst of that chaos and remaining calm in your heart.* "Never mind," Colleen said.

She opened the bottom drawer of her desk to get her purse. The bottles of vodka were gone.

"It's no bother," said Minot. "Which one is it?"

Colleen picked up the shopping bag. "Get out of my way," she said to Derek.

He moved aside and she walked down the hall, her purse on her shoulder and the depressingly light shopping bag dangling at the end of her arm. Derek walked behind her. People she knew—Ann from the Registrar's Office, Brian and Eric from Political Science—passed her, smiled tightly and looked first confused, and then—with telling swiftness—embarrassed.

Did everyone know? Colleen thought how pleasant it would be to stroke out right there and then. One could never summon an aneurysm when one needed it

Harpreet, the handsome, turbaned Sikh from the Department of Statistics, looked up from the papers he carried and said, "What's up, Colleen?"

"Not a great day," she said, and kept walking.

He looked about to say something else and then, glancing at Derek, stood with his mouth slightly agape and let her pass, as though she were a criminal being perp-walked into court.

In the elevator three students, two girls and a boy, disregarded Colleen and Derek, focused as they were on texting, their thumbs flying furiously over the tiny keyboards, their ears plugged with headphones. What did it matter? Colleen was largely invisible to the students now anyway. She was a middle-aged secretary, totally ignorable. Or, more correctly, she *used to be* a middle-aged secretary.

They exited the elevator at the ground floor. At the steel and glass exit Derek said, "Let me get that for you," and held a door open.

This small gesture of kindness created an unexpected prickling behind her eyelids and she was afraid to thank him for fear her voice would break.

She stepped out onto the open concrete plaza in front of the building. Students and professors hustled by, arms full of books and papers. Other sat on benches drinking coffee and chatting. The hot-dog cart from which Colleen had occasionally bought her lunch was already set up by the curb. The trees, encircled by metal benches, had lost their leaves and looked frail and brittle under the cloud-heavy sky.

"Do you want me to get you a cab?" Derek asked.

Did she want a cab? She supposed so, since even the idea of getting back on the subway caused a cramping panic in her chest so strong she was afraid she might scream. But where would she go? What did one do in a case like this? She saw herself standing on the Leaside Bridge, her red coat flapping in the wind. Not long ago, two University of Toronto students jumped to their deaths there. It would be quick and final, and she'd still be part of the university community.

"I don't," she said, and kept walking.

Goodbye, job.

The question now became, where should she go? What was the post-firing protocol? She didn't want to be seen just standing on the sidewalk, hopeless, lost and, she suspected, alarmingly red of face. Everyone she looked at walked with purpose; they all had somewhere to go, something to do, lives to lead. Even that crazy person across the street, wearing shorts, a T-shirt with holes in it, flip-flops and what looked like a helmet made of tinfoil, even *he* strode along with such speed—arms pumping, chin thrust forward—that he gave the impression of intent.

For want of a better idea, Colleen began walking up St. George toward Harbord and the Robarts Library. As she crossed the intersection, a gust of cold wind caught her and she realized her coat was unbuttoned. She stopped in front of the library building, put the bag down and did up her coat. *Bag lady.* Is that what she was? Is that where she was going to end up? She picked up the bag and walked faster.

All around her people went about their business and chatted with each other, jostled and joked, and not a single one knew her world had just imploded. She looked at her watch. 10:00. How was that possible? Had everything really just happened in a mere half-hour? The unfairness of it, the injustice, rushed up from her stomach and filled her mouth with an acid burn. She was going to vomit. She stopped. Leaned against a utility pole and dropped her head. She breathed through her mouth. The sidewalk dipped and swayed under her feet.

"Are you okay?"

Colleen looked into the eyes of a woman about her age, wearing what appeared to be construction-worker clothes: plaid lumber jacket, stained down vest, droopy jeans and Timberland boots. The woman's hair was cut like a man's and her face was heavily lined.

"I don't think so."

The woman put her hand under Colleen's elbow. "You gonna puke? Pass out? You need an ambulance?"

"No, no." Colleen pulled herself up and took a deep breath. "Just a bit of the flu, I think. Bit of a shock. I've had a shock." She was babbling. The woman might just call 9-1-1 if she kept this up. "I think I need a taxi. I should go home."

"You sure? Yeah, you look a bit the worse for wear, you know?" The woman grinned. "Been there myself a morning or two."

"I'm fine." Colleen pulled her elbow away.

"Right," the woman said. She stepped to the curb and whistled loudly through her teeth. "Got one." A cab slowed in front of them. The woman turned back to Colleen. "There you go. Ginger ale and pickle juice is my advice. My Polish grandfather told me about the pickle juice. Works a charm."

If she couldn't find any battery acid, Colleen vowed to try it. She got into the cab. "Thank you," she said, for she believed the rituals of courtesy functioned as a privacy screen at times like this.

The woman saluted and moved off.

The cab smelled of pine air freshener, coffee and wet wool. "Where to?" the driver asked.

She didn't want to go home. She wanted to talk to someone who would tell her everything was going to be all right and that the university was full of assholes. But everyone she knew was working. She gave the driver her address on Davisville. It didn't occur to her until they reached Bloor that she might not have enough money in her purse to pay for this. How much would it be? Twenty dollars? Twenty-five? She scrambled in her purse and found her wallet. It contained sixty dollars. The question was, did she want to spend all that on taxi fare, today of all days? The answer was, why the hell not?

"Driver," she said. "Change of plans. Drop me at Yonge and Eglinton."

"Whatever you say."

Colleen looked at the photo identification tag on the back of the driver's seat. The name was *Abdullah Elbaz*. She doubted he would approve of the stop she intended to make. She wondered if what Minot had said was true. Were her pores really secreting alcohol? Could everyone smell it on her?

She couldn't tell if this odd, distanced feeling she had now was due to shock, from which she acknowledged she must be suffering, or some remnant of the hangover. She watched the world slip by outside the taxi window almost as though it were moving and the taxi were standing still, as though the scenery—the Varsity Blues Stadium, the fractured architecture of the Royal Ontario Museum, the little Church of the Redeemer nestled against all that glass and steel, the ragtag shops, the train bridge, the apartment buildings—all of it was on some enormous conveyor belt, making the city and all it contained—every person and shrub, every building and trash can—an experience to be had but not something to which one became attached. A little bubble world. She moved along behind glass and metal and no one knew her or why she was in the cab in the middle of the morning, heading to a liquor store. This was not the way she had thought she'd spend the day. This wasn't the way she had thought she'd spend her life.

Magic Fairy Potion

The first time Colleen got drunk, she was fourteen. Danny Gibson's parents had gone away for the weekend and under such circumstances a party was practically mandatory.

Okay, maybe Colleen was only there because Tricia and Crystal—the two popular girls, one dark and curvy, the other blond and willowy—were going and they let Colleen tag along, but still, she was *there.* Daniel was sixteen, tall and athletic, and had once been accidently pierced through the calf by an arrow his next-door neighbour shot, which gave him an air of manly, warrior-like glamour.

She remembered so clearly the moment the drinking started. One minute they were all in the yellow kitchen, everyone giggling with pot-induced hilarity, as Danny displayed his talent for making the kitchen "work." He turned on the blender, the toaster, the radio; he made the oven's timer ring, and through some secret knowledge given to him by his father, who worked for the phone company, he dialled a special number and a moment later the phone rang, although no one was on the other end. The kitchen looked possessed by the ghost of Betty Crocker. Seemore, so named because he had so many holes in his jeans and you could always "see more" of him than anyone else, had apparently dropped acid and sat cross-legged on the kitchen table while examining a cut-glass ashtray with transcendent concentration.

Even though she wasn't the only fourteen-year-old at the party, Colleen felt a little bit like the annoying, merely tolerated younger sister. The week before, when she admitted to the willowy Crystal that she *liked* Danny, Crystal had smirked, stretched out her impossibly long legs and said, "I wouldn't get my hopes up; he likes the model type, not some kid with her nose always stuck in the middle of a dusty old book." Until that moment, Colleen hadn't given much thought, one way or the other, to whether she was "the model type," nor to the idea that reading was in any way unattractive. Now, watching Crystal drape her thin arm so casually across Frank Boyden's shoulder (Frank being the most sought-after boy in school, with his long black hair and blue eyes), it seemed she peered through a kind of glass separation, a sort of bell jar, like the one Sylvia Plath, whom Colleen had recently discovered, talked about. She felt dangerously close to weepy.

"You want some?" asked Brad Rogers, known to his friends as the Barbarian. He had brought a selection of bottles to the kitchen from the Gibsons' liquor cabinet. Brown ones and green ones and clear ones. He poured himself half a glass of brown liquid. "Whisky," he said. "Makes everything better." He took a drink and shivered, smacked his lips and said, "Aaaaahhhh."

"Give me one," said Crystal, stepping in front of Colleen. "Vodka. Danny," she called over her shoulder, "you have any orange juice?"

The kitchen was returning to its normal, inanimate state as Danny switched the various appliances off. "Yeah, sure, but don't drink all that. My parents will have a fit."

He picked up the phone and set it down again, silencing it in mid-ring. Strains of "Honky Tonk Women" came from the living room. Crystal slid to Brad's side and took her glass.

"Aren't you having any?" she asked Colleen, and then grinned with her perfect rosy lips and her perfect straight white teeth. "You're just a kid really, aren't you?"

For the first time, Colleen wasn't entirely sure Crystal was really her friend, or even that Crystal liked her. She suspected she might be the sort of sidekick the pretty girls only kept around to make themselves look better by comparison.

Colleen picked up a glass and poured herself some whisky, and then, just for good measure, she poured a little from the green bottle, which she recognized as crème de menthe, into the glass as well. She was quite sure the minty taste would make the whisky go down easier.

"Bottoms up," she said, which is what her father said.

"Really?" Crystal shrugged, and turned to get her orange juice.

The liquor burned going down and for a moment Colleen was afraid it was going to come right back up, but it didn't. She coughed a little, but no more. It tasted like minty fire and ice; sweet, but also smoky and earthy. The possibility that it held hidden properties and purposes flashed through her mind. It seared her tongue and the inside of her cheeks. The liquids were not completely blended and a little bright green lingered on the side of the glass like a magic fairy potion. She drank more, and that's when it happened. She heard, or rather *felt,* a tiny, but clearly audible click, and when she looked around her at the people she thought she knew, she understood all the things she hadn't understood before, including that she was perfect and pretty and just as smart as anyone else. The kitchen took on a warm, sunny glow, and everyone looked so friendly.

"I don't know if I'd mix like that," said Brad, with something in his voice that Colleen understood to be awe.

"It's perfect. I'll have some more," she said, and she did. She laughed at Brad with his pimply skin and John Lennon glasses. She saw how hard he was trying to fit in, too, just like her. Even Crystal, with her thick blond hair that fell all the way to her waist and her superior air, standing there with her chest stuck practically in Frank Boyden's face—Colleen understood she was afraid no one would like her for anything except her big boobs. Danny, who a moment before had seemed so in control of everything, even the electricity, now seemed nervous, taking tiny sips from a bottle of beer and telling a girl to use a coaster on his mother's coffee table. They were all the same and all just trying to get along and she was filled with enormous goodwill toward everyone, and she wanted to dance, and pulled Brad out into the living room so they could do just that.

Things got pretty fuzzy then. Later she remembered dancing, and stumbling back into the record player, which was hilarious, but then there was something of a break in the action, and she was crawling on all fours between the living room and the kitchen, when the side door opened and she was looking up into the astonished and furious faces of Mr. and Mrs. Gibson. Then she was sitting out on the lawn, on the curb by the side of the road, but the lawn wouldn't stay still and undulated like a riffled rug. Her mother appeared and Colleen was in the car and she didn't feel well, and someone in the back seat said she had eaten something bad at the party, and her mother glared at her and then she was sick, and it was coming out her mouth and through her fingers. There was another gap after that, and then she was in the bathroom at home, sitting on the cold tiles between the toilet and the bathtub, clutching the toilet as her mother loomed over her.

"Are you drunk?" her mother demanded, hands on her hips, a towel dangling from her fingers.

This seemed a funny question. Colleen felt remarkably dignified for someone sitting on the floor next to a toilet. With great care and enunciation, she replied, "I. Am. Plastered."

Her mother's face went white and she drew her hand back, way back, across her body to her opposite shoulder. Colleen understood she was about to be slapped, but she also remembered that if you were really drunk you didn't feel pain and so she watched in a purely analytical fashion as her mother's hand descended in a great arc toward her face. This won't hurt at all, she thought, and sure enough, it didn't, and under the force of the blow her head turned in slow motion so that she could watch the toilet tank approaching her forehead, although she didn't remember a thing after that.

The next day she discovered another couple of truths: people talked, and projectile vomiting does not make you popular in high school. And it was a long time after that before she drank again.

My People

"I'm having a party," she told Andrew, the liquor store clerk.

Andrew dyed his hair the shade of an eggplant and had a tattoo of black roses on his right forearm, which he had showed her a year or so ago, when she first saw it poking out of his long sleeved T-shirt. He had more, he'd said, but he couldn't show her those, and he winked. He also told her his girlfriend had a tattoo of corset lacings up her back. He was from Thunder Bay and had a degree in Computer Science, but couldn't get a job in his field.

Colleen knew most of the clerks at the LCBOs in the vicinity of her home and office—well, what used to be her office. She went out of her way to chat with them, as she did with most shopkeepers—the health-food store people, the bookstore owner, the dry cleaner. She liked to be part of a neighbourhood, part of a community. In the back of her mind she realized being on a first-name basis with the liquor store employees probably wasn't a good thing. It was like that old saying about how if you started getting calls on the bar phone you knew it was time to find a new bar. (Although now everyone had cell phones, that probably didn't make much sense. Yet further evidence she was old.) But with the liquor store employees it seemed particularly important. She didn't like to admit it, but sometimes she felt a little embarrassed going in to buy yet another bottle of this or that. She used several shops, and tried not to go to the same one twice in the same week, but there were times it couldn't be helped, like now. She'd been here on Friday and bought the vodka that now stood, near empty, on her counter at home.

"Not a big party," she said," just a few people over." She wondered, now and again, what they thought about how much she entertained.

"So, what do you need?" asked Andrew.

"Well, a couple of bottles of wine, I suppose. I'm serving chicken, so white. Maybe a nice Chablis. And I guess a bottle of vodka, I think they like vodka."

"No problem," said Andrew.

"It's quite the occasion, actually," she said. "We're celebrating."

"That's nice. This do?" He held out a bottle of the Canadian wine she usually bought. Inexpensive and drinkable.

He wasn't very talkative today. Not like Matt. Matt was always up for a joke, always made her feel like they were, well, almost friends. "Do you like it? What about your girlfriend? What's her name again?"

"Gretchen. It's okay, like I said. You want it?"

"Fine. I think I'll take three bottles." Between wine and vodka, she'd be good for a nice long while. Not that she'd drink much of it, but it was good to have it in the house. She'd ask Lori to come over tonight and commiserate. They'd share a bottle. She wouldn't drink any more than that. "We're celebrating my liberation," she said, following Andrew through the aisle to the vodka section.

"Oh, right. Nice. You want a 750-millilitre? Absolut, right?"

"What about this one?" Colleen pointed at a bottle that was half the price.

"Nothing wrong with that."

"I'll try it, then."

As they walked to the cash, Andrew asked, "So, what's the liberation about?"

"I've left my job." That was factual, after all. She *had* decided she would leave the stupid job. She hadn't let them call all the shots. Her dignity had demanded she quit, given the way they treated her. That was the truth, wasn't it? Of course. She refused to think about it any other way.

"Huh," said Andrew. "Well, good luck."

He put the bottles down on the cash counter, nodded at her and disappeared, just like that. It was a bit rude, really.

"Find everything you need?" the cashier asked. She was Indian, thin as a stick, with purple lips and long hair tied up in a high ponytail.

Colleen didn't know her, and although ordinarily she'd try and strike up a little conversation, exhaustion chose that moment to ripple up from her toes like a heat wave. She suddenly wanted nothing more than to lie down on the couch with a glass of wine and watch some mindless television. She could have one glass of wine, given what she'd just gone through. Anyone would. They'd have two.

"I'm good," she said, and paid. "I've don't need a carry-bag; I've got one. I'll put the bottles in here, if you can just put them in paper bags so they don't break."

It felt good to have that done, she thought as she walked out of the store. It was reassuring. She wouldn't have to worry about having wine in the house if someone came over later. And someone would, surely. Lori, probably, but maybe she'd call Helen, who lived in a basement apartment in a house down the street. Maybe Colleen would stop by Helen's. Helen was several years older than Colleen and had panic attacks so severe she'd become agoraphobic, so she was on disability. Her company, some bank, had screwed her over too, saying they weren't going to pay, or something, but Helen had sued and the company settled. Colleen should talk to her about that lawsuit. Maybe *she* should sue? She had grounds, she was sure of it. The university had tons of money.

A young man stood outside the mall entrance, begging for money. He held a sign. LOOKING FOR WORK. HUNGRY. He wore an army surplus jacket, and was so thin his shoulder blades jutted up like a hanger under his clothes. Colleen fumbled in her pocket and pulled out a loonie, dropping it into his outstretched, utterly filthy palm.

"God bless," he said. There were sores around his mouth and nose.

My people, she thought, as she imagined herself standing on a similar corner one day in the future, and then, *don't be so dramatic.*

The bag was heavy and the weather growing uglier by the minute. The clouds roiled overhead and it was certainly about to rain. She could take the subway down one stop to Davisville, and then grab the bus or walk, but getting home seemed more urgent by the moment, and cabs would be impossible to get once it started raining.

She flagged a cab and was home in minutes. There was nobody around at this time of day—all out, she thought, at their pointless little jobs. The elevator was empty, although it smelled of someone's woodsy perfume. The hallway on her floor was empty. Key in the lock, door open and then she was inside, putting her bag and purse down on the kitchen counter. She felt shaky. She didn't mean to do it, didn't intend to do it, but she took a glass out of the cabinet and into it she poured the last of what remained in the open vodka bottle. It filled the glass more than halfway.

"Hello, little fairy. Here's to new beginnings," she said as she raised her glass.

She dropped her coat on one of the four wooden chairs around the small table in the dining area, and slouched over to the couch. She flopped down and took another drink from the glass. Warm, she thought. So nice and warm. The warmth slid down her throat and when it hit her stomach it blossomed and slipped along the inside of her arms, down her thighs and behind her knees, all the way to her toes. Another sip, sip, sip.

A row of windows ran waist-high along the wall to the combined living–dining room. A door led to a tiny empty balcony she never used. It was ugly and graceless and overlooked the parking lot. Last January a fatally optimistic pigeon built a nest out there and laid eggs. She heard it chirping, loudly and insistently, but when she opened the door to see what the fuss was all about, what greeted her were four featherless, naked little birds frozen in grotesque rictus. She closed the door and hadn't been out there since.

Sitting on the couch, however, all she could see of the outside world were the tips of the coal silos and the treetops. She would have to move soon, to get busy and start doing all the familiar things she had to do when between jobs—contact Payroll at the university and make sure they sent her the necessary paperwork so she could register for unemployment benefits. She'd probably even have to talk to Minot again and get her to agree to classify her as "laid off" so she could get benefits earlier. How likely was that? Not very. She'd have to get a temp job, and fast if she was going to make the bills. A little voice in the back of her head whispered something about her mother's pension checks and bank account, which she now managed. Thank God her mother had signed the power of attorney before she'd had the mini-strokes. But no, Colleen couldn't touch that for anything other than her mother's care, neither legally or morally. Absolutely not.

Apart from her mother's money, how much cash did Colleen have in the bank? Maybe a little over a thousand dollars. Less than two thousand. It wouldn't last long. The image of the homeless man begging outside the liquor store popped up like a stepped-upon rake.

Colleen closed her eyes, took another sip, and imagined herself in a little cabin nestled at the edge of a great, evergreen forest. For years, this image had soothed her when she was distressed. She pictured nothing but horizon, and rolling hills, slightly blued by a soft mist. There was nothing in this imagined world but the trees, the birds, the creatures of the forest, and the small cabin. She knew the cabin intimately. On the wall three gauzy summer dresses with matching hats hung from brass hooks. Books lined another wall, all tidy with leather covers and gold lettering. Old books. Books of importance. A small table covered in a blue and white checked tablecloth sat by a window overlooking a tidy kitchen garden. On the centre of the table a typewriter with a stack of paper beside it waited only for her to sit down and give voice to limitless inspiration. Windows looked out onto the bucolic landscape. A deeply cushioned chair waited for her near the window, under a brass reading lamp.

Colleen sighed, and drank a little more. Peace descended.

She knew this feeling, this self-contained sense of righteous isolation. She remembered the first time she'd felt this way. She had been just a girl, really, only seventeen years old and living in Nova Scotia.

It seemed an impossible scenario, but there it was; she was seventeen and all by herself. Not that anyone had expected different, not even Colleen. After the incident with the butcher knife, which no one in the family ever talked about, and which even now Colleen avoided thinking about, getting away from home had been the most important thing in the world. And then George came along, a friend of Crystal's older brother. He was ten years her senior and talked about getting a farm in Nova Scotia, where he'd been raised, with his twin brother. Not much taller than she, he had a scraggly beard and long hair, a tight, sinewy strength and a quick temper. He wore gold-rimmed round glasses, which Colleen felt gave him an air of wisdom. That air, combined with the muscles in his arms and those narrow hips, created a potent combination of danger and sophistication, at least in her teenage, hormone-addled brain.

She graduated from high school on June twenty-third, and ran away with him on June twenty-fourth. She left a note for her parents, and when she called them later to tell them she was all right, they said, without any irony whatsoever, that she'd made her bed now and would have to lie in it. It was difficult not to giggle at that, even though her mother's fury practically melted the receiver. She had thought, maybe, that they'd beg her to come home, and although she never told anyone, and certainly not George, it stabbed her in the heart when they didn't. Her father was sober by then. Amazingly, the butcher knife incident had been the catalyst for that. He later told her he didn't ask her to come home because he felt she might be better off away from them.

Unbelievably, she'd been a virgin (one of the few she knew) until the night they left for Nova Scotia. She shuddered even now, thinking of that awful experience. The things he expected her to do. It was easy, from the vantage point of maturity, to understand what a pervert he'd been; what else would a twenty-six-year-old man want with a child of sixteen? But back then, she knew nothing.

So, she found herself with George in a rented bungalow, in a little town of just over four thousand people, on the banks of the Salmon River in the middle of Nova Scotia where she knew no one. She tried to do want he wanted, tried to reconcile her own disgust and just get on with it—until she simply couldn't any more. Until the night he brought home Dave, his friend, such a close friend, George said, that they'd share everything.

She walked out into the night, stayed in a cheap motel on the highway, took some cash out of the bank the next day and found herself an apartment on the top floor of a Victorian house near the railway track that had a little cast-iron fireplace she fell in love with, even if the place was drafty and not terribly clean. She got a job as a waitress in a diner, but planned no further than the next paycheque. George came round a time or two and tried to persuade her to come back to him. He even called her parents, and in response they sent her a letter saying they weren't surprised it didn't work out, and they hoped she'd sort herself out and get a decent job. They included fifty dollars in the letter but didn't suggest she come home. It wouldn't have mattered if they had. No matter how tough things were, at least she was on her own. She felt safe in her little apartment, not happy, maybe, but safe. After a few weeks, George stopped coming round. She heard later he'd found a new girl and moved to the Annapolis Valley.

She tried to make friends with Janet and Amy, the other waitresses in the diner, but it didn't take long to discover she was considered an outcast in that puritanical little town. "Why'd you leave George?" Amy asked. "He didn't beat you; he didn't cheat on you." They asked her to attend their church, but Pentecostalism wasn't for her. Janet wondered aloud if that was the way girls behaved in immoral cities like Toronto. No wonder, she said, Colleen's parents wanted nothing to do with her.

When she made friends with a couple of Mi'kmaq boys and a few of the black kids who came into the diner, her fate was sealed, apparently. Damned for all eternity.

Then Amy, feeling even more Christian than usual, invited her for Christmas dinner with her family.

Snow Gleamed with Silver

The doorbell buzzed on Christmas morning, right around eleven o'clock. Colleen had slept in—she slept a lot then—and she was still in her bathrobe. She went down the steep stairs to the main door and opened it to find Amy, in a black coat with a fur-trimmed collar, standing on the enclosed porch. She carried a plastic bag.

"Merry Christmas," said Colleen.

"Merry Christmas," said Amy.

Amy was tall, with broad shoulders and white-blond hair that she always wore up in a bun. Her hair was so pale she looked bald if you looked at her straight on. She wore pink lipstick, and earrings in the shape of gift-wrapped packages with gold bows. It must be a festive thing, thought Colleen. She'd never seen Amy or Janet wear any kind of makeup. Their religion frowned on it as vanity.

"Do I have the time wrong? I thought you said around four."

"I did. Can I come in?"

"Sure, sorry. I can change really quick."

Colleen climbed the stairs and Amy followed. In the apartment Colleen asked if she could take Amy's coat, maybe get her a cup of coffee while she waited.

"Oh, no, that's okay," said Amy.

"It's no trouble. It's just instant, though."

"Look, Colleen, I'm really sorry about this."

"It's okay. My fault, right? Got the time wrong. No worries." Colleen smiled and shrugged. "My fault."

"It's not that," said Amy.

She wasn't meeting Colleen's eyes. Why was that?

"Well, what is it, then?"

"It's my mother. It's just that I guess I spoke too soon, and my mother has this thing about Christmas, it's a whole traditional rigmarole, and it's all about family, you know."

"Okay. Family."

"She's kind of strict about it. I'm really sorry, but my mother's decided Christmas this year should just be for family. I feel really awful."

"Don't worry about it."

"I brought you this." Amy held out the plastic bag. "It's a roast chicken, and some mince pies."

Colleen didn't want to take it. Taking it would mean admitting how pathetic she really was. Not only uninvited but unable to feed herself.

"That's nice of you." She took the bag. If she'd had anything in the house except Tang, cream of wheat and sardines, she would have told her to stuff her chicken, pun intended.

"It's not much." Amy shifted from foot to foot and twisted her woollen gloves as though trying to wring out water. Her face was flushed and she bit her lower lip.

Colleen wondered what it must be like to have to stand there, in your good coat and holiday earrings, and tell someone they weren't welcome at your table on Christmas. She imagined the fight Amy might have had with her mother. In fact, it was the sort of thing Colleen's mother would do, and never see the irony in it.

Colleen put her hand over Amy's and said, "You don't have to feel bad, Amy. It's not up to you, is it? I'm a stranger, after all, and I really appreciate you bringing the food. Sardines for dinner don't sound really festive, you know?"

"I bought them yesterday," Amy said. "I waited, though, you know, in case Mum changed her mind." She looked up at Colleen, her eyes bright. "She should have."

"I'm okay," said Colleen. "You have a great Christmas."

Amy left. Colleen closed the door behind her and stood staring at it. Oddly, she didn't feel like crying. She was even a bit relieved. It would have been worse, being in a house where she was merely tolerated, where she felt she was intruding. She carried the bag to the kitchen. The chicken was in an oven-ready bag. The six mince pies were pre-cooked. She ate one. It was sweet and flaky. She ate another.

Colleen had a sudden urge to call home, but she didn't have a telephone—couldn't afford one—and the idea of slogging out into the snow to find a pay phone was more than she could face. She went back to bed and stayed there for as long as she could, dozing, dreaming about nothing at all, and then got up and went to the kitchen where she nibbled at the chicken. She wandered past the bathroom into the living room and surveyed the room: the cot with a couple of pillows on it that served as a sort of couch in the far corner, the worn-through carpet, the little table with a few of her things on top—a picture of Pixie the dog, a candle in a blue and white holder, a notebook in which she scribbled poetry, a little sweetgrass basket—the rickety desk with the equally rickety chair, and this chair, a comfortable old stuffed thing full of burn marks from the previous owner. Most of the furniture, except for this chair and the carpet, which had come with the apartment, she'd salvaged from things people left out by the side of the road for garbage pickup.

She picked up a cheap paperback, some crime thing about a serial killer in Philadelphia, which she'd bought at the drugstore, and tried to read it, but her mind wandered. She heard Amy's voice repeating over and over, *I'm really sorry, but my mother's decided Christmas this year should just be for family.* She put the book down and strummed her guitar, sang every song she knew—Joni Mitchell, Jim Croce, Bob Dylan—and at some point she started to cry.

She cried hard, and stuffed the end of her sleeves in her mouth so the old couple downstairs, who had made it perfectly clear they didn't approve of her, didn't hear her sobbing. The tears were hot with anger and resentment and a terrible feeling of injustice. She cried so hard she was afraid she'd drown in self-pity.

But she didn't. Instead, something else happened. Round about four o'clock, when the sun was setting and the snow on the streets turned blue, she moved her chair from beside the unlit little fireplace, and sat at the bay window watching the Christmas world go by. Kids with new sleds heading back from the slope by the agricultural college up the road; cars full of families on their way, no doubt, to Grandma's house for the annual turkey; a couple hand in hand, wearing matching green-and-red toques. Then, as though everyone who had somewhere to go had arrived at their destination and not a creature was stirring, the world seemed to settle, to take a deep breath and sigh it out again. The wind stilled, the snow gleamed with silver in the lengthening light, and the first star appeared in a cloudless sky. For a moment it felt as though she were outside her body, watching a girl in a white bathrobe sitting on a spring-sprung old chair by a frosted window. Then suddenly she was back inside her skin, but in that moment peace had washed over her. She felt as though she needed no one and nothing. It didn't matter that her parents had declined her request for a ticket home for the holidays when she'd called them collect from the pay phone in the diner two weeks earlier ("You've made your own mess, young lady, you'll have to clean it up"), or that Amy's mother had judged her unfit to sit at their Christmas table, or that somewhere George was telling everyone what a bitch she was and clearing out the bank account. It just didn't matter. She felt . . . well, *companioned* was the only word she could think of. She felt *known* by something greater than herself, some entity who knew her, all of her, and still loved her, not in spite of what they knew, but because of it. She felt clean, and utterly calm.

Flailing, Windmill Style

Colleen sat on the couch and gazed out the window at the treetops. She tried to hold onto that peaceful feeling. It hadn't lasted when she was a girl in Nova Scotia and it wasn't lasting now. Such things don't. Then, as now, she was alone: The Uninvited. Even though it didn't last, she had never forgotten the sensation of being exactly and perfectly all right, of not needing a single thing or a single person. It was the same sort of connectedness she'd felt the first time she got drunk, at Danny Gibson's house—at least before she'd gone too far and blacked out and all the rest. It was like being given a glimpse into a secret garden, and then being shut out. Ever since, she had wanted so badly to get back there.

She hadn't drunk alcohol, or not much of it, when she lived in Nova Scotia. She couldn't afford it. But she'd come back to Toronto after a year. She got the job at the university, had her own place and a decent paycheque, and she was young. Everybody drank and went to the clubs and danced and danced. Besides, she discovered when she did start drinking again that she could drink with the best of them, drink with the boys, drink like a sailor. It was a useful skill.

She soon discovered the golden warmth of the fairies-in-a-bottle. That's what she called them, those spirits who could live in just about any bottle, clever things—wine (the French fairy) or whisky (the Irish fairy) or vodka (the Russian fairy dressed in white furs) or gin (although the gin fairy was Cockney and a bit aggressive), scotch (the thistle-fairy) and certainly Grand Marnier (the fairy with pretty orange wings).

They were always there, the fairies, whenever she needed them. Whenever the day called for a celebration (and what day didn't?), whenever she needed a pick-me-up, whenever the world turned nasty and cold and cruel, as it did so often—more often for her than for other people for some odd reason. Oh, the nobility of her soul, the depth of her suffering, she would think with a snort of derision at her own self-aggrandizement. The fairies waited for her, whisking her away to a far better world. *Come away, O human child! To the waters and the wild.*

It's like she always said: They don't call it "spirits" for nothing.

And there was the vodka fairy now, all dolled up her ermine and pearls, so soothing, so infinitely kind. She whispered in Colleen's ear, telling her everything would be just fine, it would all work out as it was intended to, the world misjudged her, but the fairy understood, understood, understood. Sip, sip, sip.

The only difference between the fairies-in-a-bottle and whatever visited her that long-ago Christmas day was that the fairies exacted a price for their presence, didn't they. But wasn't that only fair, since they gave so much of themselves? And if they loosened her up, as they were doing now, urging her to reach out to her fellow human beings, to draw comfort from her friends, wasn't that only right and good?

105

The sense of peace began to fray at the edges. Doubt slipped in and nibbled with sharp little mice teeth. Colleen's hand gripped the almost-empty glass. The skin on the back of her hand was crêpey and the sinews stood out in ridges. She used to have beautiful hands, long-fingered, thin and graceful. Look at them now. Look at *her* now. This was not the life she had planned.

She should call Lori. Lori, her oldest friend and confidante, would come over and make her feel better, would help her see her way out of this mess. Colleen took her phone out of her purse and dialled Lori's work number.

"O'Toole's, can I help you?" said Lori.

"Lori, it's me."

"Hey, you, what's up? Wait, can you hang on?"

Without waiting for an answer, Lori said something to someone. It sounded as though she had her hand over the phone.

Colleen looked at her watch: 11:45. This was probably a bad time to call, with the lunch crowd starting. But this was urgent. A life crisis.

"Hey, sorry, party of eight, no reservation, naturally. Hang on. They want what? Fine, put tables fourteen and fifteen together, then. Okay? Sorry, Colleen. What's up? You coming down for lunch?"

"No, I quit my job this morning." She had meant to say she *lost* her job.

"You did what? What the hell happened?"

It wasn't too late. She could tell Lori. Then again, she couldn't tell her why they'd let her quit. She couldn't. "I'd just had enough of their bullshit, frankly."

"Really? Hey, wait, sorry. Yes, can I help you? Do you have a reservation? Parker. Yes, right here. Ruth, can you see the Parkers to table six? Thanks. Okay, I'm back, now tell me again, why did you quit?"

"It's complicated. Any chance you can come over after your shift?"

"Today?"

Of course today, what kind of a question is that? "This afternoon, this evening, whenever you get off."

"Oh, Colleen, I can't today, honey. I'm working until three and then I've got to drive Ian to work—did I tell you he slammed his car into the neighbour's mailbox? Why do we let teenagers drive?—and I promised Madeleine I'd take her shopping for a new coat and I've got to get to the grocery store . . ."

"Tonight, then, come over once Lewis gets home."

"He's working late tonight. I can't believe you quit your job. Not an easy time to find a new one, not these days, and well, I don't know, but this is, what, your third job in five years?"

"What's that supposed to mean? I transferred within the university. Was that a crack?"

"Listen, I'm really sorry, but this place is about to go crazy. Why don't I call you later?"

"Fine, whatever."

"Come on, Colleen, don't be like that."

"I'm not like anything. You're the one who apparently doesn't have time. God knows I'll be here."

There was a moment's silence. "Sweetie, listen, I'll call you later. But in the meantime, don't drink too much, okay?"

"What the hell is *that* supposed to mean?"

"Well, you're drinking, right?"

"Of course I'm not drinking. It's not even noon, for God's sake."

"I wouldn't blame you, but I thought I could hear it in your voice. If I'm wrong, never mind."

"You're wrong."

"Good. Okay, well, like I said, it's crazy here right now. I'll call you later, and I'm sorry, okay?"

"Wonderful. Splendid."

Colleen flipped the phone closed and began to cry scalding tears. Lori was her best friend, had been since they'd met back in their early twenties at a dance class. They told each other everything, even things Lori didn't tell her husband, Lewis. They knew each other's secret wounds, like the torch Lori still carried for Kent Wilde, the lacrosse-playing high-school heartbreaker to whom she had lost her virginity. Before Lori got married seventeen years ago to Lewis, she and Colleen had made the club scene together, and even dated a couple of guys from the same band back in the day. When the junkie drummer Lori had been seeing for six months told her he loved her, Lori'd almost had a breakdown, since no one (other than Colleen) had ever told her they loved her—not even her uptight Swiss parents. The drummer—a guy named Mike who reminded Colleen of Animal on *The Muppet Show*—had apparently mumbled those three magic words into Lori's neck one night, just before he ran to the bathroom backstage, puked and promptly passed out. Lori had come undone, appearing at Colleen's door in a state of near hysteria.

"*This* is how I first hear those words? *This* is all there is? He won't even remember them tomorrow," Lori had sobbed, hanging onto Colleen like a drowning woman. "I feel like the biggest thing in my life has just turned into trash, into shit, and I'll never get it back."

And maybe Colleen hadn't really seen what the big deal was, but that didn't matter. She poured Lori a tumbler full of scotch and listened to her rant and rave all night. She hadn't said she had to work the next day, hadn't said she had more important things to do. That was the way it was between them. They were there for each other when no one else was. How many nights had she listened to Lori complain about her job, or her lack of creative fulfillment? How she was too old to be a singer now and never got the right break. How she should have stayed in Paris when she

109

had the chance and become the great artist she was meant to be. Lori had her music and Colleen had her writing, and even if they never became rich and famous, at least they had each other as a cheering section. Or at least that was how it had been before she married Lewis and had the kids.

Colleen went into the kitchen, opened the new bottle of vodka and poured herself a little more. Not too much. Just enough to calm her down so she could figure out what to do next. She took a sip. She should put the white wine in the fridge, just in case someone came over later. The clock on the oven said it was nearly noon. She should also probably eat something. She opened the refrigerator. Half a loaf of bread. Some olives. Yogurt. Some cheese slices. What *was* that green thing in the back of the crisper? A lemon, wholly covered in a green-grey velvet mould. Using the tips of her fingers she carried it to the trash bin, which, when she flipped up the lid, produced some nostril-searing fumes and a small cloud of fruit flies. Colleen coughed, plucked the bag from the bin and tied it shut, hoping most of the flies were trapped within. She was going to have to clean this place, really clean it. She'd let things slide, she would admit that, but this was the start of an entirely new life, wasn't it, and she should start it by giving the whole place a good going-over.

She took the garbage bag and stepped out into the hall to carry it down to the chute. The hall was so silent at this time of day. She passed the doors of people she barely knew, but with whom she shared walls and floors and ceilings. They practically breathed the same air. She used to know her neighbours. When she first moved into the building it had been like one big party until, slowly but surely, the people she knew moved out, got married, moved on. And she was left behind. It had been a better-kept building back then too, she thought as she noticed the scuffed baseboards, the stains on the carpet, the grimy windows overlooking the front of the building, where the overhang roof was strewn with debris: plastic bags, bottles and—*what was that?*—a broken doll.

She reached the garbage room and opened the door to find the chute jammed, again, and a pile of plastic bags on the floor. She accidently nudged one with her foot as she leaned forward to place her own at the back of the pile, and as she did a swarm of cockroaches skittered out and she shrieked, dropped her bag and jumped back. She caught her heel in the threshold ridge, and staggered backwards, arms flailing windmill style, and she thought for a moment she'd be able to right herself and could even imagine laughing later at how silly it all was, just some innocent insects and everything was all right, but then it wasn't and in a great *whoomp* of air and impact she hit her head on the wall and landed on her behind.

Her eyes closed, she gripped the back of her head. She smelled the sickly, somewhat sweet stench from the garbage chute. Cockroaches running toward her! She opened her eyes. No cockroaches. She took her hand away from her head and looked at her palm, knowing there wouldn't be any blood, she was quite sure of that, but that was what one did, wasn't it? There was no blood. She looked behind her at a head-shaped dent in the wall. She must have hit with some force. Her right knee hurt and she considered it might be badly wrenched or even dislocated, and maybe she'd have to sit here until someone came home and there would be ambulances and a great deal of fuss and she'd need X-rays and maybe she had a concussion, which would mean staying in the hospital.

She looked down the hall, undecided if she wanted anyone to come to her aid or not. On the one hand, it was a shock, toppling like that, and she could use a strong arm and someone to tell her she was going to be fine. On the other hand, it was humiliating to be a middle-aged woman flat on her bum by the garbage chute, possibly smelling a little of vodka.

She wiggled her toes and that was all right, so she tried to bend her knee. She was able to do so with only a minimum of discomfort, and she chuckled at what a close call *that* had been. She'd have to talk to the super about fixing the stripping, not to mention the goddamn roaches. She'd already had to have her apartment fumigated twice in the past two years. She shuddered. She had some roach spray. She'd spray it round the floorboards right away. She rolled onto her side and then up on her left knee, bracing a hand against the wall as she pushed up with her right leg. Pain shot along the inside of the joint in both directions. "Oh, Jesus," she said, but managed to get to her feet. She rolled up her pant leg. Was the knee swelling? It looked okay, maybe a little swollen. She rubbed it.

The elevator bell rang and the door opened, letting off Charlie, the young man who lived at the end of the hall—some sort of blue-collar worker, a plumber or welder or something.

Oh, fine, now *someone shows up.*

She quickly unrolled her pant leg. Her legs weren't shaved, for one thing, and the knee-high stocking and the white skin above that—puffy around the knee, mottled with spider veins—was hardly an attractive look. Charlie wore painters' overalls (was *that* what he did?) and a down vest. He carried a shoulder bag that clanked as he walked.

"Afternoon," he said.

"There are cockroaches in the garbage room," she said, standing in front of the dent in the wall.

"In my kitchen too," he said as he walked past her. "Better get yourself a can of Raid."

Charlie slouched down the hall, his broad back and bushy hair reminding her of a pudgy bear. She didn't want to start back to her apartment until he was in his own place, for fear he'd turn and see her hobbling away. But she couldn't just stand there. She couldn't *lurk.* What would he think of her? Then again, why hadn't he asked her how she was? She put her weight down on her right leg. Not too bad. It ached, but no sharp pain. She probably hadn't torn anything. One step. All right. And then another. It was just the shock, that's all. Horrible creatures, cockroaches. Anyone would have been frightened.

She looked over her shoulder to see Charlie disappear into his apartment without even looking at her.

Well, perhaps *he* wouldn't have been scared. He probably didn't even care they were in his kitchen.

Safely back inside her own little sanctuary, her own *temenos,* she poured a bit more of the Russian fairy into her glass. Medicinal. She'd had a shock. It would dull the pain and relax her. She took her glass to the bathroom and knocked back a couple of Advil in the hopes it would stop her knee from swelling too much. In the mirror over the sink her face looked pale. She plucked a lipstick from the basket on the back of the toilet tank. *Rapture Red.* There, that was much better. She rather liked this look—the red lips, the pale skin. It was romantic, and yet bold. It was still the face of an interesting woman. Perhaps not pretty any longer, but certainly interesting. She could live with that.

Her knee was little more than an irritation, an inconvenience, and wasn't most everything, to one degree or another, just an inconvenience? G.K. Chesterton had said that, hadn't he? Or something like it? *An inconvenience is only an adventure wrongly considered.* That was it. She would rightly consider. This little knee thing didn't matter. She hadn't fallen down stairs and broken her neck. She wasn't sprawled out in front of a speeding subway train. Those were things that happened to drunks. She had merely snagged her heel. It could have happened to anyone. Look at that face in the mirror. She smiled, just slightly, so the dimple in her left cheek showed. She arched her left eyebrow. She was just in the spot where drinking made her look better, where it put a sparkle in her eye. *You still got it, kid.*

She drank and giggled. She was filled with good cheer and hopefulness. Perhaps, although she'd had a fall and a terrible shock at the morning's miscarriage of justice, she might choose to look at these things as signs that life was full of close calls and bad choices and she was liberated from a job that wasn't working anyway, and she bet she had an unfair termination case just waiting for her, an adventure rightly considered.

She raised her glass to the interesting woman smiling back at her with such confidence and such interesting lips. A woman like that could tackle anything, do anything she chose, *be* anyone she chose.

She would call the temp agency right away and get started on this new life that lay waiting for her in a glimmering slipstream of possibility. As she walked down the hall from the bathroom to the living room she was aware, although the ache in her knee was hardly noticeable, that she was just the tiniest bit unsteady. That cinched it. No more to drink today. Absolutely not. She drained the glass of the last of the vodka and picked up the phone, but what was the number? Right. Silly woman.

Carrying the phone, Colleen retraced her steps to the bedroom. Her favourite room, the room where all dreams happened. The bed, which needed making, but why bother when she'd be back in it soon enough? The bureau with her pretty music boxes on top and the leather-bound collection of books—Dickens and *The Rubáiyát of Omar Khayyám*—and, most importantly, her desk, there, under the window. It was a plain old oak desk, marred by nicks and dings and gouges that added to its character. When she found it in the second-hand store on Mount Pleasant, she had imagined it was once the desk of a newspaper man or a professor, and perhaps it still held some residue of their intelligence, their dedication to the art of putting words on paper.

She sat in the office chair she'd bought for next to nothing when the Registrar's Office was renovating (that stung, thinking about the university), and flipped open her laptop. Open the Outlook program, find the number for C&C Staffing. She checked her e-mails. Had she wanted a larger penis or to invest her money in Nigeria, she would be all set. *Concentrate. Get the number.*

"Hello, C&C Staffing. How may I direct your call?" a man's voice asked.

"This is Colleen Kerrigan calling. I'd like to make an appointment to come in and register as a temp."

"Have you worked with our agency before, Ms. Kerrigan?"

"I have, several times. I've always been very pleased with the agency."

"Let me pull your file up. Can you spell your last name for me?"

Colleen did.

"Oh, right. I have the file here. And you're looking for work again?"

"I am. Just as of this morning. I lost my job and I have to get back to work quickly. I'm the only support for my ailing mother, you see. You've always been good in the past about getting me temp work."

"Glad to hear it. When would you like to come in?"

"Can I come in today?"

"Today?"

"Why not. Take the bull by the horns, you know?"

"Okay, why don't you come in, say . . . about an hour—one-fifteen, could you be here then? We need you to take your tests over again and so forth."

"I could do that. Certainly. But I don't understand why you need me to take the tests over. You have all that, don't you, from before? Typing speeds and so forth?"

"Well, it's not so much about typing speeds anymore, Ms. Kerrigan. It's about what sort of computer programs you're fluent in, and then there's the usual aptitude and intelligence tests, just the standard tests you did last time you were here. When was that—two years ago, yes?"

Yes, it had been just two years ago. There had been that little misunderstanding in the Theology Department, but it hadn't been her fault at all.

The Soul Hunger

It had begun so innocently, as these things always did. Father Paul McIntyre was on a visiting professorship from the St. Patrick's College, Maynooth, and Colleen had been assigned as his support staff. She had resented the extra work at first, especially since he was wrestling with a new manuscript she was expected to type up, but he was such a kind person—leaving little thank-you notes and the occasional box of chocolate truffles on her desk—that she soon found herself quite liking him.

His book about early Irish Christianity from the time of Saint Patrick to the ninth century intrigued her and she found herself absorbed by its combination of science and spirituality, by the argument that science and faith were reconcilable, that the sacred could be found in nature, contrary to the Roman belief that the world and all in it was to be rejected.

One late afternoon, when he came back to the office from his last lecture, bringing with him the scent of autumn leaves and pipe smoke, she commented on how much she admired his work.

"I don't usually pay much attention to what I type up, but this is different, Father."

"Is it, now?"

Black Irish they called colouring like his, with the ruddy skin and mop of unruly black and grey hair. When he smiled, as he did now, charming little lines appeared at the corners of his wild blue eyes.

"Well, what you say about the reconciliation of transcendence and immanence, that they needn't be at odds. If I understand correctly, you're saying one can approach the question of transcendence through an appraisal of immanence . . . that it's through the hints God writes on the book of the cosmos about Him, or Herself, that we can know, or at least get glimmers of, that which exists independently of the cosmos." She felt a flush rise up her neck. She was probably blithering. "It got me thinking. I don't know, it was quite inspiring."

Father Paul sat on the ledge of the deep casement window across from her desk. "With a name like Colleen Kerrigan, you must be Catholic, am I right?"

She grimaced. "Lapsed, I'm afraid."

"Well, a faith without doubt is not worth a great deal in my estimation, Colleen, and with a name like that you're bound to have faith in your blood. To be named is to be claimed, and I feel sure God has claimed you as his own."

"I don't know about that. I don't feel much *claimed*." She said this before she knew she was going to, but as soon as the words were out she recognized them as true. "Just the opposite, in fact."

Father Paul looked serious. "Oh dear. The soul hunger, then?"

She laughed. "You have a poetic way of putting things."

He laughed himself then, a deep, rolling chuckle. "You're not the first to accuse me of having an overly poetic soul. Comes from spending too much time either with my nose in a book or rambling about a windy crag somewhere. Tell me, did you go to Catholic college?"

"I'm afraid I didn't go to any kind of college. I've been on my own since I was a teenager, working. I mean, I've taken courses here throughout the years—literature, philosophy, comparative religion—but I never got a degree." It annoyed her to feel the blush creep into her cheeks.

"Really? I would have bet money on you being Jesuit trained, the way you talk about books."

"No. Just my own reading, mostly."

"Nothing wrong with that. Wasn't George Bernard Shaw self-taught? And William Blake and George Orwell and Herman Melville and Benjamin Franklin, for that matter. But never mind. Doesn't for a second reflect on your ability to think. There's a world full of idiots"—he pronounced it *eedjits*—"graduated from universities without a decent thought in their heads. Now, back to the subject at hand. Tell me why you don't feel connected to God."

It felt odd, and yet not odd, to talk about such things with a man she hardly knew. And yet, he was a priest and she could tell from his work he was someone who enjoyed conversations about what really mattered in life, meaty things, things of substance, and not just the random small talk so many people wasted their lives on. In fact, coming to work in this department had been a bit of a disappointment. She had imagined a group of deep thinkers. What she'd found was just another faculty full of petty politics and tenure-track bickering. Until now. Until Father Paul of the beautiful, wild blue eyes.

"I don't know," she began. "It's hard to describe. It's as though there's a"—she was about to say *hole,* but saying she had a hole that wanted filling sounded entirely unlike what she intended— "a kind of hollow"—*much* better—"a blank space somewhere inside." She shrugged. "A kind of longing, I guess."

He bit his lower lip and nodded, as though she had said something profound. "It is not as uncommon as you might feel it to be. 'The Dark Night of the Soul.' Have you read St. John of the Cross?"

"A long time ago."

He closed his eyes and recited, "*Oh, night that guided me, Oh, night more lovely than the dawn, Oh, night that joined Beloved with lover, Lover transformed in the Beloved . . .*" He opened his eyes again and smiled. "There's nothing to be afraid of in the dark, Colleen."

She felt herself flush again, for a different reason. "It doesn't always feel that way."

"No, it doesn't, does it. Perhaps we should have a little chat about that then, when you've the time."

And so it began. They went out for a coffee, which turned into drinks once or twice a week, and long talks about God and the nature of the soul. His responses to her feelings of detachment, of "otherness" were always the same. "You must ask yourself, what is the invitation in my longing? What am I being invited to experience?" he would say.

One day, on his invitation, she popped into his office after she finished work. He said it was a good idea; they could talk without the interruptions and clatter of public places. He had a lovely old office with a fireplace in it, although it didn't work, and a mismatched pair of leather chairs. He invited her a second time, and a third, and it was on that third night Father Paul produced a bottle of Tullamore D.E.W. from his desk drawer. She loved the malted taste, the hint of charred oak. It became their drink. He told her that her longing for God, which up until these discussions she hadn't been aware she had, were reflections of God's longing for her.

They talked one night of Father Paul's own search for meaning, and how he had come to find God. "I was a bit of a rascal as a young man," he said with a chuckle. "I was even asked to leave the seminary for a time."

She wanted to ask why, but felt it was too personal a question. If he wanted her to know, he'd tell her.

"It was suggested I might take a walk in the world, just to be sure I could manage the balance of the office, you know, to be sure there were things I could deny myself, in return for serving God's glory."

She imagined women, red-haired, smelling of freshly baked bread, dressed in loose linen shifts, glowing by firelight. (There was an Irish shop on Bloor Street. They sold linen clothing, linen nightdresses.)

Father Paul rolled the glass of whisky between his palms. "They asked me to pray on my calling, which I did, and I found Christ waiting for me on the mountaintops and in the fields and by the sea, singing in every stone and seashell. I realized there was nothing in the world to fear, all of it being visioned from the mind of God Himself."

She loved the way he talked.

"Call me Paul," he said. "I'm not *your* priest, am I. I'd be glad if you thought of me as a friend. A friend is a good thing to have and doubly so when a man is far from home."

"Paul, then," she said, and thought what lovely long legs he had, stretched out there in front of the fire— although of course it wasn't a fire, just a couple of candles he'd lighted in the hearth. That was the second of the university rules he broke, the first being the drinking of whisky.

On the fifth night, a Friday, over her third whisky of the evening, Colleen confessed how very lonely she was, and Paul took her hand in his and kissed her palm. It was as though he'd poured warm, melted honey on her skin.

Oh my, she thought, oh my.

In her mind she saw a white, thatch-roofed cottage by the Irish Sea. Paul stood in a patch of garden by the door, his hair lifted by the salt-laden breeze. He turned, smiled at her, his eyes full of laughter in their nest of crinkles and . . .

When he leaned over the little table between their chairs to kiss her, she thought how she should resist, how wrong this was on so many levels, but then she thought she would wait to resist just a moment or two, and then the moment of resisting passed and she thought only of the taste of smoky peat and honey on his lips and how assured and knowing his fingers were.

The next night she told him about her financial troubles and how she feared becoming a penniless old lady—homeless even, unloved and abandoned. She shed real tears, encouraged, perhaps, by the drink, but no less sincere for that. She did not say that in a small corner of her mind she was afraid it was the drink itself that would cause this horrible fate to befall her.

As Paul buttoned his fly he smiled and said, "You'll never be old or unloved, Colleen, for you are beloved of the Lord," which is not exactly what she hoped he'd say. "And as for penniless," he continued, "I believe I have a remedy for that as well."

He opened his drawer, took out an overtime sheet and filled it in with a generous number, signing it with a flourish. "We'll say you're helping me with invaluable research, shall we?" He crossed the floor to her and pulled her down onto the oriental rug beside him. He nuzzled her neck. He smelled of whisky and damp wool. "And we wouldn't be fibbing for I've learned a great deal from you, my Colleen."

His Colleen. She was claimed.

And so it continued for two happy months, until that night Professor Roach came looking for Paul. If only they'd remembered to lock the door.

Paul did not come to the office the next day, and the day after that the Dean summoned her into his office. Father Paul, it seemed, had been called back to Ireland unexpectedly.

"Is there anything you'd like to tell me?" asked the Dean, from behind his cluttered desk. He drummed his fingers on a surprisingly thick wad of timesheets.

Perhaps she'd been greedy, padding her overtime that way, but it had been Father Paul's idea.

"Not a thing," she said.

She took some time off, intending never to return, and worked several temp jobs while she "considered," much as Father Paul once had, her calling in the department. But in the end they hadn't wanted a scandal, especially not when it turned out there were two female students as well

125

who were broken-hearted at the good Father's sudden departure.

Yes, those girls. Coltish, smooth-skinned, pert of bottom and breast. He had never said she was the only one; the assumption had been hers. Had he talked with them the way he talked with her? All that poetry of wind-swept barren crags where God waited for the supplicant with berry-stained lips, and heather-scented skin. That, more than anything, more even than the lack of a goodbye, seared humiliation into her heart like a branding.

It was suggested she look for a job somewhere else in the university. Fair enough, she'd thought, her evening bottle of wine salted with tears. Very well. A fresh start.

A Prudent Idea

And now there was to be yet another fresh start. "Fine," she said to the man at C&C Staffing. "An hour. I'll be there."

"See you then."

Colleen pressed "end call." Computer programs? She knew Excel, Word, PowerPoint, but didn't remember being tested on those last time. She checked her watch: 1:17. The C&C offices were on Eglinton Avenue. She could walk there, but she'd have to leave in about twenty minutes to be there on time.

Next to the laptop lay four notebooks full of Colleen's writing. A journal, two old scribble-books of poetry that she knew wasn't any good, and another book full of jottings for a novel she planned to write one day about a young girl in the 1930s, whose mother was mentally ill and whose father was an alcoholic. It was her life, of course, but under the guise of another time, another place, in order to protect the guilty. She'd read a few books on the Great Depression and she would start the actual writing anytime now.

She picked up the journal and realized it had been almost six months since she'd written in it. She felt the urge to write in it now, to pour out her pains. But she couldn't. Not now. She'd go and see the temp agency and get that squared away, and then she'd come back and write.

She went to the bathroom, brushed her teeth and rinsed her mouth out with Listerine. She knew some people, *real* alcoholics, drank Listerine for the alcohol content, but she couldn't imagine doing such a thing. Perfume, cleaning products . . . that would really be the end of the line.

She reapplied her lipstick and noticed her face had become shiny, the pores a bit large. That happened sometimes when she drank slightly too much, but she was still in that pocket before the booze made her look awful, and that wouldn't happen today, not with a little discipline. Still, she'd have to fix the shininess. She wiped off the lipstick with a piece of toilet paper and washed off her makeup. She ran the water until it was really cold, then splashed her face several times. So bracing. She reapplied her foundation, and for a moment considered using eyeliner, but decided against it. She didn't want to look like she was trying too hard. Just the lipstick, that *interesting* shade of red on a pale face.

She was already in her coat and just about out the door when she thought she might like a little nip to keep her warm on the walk to Eglinton. Her lips left a red imprint on the bottle, which she wiped off. Perhaps she'd take a little something with her, just in case she got nervous. That seemed prudent. What to take it in? A salad dressing bottle would do nicely. Just the right size. She dumped the contents (past their sell-by date anyway) into the sink and with a fine, almost surgical, steadiness she poured vodka into the bottle. Not all the way—she would leave room for something else, something that looked dressing-y. She opened the fridge. What would look like dressing? Well, nothing, since she wasn't going to put milk in it. Just a splash of cranberry juice, for colour. Not that it mattered, she couldn't imagine drinking out of it, but it was comforting to have it within reach.

At the last minute it occurred to her she should change her purse to a larger one. How embarrassing it would be to reach into her purse to get a pen, say, or her social insurance card, and have the young man with whom she'd spoken see the salad dressing bottle. She rummaged around on the shelf in the coat closet and found her black hobo bag. A little large for a truly professional look, but that couldn't be helped. She switched the contents of her bag, nestling the salad dressing bottle in the bottom. She checked that the lid was on tight, and felt moisture. Oh dear. What if it leaked? What if she left a trail of cranberry-coloured vodka after her as she walked? She took the bottle out and wrapped it in a plastic bag before resettling it carefully in her bag.

She walked along Mount Pleasant, past the Bread and Butter, George's Trains, the Longest Yard Sports Bar and the Regent Theatre. The sky had cleared, which she took to be a good omen. She smiled at the woman in the green coat walking her pug, wearing a similar green coat. The woman smiled back.

"Turned quite nice, hasn't it?" the woman said.

"Oh, yes, a great day," said Colleen.

It *was* a great day. She breathed deeply. Wasn't autumn her favourite season? While others said it was depressing, with the bleak mid-winter right around the corner, to Colleen it was the time of going within, of bracing, clean weather after the filthy humidity and lung-clogging heat of summer. The first days of school and crisp, clean, as-yet-unmarred new notebooks came to mind. Good things could happen at this time of year. They *would* happen. A gust of wind swirled round her, so that she clutched the collar of her coat and took a little two-step. *Blow, winds and crack your cheeks!* She laughed. She imagined Nanabush, the trickster spirit, dashing round her life, stirring things up. The Holy Ghost by any other name. The spiritual hurricane. Just when one's life seemed all set and staid and boring beyond bearing, there was that big *whoosh,* and who knew where one might land? Losing her job might all be part of some great plan after all.

That was something Father Paul had said about the Holy Spirit—it was the essence of change, that Big Wind that comes in and blows everything in our lives topsy-turvy. She chuckled. She could think of poor Father Paul with some affection now. She Googled him now and again. There was no evidence he was still teaching. In fact, he might not even be a priest any longer. There was a Paul McIntyre who popped up on Facebook, but the only public photos were of the Irish countryside, not a single picture of his face—then again, that would be just like him. She hadn't sent a "friend" request yet, but she might. Why not? All was forgiven, and loneliness came in so many forms.

She could understand, now, how it might have led him to his own follies.

She walked past the Chick 'n' Deli. ALWAYS IN GOOD TASTE, the sign read. A large white rooster perched on the roof, looking ready to crow. Yes, well. There had been some marvellous nights there, and one spectacularly bad one. She wouldn't think about that right now, not with all this tingle of good luck in the air. She wouldn't. One foot in front of the other. Just keep walking.

You're Going to Have Bruises

Lori and Colleen had gone to see a band called Bitter
Grounds. Colleen had become totally infatuated with Craig,
the bass player, and was sure they would take things to the
next level soon. They hung out a few nights after the gig,
getting coffee and a greasy late-night breakfast at People's
Foods, talking about Céline and Bukowski and Coltrane
and Miles. Not only was Craig as beautiful as a Nubian
king, he was smart and, just as important, between
girlfriends. Lori had just broken up with Mike, the junkie
drummer from Book of Days, and wanted diversion and,
she said, "a very large gin."

The Chick 'n' Deli was packed, as it always was on
Friday nights. Overhead the drop-ceiling lighting of faux-
Tiffany stained glass cast blue and green shadows on the
oak-style bar and black café tables. Girls with big teased-up
hair and young men with pastel jackets, sleeves rolled up to
the elbow, flirted and ate the chicken wings for which,
along with the music, the Deli was rightly famous.

Bitter Grounds played funk—sexy, Prince-style funk
with Craig's slap-style of bass front and centre. You
couldn't *not* dance, and Colleen loved to dance. She was out
on the floor with Lori, who could do some mean neck rolls
and moon walks herself. Colleen wore fingerless lace gloves
and ripped jeans with an off-the-shoulder torn sweatshirt.
A little Roger Rabbit, a little *Running Man*, some Jamaican
hip-slides. She knew people watched her, knew she looked
good. She caught Craig's eye and he winked.

Someone bumped her, hard. She was knocked off balance and looked around, ready to laugh and apologize. Staring daggers at her was a black girl in a leather jacket with a wild halo of hair tied back with a big white bow.

"What the fuck do you think you're doing?" said the girl.

Lori stopped dancing and came to Colleen's side, taking her arm. "Come on," she said, "let's go sit down."

"Why the hell should we sit down? What's her problem?"

There were three black girls now, not dancing, in front of Lori and Colleen.

"You want to know what my problem is, bitch, do you?" said the girl.

Lori, ever the sensible one, pulled Colleen away. "I don't care what her problem is," she said. "I just want to sit down."

Colleen allowed herself to be led to their table near the railing that rimmed the dance floor. She felt shaky and humiliated, although she hadn't done anything wrong. "What was *that* about? I just don't get it," she said. "I don't even know that girl. Do you know her?"

"No, but I think Craig might," said Lori.

Two of the girls now danced right in front of Craig. One had her back turned to the other, grinding into the other girl's pelvis. The third girl, the one with the bow, rolled her sinuous body in a wave, letting her palms outline the movements of breasts and belly and hips.

"Fucking bitch," said Colleen. She slurped the last of her Long Island iced tea through the straw.

A waitress passed and Colleen said, "Bring me another and a couple of tequila shots."

"Is that a good idea?" asked Lori.

"It's an excellent idea."

"You want anything?" the waitress asked Lori.

"I'm good." Lori nursed her gin and tonic. She shrugged when Colleen made a face. "I have to drive home."

"You can stay at my place."

"I'm good."

The drinks came and when Lori refused the shot, Colleen knocked back both of them. She watched Craig, who wasn't meeting her eye anymore, so fixed was he on the trio dancing in front of him.

"Forget it, Colleen," said Lori. She used her hands to scrunch some volume into her blond hair. "It's probably a racial thing."

"Oh, come on."

Lori rolled her eyes. "You mean that hasn't occurred to you? Black girls don't like their men going out with white girls."

"*Their* men?" The injustice of this flared in Colleen's stomach. Either that or it was the tequila. "That's completely unfair. What about Jake? There's not a racist bone in my body."

"Hardly the point."

The music got louder. Craig and the guitar player riffed off each other, leaning first toward the crowd and then away from it. The three girls did the same, connecting themselves to the band in a way Colleen didn't like at all. She drank some more. The liquid was silken and full of flame. She wanted to get back out there and dance. She said so.

"Why should I be up here and them down there? They don't own the goddamn floor."

The girl with the bow turned and looked at Colleen. She smiled in a smug, proprietary way that made Colleen want to rip the bow off her head and half her weave with it. She thought of all the lovely talks Craig and she had had; how he ran his long fingers, the pads callused but his touch still so soft, up the inside of her wrist. How he'd kissed the spot where her neck reached her shoulder and said he wanted to see more of her, *lots* more.

Lori said something, but Colleen couldn't make it out over the music and she cupped her ear. Lori leaned in and repeated it. "Keep your voice down and, you know, you might want to slow down. You're slurring."

"I'm not."

Colleen drank some more, watching the girls dance and trying to will Craig with the power of her mind, with the power of her *allure*, to look at her, but he didn't. And then, just below the tumour of umbrage taking up so much space beneath her breastbone, her stomach began to feel queasy. She thought she might like to stand up, but wasn't quite sure she could. Maybe Lori was right. How many drinks had she had, apart from the shots? Three? Was this her third or her fourth? She felt quite hot. Sticky. Her stomach gurgled. She stared at the mound of chicken bones and sauce in the middle of the table and it looked less like the remains of her dinner than of something hit by a car. She looked away. Someone passing behind her jarred her chair, and the action seemed both violent and yet at the same time to happen in slow motion.

"Are you okay?" asked Lori. "You don't look so good."

The band was saying they were going to take a break and be back, so don't go anywhere.

"I think I'll go splash some water on my face," said Colleen.

"What?" said Lori.

She stood up and the room did a fancy dip and roll and she grabbed the back of her chair.

"Uh-oh," said Lori. "I better come with you."

"I'm fine," Colleen tried to say. If she could just hold onto the railing as she walked, she was quite sure she'd manage, although she did feel a slight panic. There were

136

three stairs down. The bar had turned into an obstacle course. It was important to concentrate on such things as mechanics. Stairs could be so mischievous. Lift the leg, bend the knee, place the foot. Repeat.

A lot of people were coming off the dance floor, and she imagined herself as a salmon fighting its way upstream. "'Scuse me. Sorry." There was Craig and the band's singer—what *was* his name? They descended the stairs by the stage and made their way to the bar. Colleen didn't want to talk to Craig right now. She just wanted to get to the bathroom. It was *imperative* she get to the bathroom. "*Excuse* me," she said again.

She stumbled, just a little, but reached out and with enormous gratitude felt the solid back of another person, which blocked what might very well have been an embarrassing tumble. "Sorry," she muttered. There was quite a dreadful taste in her mouth.

"You stupid bitch," a voice said.

Colleen found herself looking into the face of the girl with the white bow. At almost any other time, Colleen would have been open to a discussion about the intricacies of interracial dating and the tragedy of *any* sort of racism, but at this moment, she really, really had to get to the bathroom.

She put her hand up not only in the hope that doing so would stop the room from wobbling and gliding as it was doing, but also to indicate to the girl with the bow that

Colleen wanted only to pass, to get by, to move forward without incident.

The girl did not take it that way. She slapped Colleen's hand.

"You fucking raise your hand to me? You're crazy!"

She stepped so close, with her nose practically between Colleen's eyes, that Colleen couldn't see anything at all. She could only smell the beer and cigarettes on the girl's breath.

Her stomach lurched and sour matter rushed into her mouth. Her cheeks popped out and she jammed her palms against her lips, hoping, *praying* it might be enough to avert catastrophe. The girl with the bow, at last grasping the severity of the situation, jumped back. She was not, alas, quick enough. Colleen doubled over, craning her neck forward quite involuntarily, and when a torrent of vomit exploded from Colleen's mouth, the girl with the white bow got covered in a good deal of it.

Colleen's eyes were closed by then, but she felt an impact on her shoulder and understood that she had been kicked or punched and that she was falling and was on her knees. It was all sensation then—burning in Colleen's nose and mouth, watering eyes, convulsions in her stomach, and worse, urine escaping; she could feel it escaping and was powerless, in the violence of her spasms, to stop it. There was a good deal of yelling. The voices were male and female. Someone's hands where on her then, lifting her by the shoulders.

"Colleen! Walk. Just walk. I've got her. Let me get her to the bathroom. I'm so sorry."

"Get her cleaned up and get her the fuck out of here," a man's voice said. "Take the other one into the men's room."

There was some laughter.

In the bathroom Colleen vomited again, twice, but at least now it was in relative privacy and in, as her mother used to say, the proper place. Lori, best of all possible friends, held her hair and said it could have happened to anyone and not to worry and it would be all right.

After Colleen returned, more or less, to herself, she began to cry. She washed her face and rinsed her mouth and cleaned up her clothes—she had to take her jeans off, wet them down in the sink and dry them using the hand-blower, which took quite a bit of time.

"I can't go back out there," she said. "I can't."

"You're going to have to," said Lori, and her voice was a little less sympathetic than Colleen wanted it to be.

"I want to kill myself." Her shoulder hurt.

"Come on, Colleen, you're not the first person to puke in a bar."

Colleen supposed it was kind of Lori not to mention the fact she'd wet herself. "But in front of Craig!"

Lori shrugged. "Yup."

"And what if that girl's still out there?"

"She's not."

"How do you know?"

Lori winced and brushed something off her lace-tiered miniskirt. "When you threw up on her she threatened to punch the crap out of you. She was pretty crazy. The bouncer pulled her off you, but she got a couple of kicks in. I think they made her leave after she cleaned up in the men's room. I'm sure they did. We have to leave too."

Colleen had, it seemed, been so far inside her own personal apocalypse that she hadn't even noticed the violence done to her, apart from the dull impact on her shoulder. She remembered that time, so many years ago, when she'd been sick-drunk and her mother had slapped her across the face. She hadn't felt anything then either. There was something to be said for being blotto.

"I felt somebody hit my shoulder." Under her fingers it was tender.

"She kicked you first, then her friends joined in. You don't remember?"

"Not really."

"You're going to have bruises."

They waited until the band began playing again and then snuck out, or almost did. The manager caught them and Colleen had to pay not only for her bill, but an extra fifty for cleanup. She didn't argue.

The next day, she awoke with bruises up and down her ribs and arms.

She never went to see Bitter Grounds again, and it was weeks before she went back to the Deli.

A Woman of Quality

Colleen turned left onto Eglinton. Remembering all that
about the Deli and beautiful Craig had brought her down.
It seemed her whole life was a series of missed
opportunities, of things *almost* turning out right and then
some stupid twist and it all went wrong. She caught sight
of herself in the window of a dry cleaner as she passed. She
paused, pretending to examine the pricing signs. EARLY
BIRD SPECIAL! IN BY 8:30, OUT BY 5:30! 25% OFF!

She looked like a dressed-up waif, albeit a not-quite-
young one. Her height always surprised her. She thought of
herself as taller than she was, just as she thought her hair
wasn't quite that stringy. How she used to envy girls whose
hair went all fluffy and frizzy in humidity. Under such
conditions, hers looked like nothing so much as seaweed on
a rock. It occurred to her that this red coat, this Little Red
Riding Hood coat, might be just a little too young for a
woman of her age. But it was Audrey Hepburn elegant, like
the slim black pants and ballet flats Colleen had once worn.
She had never quite managed the hats, however, nor the
cigarette holder. Now it was probably too late for
interesting hats. Young women in fabulous hats were
intriguing and bold, old ladies in such hats looked like
either church ladies or Quentin Crisp, that gay British man
who made a career out of looking like a sad old lady. The
woman in the window reflection wasn't an old lady yet.
Although she wasn't as delicate as she once had been,
although her smile might not be as dazzling as it once was

142

(everyone bleached their teeth to marshmallow these days; how did they afford it?), she did have that interesting lipstick and, when she remembered to hold her mouth in a slight smile so it didn't droop and deepen the lines by her nose, she could pass for five years younger, surely. But there were those eyes to contend with. They were puffy, and although it was almost certainly a trick of the reflected light, the whites looked just the slightest bit yellow.

It wasn't a bad reflection, not a revolting reflection. It just didn't look like her. Where had she gone?

She sighed and raised her chin, walking on. Philosophical questions would have to wait. Where was she *going?* That was the question of the moment, and the answer was this: she was going to a new beginning.

C & C Staffing. She would go in. She would smile, and make the best of it, and prove them all wrong. There was something noble, heroic even, in that.

She marched into the lobby with a long stride that bespoke confidence. A woman of quality, with wisdom and experience. In the elevator on the way to the fourth floor she hummed, thinking how much good the walk had done her. It had cleared her head and put some colour in her cheeks.

The door to C&C Staffing was directly in front of the elevator. The silver lettering on the wooden door was missing the *a* in "Staffing" and some wit had inserted a *u* in its place with a black marker. Inside, two chrome-legged green couches, with a brass lamp on an end table where they met at the corner, formed an L-shape to the right of the doors. Gossip magazines were scattered on a coffee table and a water cooler with no cups stood near the hallway leading to the offices. Motivational posters adorned the walls. LOVE WHAT YOU DO. DO WHAT YOU LOVE. A photo of a snail crawling up a rock with the caption IF YOU DON'T MAKE IT UP THE MOUNTAIN, TRY AGAIN. Another of a man standing on a mountain peak, high above the clouds; underneath it said, AMBITION: ASPIRE TO CLIMB AS HIGH AS YOU CAN DREAM. Stains, probably coffee judging from the colour, marred the carpet. The reception desk, behind which a young man sat, was scuffed and a corner of the veneer peeled.

Colleen smiled brightly, gave her name and said, "I think we spoke on the phone a little while ago."

"Hi, Colleen, yes?" the young man said.

How old was he, twenty? And why did he put those dreadful white streaks in his black hair?

"I've got your file here, and there are just a few forms and things I need you to fill out. They're on the top and the tests are on the bottom. When you've filled out the forms, bring them back to me and then you can use one of the carrels in the back to do the tests. When you've finished the IQ and aptitude tests, we'll get you set up on a computer for the typing and program tests." He handed her a clipboard with a thick pile of papers on it. "Do you need a pen?"

What a lot of paper. "I have one. Is all this really necessary? I've been registered here before. You do have that, right?"

He smiled in the way one might to a simple child, with his head cocked and his lips pressed together. "Well, we like to keep things current, dear—get the records up to date."

Dear? Dear was what you called old ladies in nursing homes.

"Thanks, sweetie," she said, perhaps just a little archly, and took the pile of papers to the rickety couch. The place had certainly gone downhill in the past couple of years. This used to be quite a high-end agency.

Colleen opened her purse and rummaged for a pen. There was the friendly little bottle. She let her fingers rest on it for a moment. Wallet. Phone. Keys. Makeup bag. Old grocery store receipts. Two loose mints slightly furred with lint. A baggie of almonds and apricots. How long had *they* been in there? No pen.

She returned to the reception desk. The young man, who hadn't even been polite enough to tell her his name, talked on the phone with the chair swivelled so his back was to her. She waited, listening to him talk about meeting someone later for dinner. She coughed. Nothing.

"I'm sorry," she said. "I don't seem to have a pen after all."

He turned without putting the phone down. He raised his eyebrows in her direction.

"Excuse me," she said. "Pen?"

He pointed to a mug filled with ballpoints at the corner of the desk and immediately went back to his conversation.

Pen in hand, she began to fill in the forms. Name, address, date of birth, Social Insurance Number, all the usual stuff. And then the employment history.

Begin with your most recent position.

Duties and responsibilities?

How long were you there?

Colleen paused. The next question was "Reason for leaving" and then "List references." What should she say? This was like a divorce, wasn't it, but there was no "irreconcilable differences" box to check. Someone had to be at fault, and as usual, that someone was her. What would sound appropriate? What would sound positive? She needed to spin a story that would be plausible, and one that painted her in a good light. All those years at the university, that would be it. She felt she needed a new start, a more challenging position. The last time she was here the woman processing her application had been impressed with her test scores, saying she scored within the top ten percentile on the intelligence test. She'd even let slip that she was rather surprised to see someone with

Colleen's scores looking for temp work. And her typing was lightning fast, always had been.

Colleen wrote, *I felt I need more responsibility than I had in my last position.* She looked again at the "Ambition" poster on the wall. That's it; she was dreaming bigger, she was finally giving herself permission to be all that she could be, so to speak. References were admittedly an issue. But surely Harry Barnes and Michael Banville would speak well of her, given the circumstances—perhaps especially well, since she knew they had a soft spot for her. She put down their names with only a sliver of doubt.

She sighed, unclipped the pages and tapped the edges against the clipboard so they were nice and neat. She'd always had an eye for details. She handed the information forms to the receptionist, who had stopped talking on the phone and was now doing a crossword puzzle. *Seven letters for* idiot, *starting with* a *and ending in* e, *perhaps?*

"Carrels are through there," he said. "Let me know when you've finished the aptitude test and I'll give you the IQ test. That's timed."

The door opened and in walked a girl of about twelve, Colleen thought, albeit a tall one. She was sausaged into jeans of the skinny-leg variety that had been popular when Colleen was that age herself. The ones you had to lie down on the bed to get into and pull up the zipper using a pair of pliers. *If you wore something the first time a trend came around, you're too old to wear it again.* Over this she wore a baggy white sweater and, in apparent disregard for the weather, she balanced on a pair of high-heeled strappy sandals that made Colleen's feet hurt just looking at them. The girl tossed back her brunette curls and smiled at Colleen, flashing exactly the sort of alarmingly white teeth Colleen could not afford. Colleen smiled back, in what she hoped was a non-hostile way.

As Colleen walked to the carrels, clutching her papers and her purse (affable little bottle inside), she heard the receptionist say, "Hey, Brenda, how's our favourite girl?" This was followed by the sound of kissing and the girl saying, "Just came in to pick up my check, Kev. There's a pair of shoes at Holt's with my name on 'em."

"Want to meet up for a drink later?" said Kev. "I'm having dinner with Louis. You should join us."

The girl said something and they both laughed.

Colleen settled into one of the three carrels. She didn't remember that last IQ test being timed, but she wouldn't think about that now. One thing at a time. Besides, she aced these sorts of tests. She always had.

"Personality & Aptitude. Part One. Indicate, on a scale of one to five, one being the most accurate and five being the least accurate, where you fall in terms of the following questions": *I am the life of the party. I keep my thoughts to myself. I am comfortable with my feelings. I start conversations. I love large parties.*

She ticked off the boxes—five, three, two, three, four. After all these years, she knew what employers were looking for. Social, but not *too* social. No gossiping. Confidence. She plowed on for fifteen minutes. *I push myself forward. I like to lead.* It seemed so ridiculous. She looked at her watch: 1:35. She'd be here all afternoon. *I need a lot of time to do things.* Five. *I come up with solutions easily.* Two. Page after page after page of utter inanity.

Finally, at last, two hundred questions. Done.

She handed the papers in to "Kev" and he passed her the IQ test.

"You have forty minutes for this one. So, that's about three o'clock, right?"

"All right." She returned to her carrel. It didn't feel all right. It felt too fast. She was nervous. She flipped ahead. Only thirty questions here.

First one:

"Car is to road as train is to_____."

She was tempted to put in *aardvark* or *fruitcake* just for fun. But she wrote, *Rail.*

Which is the odd one out?

Hockey, Exercise, Tennis, Football?

So easy. Two more, just the same, and a series of squiggly lines—pick the next in the sequence. Fair enough.

When Jack, James, Jim and Jane stand by age, Jack being the youngest stands first, while James brings up the rear. However, when they stand by height, Jim being the shortest stands first, while James comes to the third spot. In both lines Jane remains at the second position. Who is immediately younger than James?

What? Read that again. Jim. Yes, that must be right. The questions were getting harder.

Which number should come next in this series? 25, 24, 22, 19, 15 . . .

Think. All right. 10.

And then this:

Which number should replace the question mark?

8	5	21
35	32	12
32	28	31
4	?	28

a) 3

b) –2

c) –6

d) 48

There was some pattern to this problem. She could almost see it, but it slipped away. Add the second column to the first, and then subtract? No. The first row by the second? No. She felt a mind-cramp coming on. Skip this one and come back to it later. She moved on, but the skip ruined her rhythm, shook her confidence. She went back and read it again. She stared at the numbers but nothing seemed logical.

It was hard to concentrate and her mouth felt dry as ash. It was altogether too hot in here. She thought of getting water but remembered there were no cups at the cooler, and besides, she was being timed. Her heart beat too quickly. Abandoning that problem, she moved on to the next— but couldn't get the gist of that one either.

At the end of a banquet 10 people shake hands with each other. How many handshakes will there be in total?

a) 100
b) 20
c) 45
d) 50
e) 90

Ten times ten, yes, so *A*. The correct answer is *A*. Or is it? Certainly. Don't get stuck, forge ahead. She could hear the timer ticking in her head. She glanced at her watch: 2:30.

The next question:

Select the number that best completes the following analogy—10 : 6 : 3 : ?

a)   2
b)   1
c)   −1
d)   12
e)   4

What did those colons mean? Why should she have to know that? She could only guess. She circled *B*.

She put her pen down. She was thirsty and hot. She picked up her purse and returned to the receptionist area. A woman Colleen recognized from the last time she was here, one of the placement officers, stood talking to another woman, presumably another client, who wore a grey wool wrap dress and expensive-looking burgundy boots and whose hair was tousled in a professionally styled sort of way. Kev had disappeared.

The placement officer, her hair in a neat bob, wore a white jacket over a grey skirt, which made her look as though she ought to have a stethoscope around her neck. She turned to Colleen.

"Did you need something?"

"I wonder if you could pause the test. I need to use the facilities."

"Oh, yes. It's Ms. Kerrigan, isn't it?"

"How nice you remembered. Yes, Colleen Kerrigan. But I'm sorry . . ."

"Nancy Fischer." The woman held out her hand.

Colleen shook it. "Sorry."

The woman leaned in and chuckled. "You don't have the benefit of being handed a file. Excellent memory booster. Colleen, this is Diane Harding."

"Nice to meet you." Colleen was aware the clock was ticking. "So, would it be all right to pause the timer?"

Nancy Fischer turned to the other woman, who was not much older than the girl who'd been in to claim her cheque. "Hang on just a minute, Diane." She picked up the timer from Kev's desk. "Twenty-five minutes or so left. I'll make a note and start when you come back. It's down the hall to your left, first door round the corner."

"Thanks."

In the bathroom, Colleen ducked into one of the three stalls and sat down with her purse in her lap. She found the friendly bottle, unwrapped it from its plastic overcoat, opened it and tilted it to her lips. Just a little and she'd relax. She smiled. Colleen had never been a great test taker. The vodka slipped down her throat and skipped along her nerve endings. She took three, four more drinks.

Good Lord, was that half the bottle? But she hadn't filled it, and there was the cranberry juice to consider.

The bathroom door opened. Someone came in and walked to the stall next to the one Colleen occupied. Colleen stood, replaced the cap on the bottle, and flushed the toilet, even though she hadn't used it. She thought a breath mint might be in order. She tucked the bottle under her arm and poked around in her bag. Yes, there was a blue plastic container of mints in a side pocket. As she reached for it she moved her arm a little. It didn't take much, just a small unthinking adjustment, and the salad dressing bottle slipped. She felt it go and snatched at it, but was too slow. She watched it fall to the tile floor and as it fell she thought, Maybe it won't break. Maybe it will just fall and I'll be able to nab it and stuff it back in my bag with no one the wiser. Maybe it will be all right.

The corner of the bottle hit the unforgiving tile and didn't merely break, it exploded. Pink vodka flew everywhere. The woman in the other stall yipped, and for a moment Colleen feared a piece of glass might have struck her.

Then the room went still. Fumes rose to Colleen's nostrils, acrid and unmistakably alcoholic.

"Is everything okay?" a woman's voice said.

"Fine, thanks," said Colleen. The woman, whoever she was, didn't respond, and Colleen felt obliged to explain. "I dropped a bottle of salad dressing."

A moment's silence, and then "Bummer," followed by a flush.

Colleen looked down at the mess at her feet. A hunk of the bottle, with some fluid still inside, rested near her foot. She could actually picture bending down and lifting that unholy vessel to her lips, draining the last drop. She wouldn't do that—she considered the possibility of glass in her gut and the horrible death that would result. She even understood how simply thinking such a thing was evidence of a certain degree of madness, but this had been, and continued to be, such a very bad day. A little madness could be expected. In fact, a little madness was kind of attractive just at that moment.

Come and Get It!

It was mid-October, three weeks after Colleen's fourteenth birthday, and it had been a bad week. The bank had called every day, asking questions about unpaid mortgage and car payments. Colleen's father stayed away four nights, from Monday to Thursday, and every night her mother sat in the basement TV room, smoking cigarettes and telling Colleen stories about what a bastard her father was, how he spent every paycheque on booze and other women and how, given his job as an airline executive, they should have been living high off the hog, but because of *him,* that weakling, they'd probably lose the house and Colleen would be sent to a foster home because she certainly wouldn't be able to take care of her. This last comment was meant as a threat.

Late Friday night of that week, Colleen was getting ready for bed in the upstairs bathroom, which always smelled of the bleach her mother applied to the surfaces each morning, vigorously trying to wipe out any trace of the pathogens she maintained lurked in every crevice. She heard her father's key in the front door and the scramble of Pixie's feet on the stairs followed by her yelps of greeting.

"Well," said her father. "Somebody's happy to see me."

Colleen wondered if her mother would come up from the TV room and confront her father but she didn't, so Colleen went to the top of the stairs and waited. It would not please her mother if she went to her father, but she would stand where he couldn't fail but see her. Pixie, butt wiggling, stumpy tail a blur, sidled from the vestibule and looked up at Colleen, mouth open, tongue lolling, as if to reassure her everything would be all right now.

Peter Kerrigan stepped out after the dog, glanced around and caught sight of his daughter. He looked a little oily. His hat had flattened his dark, thinning hair and left a ridge on his forehead. His suit was rumpled.

"Hey, pet, how's my girl?"

Colleen came down the stairs and hugged him. He smelled of whisky, cigarettes and the musty scent of commuter train and musk-laden perfume, which was so familiar. "Dad, where have you been?"

"Had to stay in the city. Big labour dispute with the baggage handlers. Ramp rats always wanting more than their fair share. You know how it is. Your dad's the one who has to go in and mediate. Averted a big strike this time."

Colleen raised her eyebrows and tilted her head. It didn't sound convincing to her, so she doubted her mother would buy it. "Mum's in pretty bad shape." She chewed her upper lip and then said, "We've been getting lots of phone calls. You know, money calls."

Her father's smile, which up until that moment had been resolute, now faded. "Where is she?"

"Downstairs."

157

"You should go on to bed, pet." He kept his eyes on the shadowy stairs leading down to the TV room.

"What are you going to do?"

"Oh, I'll just settle in for a few minutes and then I might just head on up to bed myself."

"I don't think you should have any more to drink, Dad."

"You go on to bed, sweet pea." He gave her a kiss on the top of her head. "Go on, now."

She did as she was told, and it wasn't long before her mother clomped up the stairs. Pixie scrambled along the hall to Colleen's room and jumped on the bed. The dog turned around in circles a few times and then plunked down with her head on Colleen's stomach. Colleen stroked Pixie's soft fur. She put her transistor radio up against her ear, turned low, trying in vain to block out the voices.

You've never been any good. I don't know why I married you.

You've got what you wanted—got the house in the suburbs and the kid and the dog. You can't say I don't provide.

You better not have asked my father for any more money.

Don't tell me what to do. I'm dying in this suburban hell.

If you take another drink I'll kill you myself, I swear I will.

And so on.

In the morning, hunched over black coffee at the kitchen table, her father was pasty, sweaty, with trembling hands. His lips were purplish and his eyes red and watery with crusty yellow bits in the corners. He smiled weakly when he saw her. Pixie was under the dining room table on the other side of the kitchen, where, presumably, she could keep an eye on things while staying clear of everyone.

"I think your mother's sewing," said her father when she asked.

Her mother's sewing room was just a cleared-out space in the unfinished basement next to the TV room. Surrounded by damp hanging laundry, she sewed with furious intensity on an old pedal machine that had been her mother's. The fact she was already down there was not a good sign.

"What are you doing today?" asked her father.

Colleen got herself a glass of orange juice and shrugged. "I don't know."

"Your mother's just a bit nervous. She gets her moods."

"I know." Colleen leaned up against the counter. "I think I'll get dressed and take Pixie out into the woods."

"Good idea." Her father sipped his coffee, holding the cup with both hands.

The woods behind the house were a refuge for Colleen and she was grateful the day was dry and sunny. Crimson, garnet and amber leaves fluttered from the trees. Pixie bounded after squirrels and then ran back to Colleen. When they came to the stream with the big rocks, Colleen sat down and Pixie flopped beside her, resting her chin on Colleen's leg.

"Heffalump," said Colleen, affectionately.

All around them water gurgled, birds sang and leaves rustled in the breeze. Pixie heaved an enormous sigh. "Yeah," said Colleen, rubbing the dog's ear. "Me too."

Colleen had brought cheese and crackers, a handful of chocolate chip cookies and an apple. She had also brought *The Hobbit* and so had something to occupy her between throwing sticks for Pixie and watching the dog chase rabbits. They stayed on the rocks by the stream for a long time, and then they walked through the woods to the horse farm. Colleen shared the apple with the big chestnut horse that ambled over to greet her. His nose was like velvet and even Pixie liked him. The horse hung his head over the fence and Pixie reached up and they had a nice long sniff. Colleen climbed the fence and sat astraddle the rail while the horse rubbed his long head against her shoulder. He almost knocked her off once, and she laughed.

The shadows were starting to lengthen by the time she said to Pixie, "I guess we better get back."

Why did the walk back home feel so short? She always imagined she'd managed to get farther away than she had. The ground she'd gained in an entire morning and afternoon was lost in the brief hour it took to retrace her steps.

From the outside, the house seemed quiet. Maybe her father had gone out, but where would he go? If he didn't go golfing—and it was too late in the season for that—he didn't go much of anywhere on the weekends. The hardware store sometimes. He puttered in the garden, or watched sports on the television.

Colleen climbed up the steps, Pixie behind her. She waited a moment before ringing the bell (she wasn't allowed to have her own key), listening for raised voices. Nothing. That could be a good thing, but then again, it might be her mother had locked herself in the bathroom again, or barricaded herself in her bedroom. Her father slept in his own room, halfway down the hall between mother and daughter. Her mother's room, the master bedroom, had big white and gold dressers, and blue carpets. It held twin beds, so nobody would know her father slept in the other room, the one like a motel, with the narrow bed, the plain bureau, the gooseneck lamp. Sometimes he took long naps on weekend afternoons in his little room, with the door ajar, because her mother couldn't abide a closed door, not even if you were in the bathroom on the toilet.

She waited a minute longer, until Mrs. Baker drove along the street. She slowed down, and Colleen knew she was about to ask her if everything was okay, so she waved and smiled and rang the bell. Mrs. Baker drove by. It took a long time, but eventually her mother came to the door. She flipped the lock on the screen door but didn't open it, so Colleen let herself in. The whole house smelled of cigarette smoke. That wasn't good. Pixie scampered up the stairs to Colleen's bedroom and disappeared.

"Where have *you* been all day?" Her mother puffed a cigarette, burned down almost to the filter, and blew the smoke at Colleen.

"No place, just out in the woods. I went to see the horses. The big one had burrs on him so I picked those out. He's a good horse. He stood really still and didn't even stomp when I pulled them out of his mane, which I bet hurt, you know, like having knots combed out of your hair, and I gave him some apple." It was important to keep talking, because as she talked she could try to see where her father might be, and figure out what her mother had been doing just before she came in. Apparently she had been in the kitchen, because that's where she headed now. Colleen wiped her sneakers off on the mat and followed her without taking off her corduroy jacket.

In the kitchen her mother stood behind the speckled white and gold laminate countertop and butted out her cigarette in an overflowing ashtray positioned next to a bottle of scotch and a half-empty glass.

"Your father's downstairs."

Colleen knew she should acknowledge the bottle of scotch and the fact her mother was drinking during the day, which she never did; daylight drinking was Peter Kerrigan's province. She knew this, and yet she didn't want to say, *Why are you drinking, Mummy?* The whole room looked like a stage set, the props arranged just so, for maximum effect, and way down deep inside Colleen's stomach curled a teensy worm of contempt. All that drama, it got tired after a while, and seemed cheap.

"Do you want help making dinner?" Colleen asked.

Her mother lit another cigarette. "What makes you think I'm going to make you and your father dinner?" She blew the smoke from the side of her mouth and screwed her eyes up as she did.

"You don't have to make dinner."

"Well, thank *you,* Your Highness. I'm delighted to have your permission."

"I didn't mean it like that." When her mother was sour and snide like this, Colleen knew it wouldn't be long before she really blew up. Her mother was never really satisfied until everyone felt exactly as she did. Colleen didn't want to feel like her mother.

"How *did* you mean it?" her mother said.

"I just meant that if you're not feeling well, I can make dinner."

Colleen's mother knocked back the scotch in her glass and poured more. "What makes you think I'm not feeling well? Do I look unwell?"

The turquoise kitchen walls reflected coldly in the light from the overhead fixture and her mother's skin looked clammy. "You look fine," Colleen said.

"Then why say I'm not feeling well?"

"Mum, I only meant—"

"Oh, I know what you meant. You need somebody to take care of you. Everybody needs somebody to take care of them, don't they?" She reached over to a bowl of onions sitting on the counter and picked one up. "Fine. I'll make the dinner. Yes, that's exactly what I'll do. Sit and keep me company like a good daughter. You can pretend to be a good daughter, can't you?"

For a moment Colleen thought her mother might throw the onion at her. She sat. The brown plastic of the chair seat squeaked.

Colleen's mother opened the Lazy Susan and pulled out a big wooden cutting board. She slammed it on the counter before reaching into a drawer and snatching a large butcher knife from the cutlery tray. She hacked at the onion without peeling it. She put one hand on her hip and with the other she whacked and whacked at the onion, sending pieces flying everywhere. *Bang!* went the knife on the wooden board. *Bang! Bang! Bang!* From the corner of her eye Colleen saw Pixie slink from her bedroom and huddle by the stair railing. *Don't come down, puppy, don't come down.* The knife was very sharp and the smell of onion was bitter in the air.

"How's that? No, we need something else, don't we?" She spun round to the refrigerator, the knife still in her hand, opened the door and grabbed a bunch of carrots. She threw them on the counter. They hit the remains of the onion and onion bits fell to the floor. "What about this?" She held a raw chicken aloft. "Chicken! *Brak-brak-brak-brakkkkaaaa!*" She made chicken noises and then laughed in that madwoman way she did sometimes, the laugh that warned Colleen the funnel cloud was forming. Then she threw the chicken to the floor and stalked out of the kitchen.

Colleen grabbed the chicken and tossed it into the sink. She had to do this right away, she thought, because she didn't know what would happen next, and if things went really bad she'd forget about the chicken and Pixie might eat it and chicken bones would kill a dog. She knew this was an odd thing to be thinking and that it was odd she had time to think it. Her mother's crazy chuckle slipped around the corner. In the sink the chicken looked obscene, its legs flopping, the hole in its middle gaping. Time had slowed down, as though folded over on itself.

"Hey, Peter!" her mother yelled. "Peter, come here and tell me what you want for dinner! Peter!"

Colleen followed her mother and found her standing at the top of the stairs leading to the landing where the door to the garage, Colleen's playroom and the powder

165

room her father used were, and past that the second flight of stairs that led down to the television room.

"*Brak-brak-brakkkaaa!* Come on, Peter. Come and get it!"

Colleen's father appeared on the landing and looked up at his wife standing above him, waving a butcher knife. His face was grey except for red patches on his neck and under his eyes. Colleen couldn't tell if the patches, especially those on his neck, were just from fear or if they were marks of some earlier violence.

"What are you doing, Deirdre?" he said, and his voice held something like awe. "What the hell are you doing?"

"Come and get it, you chicken. Come and get it, big spender!"

She stepped down two stairs, jabbing at the air with the knife. With her left hand she gripped the banister, as though for traction, and her knuckles were white and purple.

Colleen locked eyes for just a second with her father, and then he bolted out the door to the garage, not even bothering to close it behind him. Colleen assumed her mother would go after him, but Deirdre Kerrigan turned and walked toward her daughter. Pixie barked and dashed down the stairs from the upstairs hall.

"Do *you* want it? How about it?" She moved her arm sinuously, making the glinting blade move like a snake. "Do you want *this?*"

Colleen backed up, Pixie beside her, barking.

"And your little dog too," her mother said, and laughed at her own joke.

Colleen lunged for the front door and pushed Pixie out in front of her. "Come on, Pixie. Run!" They ran down the steps, across the driveway and around the corner of the house.

Her father leaned against the brick near the garage's side door, doubled over, his hands on his knees.

"Daddy!"

She wanted to throw herself in his arms, but he stood up and held his hand out, warding her off. He looked past her, the fear still in his face.

"Is she coming?" he asked.

"I don't know."

He fumbled in his pockets and pulled out his keys. "I was coming to make sure you were okay. You go to a friend's house or something, pet. I have to go out."

Go out? "Where are you going?"

He walked back into the garage.

"Where are you *going?*" she cried after him. He couldn't be leaving. He couldn't leave her, not with her mother like this. He wouldn't.

The garage door opened and then she heard the car door close and the engine start up. She walked back around to the driveway. Sure enough, there was the car, the white Skylark with the red interior, backing out onto the road. She watched her father drive away.

Pixie whined and nudged her leg. "Okay, puppy, okay." She stroked his head and he mouthed her fingers, not biting, just holding on. Colleen turned and saw her mother in the master bedroom window over the garage. She had a cigarette between her lips. She, too, watched Peter Kerrigan drive away, and then she looked down and smiled at her daughter. A second later the curtains closed and Colleen was left standing in the driveway.

Colleen was glad she hadn't taken off her coat when she came in the house. Where should she go? She realized she was shivering. In fact, her teeth began to chatter and she knew she would, if she gave herself half a chance, start crying. She would not cry. She would not. She'd go to the park. She'd sit on the swings or on the bench and she'd wait until it was late at night and then she'd go back to the house and see if the car was back in the garage. First, though, she'd go down to the gas station and get some chips and cookies for supper.

"C'mon, Pixie." She tucked her hands under her armpits as she walked away. She didn't look back, and slowly the chattering and shaking subsided.

A Dangerous Current

Standing in the toilet stall, Colleen realized she probably wasn't going to be able to will herself insane right here and right now, although she acknowledged the possibility remained on the horizon. She stepped out of the stall. As she moved, she noticed the bottom of her left pant leg was soaked in vodka and cranberry juice. She looked up just as the other woman exited her stall. It was Diane, of the expensive burgundy boots, the dove-grey wrap-dress and perfectly tousled hair. The smell of alcohol wafted round the bathroom like a malicious spirit.

They don't call it "spirits" for nothing.

Diane blushed. "Are you sure you're all right?"

"Of course. I'm fine. Absolutely fine. I'll clean that up if there's a broom or something. Silly carrying salad dressing in my purse. I just picked it up at the market and didn't want to lug an extra bag around, you know?" The vodka sloshed against the inside of her skull and she realized full well she was talking too much, but maybe, just maybe, she could walk out of this bathroom and Diane wouldn't say anything to C&C and Colleen could go back to taking that stupid fucking test.

Diane washed her hands at the sink. "Don't worry about cleaning it up. I'll call down to Maintenance."

Why would she call Maintenance? Colleen thought she should wash her hands as well. That was what one did.

169

That was what well-mannered people did. She pumped the soap dispenser, but it was empty. She pretended it wasn't and rinsed her fingers under the water.

Diane pulled a paper towel—just one—from the dispenser and carefully dried her well-manicured hands. "I think I should tell you," she said as she tossed the used towel into the bin, "I'm a C&C placement officer. I was assigned to work with you."

Colleen's stomach pinged. "Lovely. I'm almost finished the tests." She reached for her own towel as Diane stepped closer to the door.

Diane looked at her watch. "It's nearly three. Perhaps it would be better if you came back tomorrow. You know"—she crossed her arms and looked down for a moment, then up again—"perhaps you should come back when you've given this some more thought—when you're . . . refreshed."

Colleen stiffened. "I don't know what you mean."

Diane's gaze was level and she looked as cross as a schoolmarm, but just a little sad too. "I have a sister with a drinking problem."

"I'm sorry to hear that."

"She got sober, though. She went to AA."

"Good for her."

"Perhaps you should try going to a few meetings."

"I appreciate your advice, and if I had a problem with alcohol, I'm sure that's the first place I'd go, however, I think it's presumptuous"—*Did I slur on that? Did I say "prezuptious"?*—"of you to say something like that to a perfect stranger in a prefeshonal . . . *professional* setting. I've had a bad day is all. A very bad day."

Horrified, she realized she was crying. Hot, stinging tears oozed from her eyes and dripped off her chin. She slapped at them with the palms of her hands.

Diane was looking at Colleen, her lips in a little moue, her head cocked, her brow furrowed. She placed her hands in the prayer position, just under her small sharp chin, and opened her mouth to say something.

Colleen pre-empted what she presumed would be the woman's self-satisfied pity. "Oh, to hell with it," she said, and hurled herself toward the door. Diane hopped aside, her hand to her throat.

In the hall, Colleen realized she'd have to go back into the office and get her coat, her lovely red coat. But the hallway seemed at an odd tilt, and she put her hand against the wall to steady herself. Panic rose in her chest like a black eel, slithering and squirming. She had drunk too much, had slipped over the line and was in real danger of careening out of control. She could fall, or pass out. She closed her eyes and for an instant it was impossible to tell what was up and what was down. Behind her, the door to the washroom opened, and she knew Princess Diane was about to parade her perfection up the hall, tossing judgment like coins to beggars.

Holding onto the wall, Colleen ducked round the bank of elevators into the hall beyond the C&C offices. Safely out of sight, she leaned back and tried to breathe deeply. It wasn't the drink, was it? This was an anxiety attack. Oh, the humiliation. It rose up in waves, along with the alcohol fumes. She looked around her. She stood in front of a dentist's office—Dr. Lipshitz—what kind of name was *that* for a dentist? Now she was laughing and crying at the same time, although laughter was definitely winning, which was a good sign.

After a few minutes she began to feel better; her chest was less constricted and the hall wasn't doing the old dipsy-doodle anymore. She could go back and finish the test probably—but she wouldn't, would she. Look at this place. The linoleum was stained and peeling in spots. A dead fichus tree rotted in a chrome planter by the dentist's door. The glass shades of the overhead light fixtures sported a spatter of dead flies. What kind of a job would she get from an agency housed in a dump like this? Another cheap lawyer's office in need of a fast typist, or some executive looking for a body to sit in front of his door while his secretary was on vacation lest an empty desk indicate how unnecessary the position was. Maybe she'd get lucky and work for a few weeks at some dismal, third-rate marketing agency and they'd want to hire her full time at less money than she made at the university. Lucky her.

This was not the new start of which she had dreamed. She was wasting her time. It was only the shock of the day that had led her here at all. She should give herself a few days to figure out her next move. Something in the film world, perhaps, or the music business. She'd enjoyed working in a music management office back in 1985, even if the boys in the band were divas. Tony Madison, that was the name of their manager. He'd liked her, and told her when she left to go back to the university (so sure she'd get her degree that time around) that he'd be glad to have her back if she changed her mind. There were people in the music business who would remember her. Maybe she could get a job in a recording studio.

Colleen felt better. She strode back into the offices of C&C Staffing. Kev was at his desk again and looked up from his crossword puzzle as she walked in. He blushed red as a radish. So, little Princess Di hadn't been able to keep her perfectly lipsticked mouth shut. Exactly what you'd expect in a place like this.

"We didn't know if you were coming back. Are you going to continue your testing?"

Colleen walked past Kev and snatched her coat from the back of the chair by the carrel at which she'd been working. She also picked up her test papers and stuffed them in her purse. She didn't want anyone looking at them and sniggering at any questions she'd answered incorrectly. Kev watched her leave, but didn't say a word. Not even *Will you be back?* Not even *Goodbye.*

Who cared? Out the door she went. Elevator down. Across the lobby and back onto the street.

And now what?

People flowed around her like schools of fish. Cars and buses zoomed past. Bicyclists, too, and a man on a silver scooter going faster than the cars. Where was everyone going in such a hurry? Colleen realized she had no destination. There was nowhere she needed to go and no one who cared if she got there or not. Where was her life?

Over and over again, she saw that bottle of vodka crash to the floor. She had been caught. She had done what she never thought she would: she had huddled like a fugitive, drinking out of a hidden bottle in a bathroom stall. But was that true? No, it wasn't true. She had drunk from a hidden bottle in a number of bathrooms—at work, in movie theatres, at her mother's nursing home (quite often there, in fact), in people's homes when the booze wasn't flowing fast enough to suit her, in restaurants when she deemed it more economical to bring her own . . . She'd just never been caught before.

This was not who she was, though. She was not a woman covered in vodka in a bathroom stall. This was not the Colleen Kerrigan who loved James Agee and Gabrielle Roy and Graham Greene and Thomas Hardy and all those other wonderful writers. Not the Colleen Kerrigan who had her first poem published in the school yearbook and who even though she never had anything else published surely would, one day, she surely would. She was a bluestocking, a woman of the mind, who lived in her thoughts, and who read books on God and science and history and understood all of it. I didn't matter she'd never graduated from university. Neither had Ray Bradbury nor Truman Capote. Everyone had always said how smart she was. Even Jake, who was about as cheap with a compliment as ever a man could be, said she had brains.

So how had she let that terrible moment happen? How? She drank too much—hadn't she vowed just this morning not to drink at all today—and in a hideously, fluorescent-lit moment of clarity she understood she was probably exactly what Princess Diane had said she was. A little cry escaped her lips and a man passing glanced at her. She put her fingers over her mouth. It was true, wasn't it, and not the first time she'd thought it either. The problem was, she couldn't possibly stop drinking today, and it had been that way for a long while, hadn't it.

She felt lost, adrift. What a desultory sort of life she'd been leading, rambling, meandering, being knocked from one place to the next, led not by any map or plan, but merely in reaction to one damn thing after another. She was a little boat that had slipped its moorings and was floating off into a dangerous current leading to a turbulent open sea. She could not help thinking of safe harbours and whether or not she would ever find one.

The air stank of car exhaust and dust. The whole neighbourhood, which used to be so trendy, looked down on its luck. Plastic bags fluttered by the curbs. Garbage cans overflowed. The never-quite-solvent businesses that changed every year or so . . . a spa, a laser treatment centre, an answering service (who used *those* anymore?). The public school looked like a refugee from 1960s Russia. That was the problem with this city; it tried so hard, but never quite managed to live up to its potential.

Colleen wanted to get away from the C&C building in case Kev or Diane came out and saw her just standing there like a piece of battered driftwood. She walked toward Mount Pleasant, reached into her purse and pulled out her cell phone. Maybe someone had called her. She flipped it open. *You have two missed calls.* Colleen's heart did a little Texas two-step. She dialled in to her messages and listened.

"Ms. Kerrigan, this is Carol from Spring Lake Place. Can you give us a call when you get a minute? Everything's fine, but your mother's had a bit of a fall and we've sent her off to St. Mike's just to be sure."

Shit. Colleen was about to call them back, but then thought she should listen to the second message. Maybe it had all worked out without her. She could *not* handle her mother today. Of course she fell, *again.* She fell all the time, because she refused to use the walker that everyone, except Deirdre, agreed she needed. She kept saying she just wanted to fall down and be dead. Eventually, Colleen assumed, she'd get her wish, but not without causing a great deal of trouble beforehand.

Ah, that was a terrible thing to think, and she knew it. But it was the truth. For Colleen, her mother's death was something she both feared and desired. For forty-nine years she had lived under her mother's cloud, and the possibility that she might one day be free of it was incontestably attractive. On the other hand, when Colleen thought of her mother she was filled with regret, for even though Deirdre was the cause of so much wanton destruction, so much slash-and-burn, Colleen understood her life had been a miserable one, and when it was finally over she knew she'd grieve for all the things that might have been and never were.

She listened to the second message.

"Hey," a deep male voice said. *He* said. Jake. "It's me." Of course he never gave his name, always assuming she'd know. Cocky bastard. "Give me a call. I want to talk to you."

She should call the nursing home back. But they said everything was all right. There was nothing she could do. And besides, this was the worst of days and she couldn't cope with one more goddamn thing. She was disappointed. Lori hadn't called, nor had anyone from the university. What did she expect? Well, she had hoped maybe one of the profs would call to see if she was okay, to see if there was anything they could do. They would have heard by now.

She didn't want to call Jake from the street because she knew talking to him, the person who maybe knew her better than anyone else in the world, and from whom it was impossible to hide, could lead to tears. She hurried back down Mount Pleasant and by the time she reached Davisville she was nearly sober again. In fact, she had the post-drink droops, all energy gone, mood plummeting to her heels. She might need a nap. She was also hungry. Her stomach growled as she stepped into the empty lobby and she realized she hadn't eaten since that breakfast sandwich on the way to what-used-to-be-her-job. The elevator was as deserted as the lobby. She imagined a post-apocalyptic city with all the people gone, just her and the plastic bags tumbling down the forsaken streets. It was almost comforting. What would it be like to never have to worry about what other people thought of you?

As she opened the door to her apartment she was struck by how still it was. A miasma of loneliness thickened the air. She snorted at her own sentimentality—either what she smelled was a miasma of loneliness or the milk was off. She dropped her purse, took her coat off, hung it in the hall closet and went into the kitchen. Whatever she had smelled when she came in was gone now. Perhaps it had been a ghost, or perhaps she was becoming more like her mother than she wanted to admit. Her mother's condo, the one she'd moved into after Peter Kerrigan succumbed to lung cancer seventeen years ago, had this *smell* in it— pungent and cloying—an old-lady smell it had taken Colleen weeks of cleaning to eradicate before she put the place up for sale last spring. Deirdre never seemed to notice it. Maybe this was how it started: you walked in one day and there it was, an odour so sharp it peeled the wallpaper, and then, as quickly as you started smelling it, you stopped smelling it. It just became the smell of your own house, which no one really smelled, did they? She vowed to watch the faces of those who crossed her threshold for signs of sniffing, and if they appeared she'd drown the whole place in bleach and burn sage for a month.

There was nothing in the fridge she wanted: yogurt, stale bread, two apples, a jar of olives, celery. The white wine bottles stood in a tidy at-attention row in the fridge door. How clean and cool they looked. She had to call Jake back, and she couldn't do that without a glass of wine in her hand.

She chose a packet of cheddar cheese slices, and the stale bread. She toasted the bread and made herself a sandwich. Then she poured herself a glass of Chablis. The taste on her lips was as refreshing as a dip in a mountain lake. The perfect accompaniment, she thought, to a cheese sandwich. There she was, the little French fairy, all decked out in verbena leaves, released from her bottle, flitting around the room.

Colleen brought the sandwich and the glass (not the bottle, just the glass) to the couch. The apartment was too quiet. She turned on the television and listened to a big old bald Southern boy with a cheesy moustache telling a crying woman this wasn't his first rodeo and something about a pancake having two sides no matter how flat it was.

"Fucking genius," Colleen said to the screen.

She turned the television off and when she did the silence rushed back in to fill up all the available space. The room looked the same—the blue sofa, the black coffee table, the television, the battered leather chair under a reading lamp by the window, the shelves of books (most bought from remainder tables), the small table and four chairs in the dining area no one ever sat in—but the objects looked slightly askew, as though someone had come in while she was out and moved everything an inch to the left. This sinister silence, whatever it was, invaded her home with intent. *They don't call it "spirits" for nothing.* She finished her sandwich, refilled her glass and called Jake.

"Yeah, hey," he answered, because of course her number came up on his phone and that was how he spoke to her, casual, almost bored. She understood this was because he didn't want her to know his true feelings. The old game.

"I'm having a bad one, a really bad one," she said. She hadn't meant to start like that. She hadn't meant to sound so needy. Why did just the sound of his voice turn her into Imperilled Pauline? Not that what she said wasn't true.

"Yeah, I thought you might be."

Why would he think that? Last night? The phone calls? She didn't want to ask. She'd learned the best way to handle what she called her "grey-outs" was to pretend nothing at all had happened, but to listen for clues. "Really? What are you now, psychic?"

"You were pretty upset last night."

The blunt statement gut-punched her. It was important not to let on that memories of the night before were little more than vapour. "Things are piling up, you know."

"You had me worried."

"Nice to know you still care."

"Don't be cute, Colleen. You said some pretty wild stuff last night. Look, I know you'd had a few, and that's no big deal, but maybe, I don't know, maybe you should find someone to talk to."

"I'm talking to you." What the hell had she said? Snippets of talk hovered at the edges of her memory. *Can't take much more . . . might as well . . .* yes, she'd been crying last night. She'd been pacing, phone in hand, crying. Had she said that? *I miss you . . . empty life . . . pointless life.* Jesus. "I was upset last night, that's all. But today . . . Jake, I don't know if I can take much more." Why had she said that, *again*?

He sighed. She would bet he was pinching the bridge of his now, bowing his head. His special expressions of impatience.

"Sorry, am I a burden? Maybe this call was a mistake. I'm returning *your* call, you know. I just thought . . . you were going to be there for me, a friend. My mistake."

"Babe, take it easy. I am your friend."

"It doesn't feel like it."

"Okay, what's up?"

She pictured him at his desk, tie loosened, chair tilted back, Bluetooth in his ear. Maybe he was pulling on his lower lip the way he did. Amber eyes scanning the room. His eyes were never still.

"I'm out of work."

"You get fired?"

"Why would you say that?"

"Well, did you?"

"No, I didn't get fired. I had to quit." Her chin was trembling and now she really was going to cry. She gulped down the white wine. Empty glass. The pretty French fairy disappeared like a burst soap bubble. "They were accusing me of all sorts of things I didn't do."

"Like what? Anything interesting?"

She knew that tone. Jake was a great smirker. It was part of his armour against the world and she knew that but it didn't stop her, from time to time, from wanting to rip it off his face. Their relationship had always been like this, and worse. He'd slapped her a couple of times. She once threw a chair at him.

"Sylvia's been taking work off my desk and then I get accused of losing it or not doing it. I told them. She even had a bunch of stuff right there in her hand, papers Harry had left for me to make copies for his class, but she took them and when he came looking for them, of course I didn't know anything about it and David was there and Sylvia's grinning away and *presto* she produces the copies and I look like an idiot. I don't know why that little bitch had it in for me. I never did anything to her. When she first came to the department I took her out for lunch and tried to get to know her, but she thinks . . . oh, I don't know what she thinks."

Tears ran down Colleen's face. She had taken Sylvia out to lunch, taken her to a little restaurant down on John Street. Colleen had ordered a carafe of wine but when she went to pour some for Sylvia, the stuck-up bitch put her hand over her glass and said, "Do you always drink at lunch?" *Really?* What kind of manners did that show? Colleen had only drunk a single glass and left the rest sitting on the table, which was a stupid waste, and they'd never had lunch again. Sylvia had asked her a couple of times, but Colleen didn't trust her.

"Hey, I'm sorry, babe." Jake's voice was softer now. He could be so sweet. "What are you going to do? You'll be all right. You've got the money from your mother's condo, right?"

"I'm the legal guardian, but I have to pay for the nursing home and anything else she needs. I can't spend her money on myself. Not until she dies. I don't mean it like that. You know what I mean."

"Yeah, I do. But she's what, ninety? She's not going to need all that money. How much is it? Two, three hundred thousand? She owes you. You can use some if you need to."

"I need another job. Listen, can you come over? I'm so down."

"I'm working."

"I know that. After work."

There was a pause. A longer one than Colleen liked. "Problem?" she asked.

"No. Sure. I can come over for a minute. I wanted to talk to you anyway."

"About what?"

"I'll see you later, okay? Couple of hours. Around six. Take it easy this afternoon, okay? Take a bubble bath or something."

"I wish you'd tell me what you want to talk to me about. You sound serious."

"We'll talk when I see you. I gotta go. And Colleen . . ."

"What?"

"Just take it easy, for me, all right?"

He was worried about her; that was all. "I think I'll take a nap."

"Great idea. See you." He disconnected.

Colleen sat looking at the phone in her hand. Several things buzzed through her head. First, she was going to have to start hiding the phone from herself. No more drink-and-dial calls. But it always happened. She'd feel down and have a drink and then the booze would lift her spirits and she'd feel like all was right with the world, but then the happy turned to sad again and she'd *need* to talk to somebody and the next thing she knew she was scrolling through her phone list and dialling away.

Admit it: fewer people were answering her calls these days. She had fewer and fewer numbers in her phone list.

Colleen clasped her hands between her knees. She looked around the room. The parquet floor under the air conditioner was water-damaged. Dust balls looked like dead mice in the corners. The furniture was variously faded, stained and chipped. The venetian blinds on the long wall of windows hung unevenly, the slats bent in places. The light was harsh, late-afternoon, sharp and autumnal, promising only oncoming darkness and months of colder, bleaker light to come.

When she first lived on her own, sometimes at night she'd imagine sounds in the hall, or claw-like hands reaching around the door frame. She'd dream of malicious spirits that half woke her from sleep, but held her down so she couldn't move, couldn't scream. The struggle to wake up seemed to take hours. Then, shaking and chilled with sweat, she'd crouch in the corner of the room so nothing could sneak up behind her. It took years before the night-terrors went away, and only with the help of her fairies. She hadn't thought about that in ages. She glanced toward the hallway. If she let herself, she'd conjure the vision of those bony, grasping claws again. She brought her clasped hands up to her mouth and bit her knuckles to stifle a cry.

It was just after four.

Colleen stood and went to the shelf behind the table and chairs. She ran her fingers over the books. They were friends who never failed her. Shakespeare, of course, Mark Twain, William Wilberforce, James Baldwin, Tim O'Brien, Madeleine L'Engle, Julian of Norwich, Pema Chödrön, Celtic prayers, Dietrich Bonhoeffer, histories of various periods, Austen, Dickens, Thomas Wolfe, memoirs by people who had survived dreadful childhoods, the sagas of Iceland, Eudora Welty, Dorothy Parker, Hemingway, Cheever, and Auden . . . They weren't the books she wanted. What did she want? Something. Something she wouldn't leave out in the open. She walked, a little unsteadily, to her bedroom. In the closet, in a box on the top shelf. All the books of her secret self—*Drinking: A Love Story, Under the Influence, The Vitamin Cure for Alcoholism, Alcoholics Anonymous, The Easy Way to Stop Drinking, How to Change Your Drinking, Overcoming Addiction without AA, My Way Out, Seven Weeks to Safe Social Drinking, The Alcohol Cure, Cool Water: Alcoholism, Mindfulness, and Ordinary Recovery . . .*

She'd read them all. Tried them all. Gone to therapy even, which hadn't helped a bit. The first therapist, who had just recovered memories of her own childhood sexual molestation, kept insisting Colleen had probably been molested as well, and that her lack of memory around the events was evidence of their existence. Jesus, Colleen had said, I remember enough bad shit, can't we deal with that? The second therapist (or *analyst,* as she corrected Colleen) was a Jungian, but Colleen generally went there half sloshed. When she finally admitted that and the analyst suggested she come back sober next week, she hadn't returned.

Everyone had an answer, but none that worked for her. *Surrender. Fight. Take a pill. Make a graph and monitor your drinking.* Did non-alcoholics need such graphs?

She picked up the *Alcoholics Anonymous* book. She looked for the passage she had underlined, about the movie publicist who wanted to be a writer. There it was. Alcohol, the man said, had first given him wings, and then it took away the sky.

She said the sentence aloud, closed her eyes and said it again. She wished she had written that line. She went to the desk under the window, picked up her journal and a pen and began to write, but it was nothing but whining and complaint, the lines on the page all scraggly. There was nothing to say except that she was fucked and yet she wanted those wings, wanted them so badly. She threw the pen on the floor and ran down the hall to the kitchen. She opened the refrigerator. Next to the two full bottles, the third was less than half full. She lifted it to her mouth and drank straight and true and deep.

Little French fairy*, bonjour, encore. Restez, je vous supplie.*

The hollow centre of Colleen's soul filled with honey, the nectar of the gods who knew the truth of all things and would, at any moment, share them with her. But then, as though she were a ship hit by a rogue wave, the room spun

187

and her stomach pitched and rolled. She had to lie down. She edged to the couch and flopped into the squishy pillows. The room twirled. She put her foot on the ground. She was cold, chilled to the bone, and pulled the smelly old green throw over herself. She mustn't be sick. God, that was it for today, no more drinking. She had wasted yet another day, another chance. She saw the look on Princess Diane's face, the falling vodka bottle, the splatter, and smelled the fumes. Shame swam through her gut like an acid shark. She bit the corner of the green throw and made promises to God. Never again. She was done. She'd had her last drink. She would be better, cleaner, purer. If only she wouldn't throw up now. If only she'd be sober now. She had to concentrate on something other than the watery, sloshing sensations in her gut. She reached for the television remote control. Oprah and her favourite things. Hair care products. iPad by Apple (a name no woman would have suggested). Those goddamn ugly boots Sylvia wore. Change channels. *Law & Order.* God bless *Law & Order.*

She concentrated on her breathing. In and out. Stare at a fixed point. Watch the detectives . . . The criminal reminded her of her cousin, Liam. Poor Liam, now there was an addict, poor bastard. She wasn't anywhere near as bad as that. Colleen felt herself drifting off. Oh, blessed sleep . . . *In peace will I both lay me down and sleep; for thou, Lord, alone makest me dwell in safety . . . Keep watch, dear Lord, with those who work, or watch, or weep this night . . .*

Just Keep Walking

Liam, Colleen's cousin, was five years younger than she. A long, gawky kid with a shy smile and a floppy mop of brown hair he either hid under or blew out of his eyes, he was the black sheep of the family, the one they all tut-tutted about, starting as far back as when he was fourteen and he dropped acid, then spent the night sitting in a farmer's field with a shotgun under his chin. He'd spent a year in the mental institution after that, where he drew thousands of pictures of fantastical birds and beasts of his own imagining. Everyone said he could have a career as an illustrator if he wanted. Maybe he did want, but he wanted to get high more.

He was what they called a "garbage head," meaning he'd take anything to get high, from booze to pot to pills to crack to meth. When he was around thirty he told the story of how he found a red capsule on the sidewalk and popped it into his mouth, delighted at the mystery.

"But it could have been *anything*!" Colleen had shrieked.

"That's the fun part," he replied.

He couldn't hold a job. He mowed the lawn at a golf course for a while, and worked as an orderly on the palliative care wing of a hospital, which, Colleen thought, was a spectacularly bad place for a drug addict to work. Sure enough, he was fired for pilfering opiates. He did day-labour and delivered pizzas and worked for a lawn service and a dry cleaner and a variety of fast-food joints. He got

189

fired from or quit them all. For a while he lived with a woman, fifteen years older than he, who had four kids. If nothing else, they shared a love of the pipe. His parents, Colleen's paternal aunt and her husband, made sure he had groceries, and when he wasn't living in their basement transferred twenty dollars a day into a bank account they'd set up for him.

He got clean when he was in his early thirties, and it seemed as though he might just be all right after all. He visited Colleen now and again. They went out for lunch, and although he said he didn't mind if she had a glass of wine, she didn't drink around him. Once she let him sleep on her couch for a week when he was between places. The second night he was there, just after they'd shared a dinner of lasagna and salad, he said he'd like to go to a meeting, and did she want to come.

"A meeting? What, for addicts?"

He grinned at her over his coffee cup. "Addicts and alcoholics, yeah. There are some really nice people there. You might even meet someone, you know?"

"I don't think so." Looking for a date at a meeting of alcoholics and addicts seemed akin to looking for one in a mental institution.

"Okay, forget romance. Aren't you curious?"

She considered this. She was a bit. Liam had been such a horrible mess six months ago. Now, here he sat in a crisp white shirt and new jeans. He was shaved and his brown hair—still floppy—was clean. His hands didn't shake and he didn't smell like a backed-up sewage pipe. Although he was still thin as a whippet, he no longer had that gaunt, starved look. Sores and scratches no longer marred his skin.

"Speaking of romance, maybe you have a new girlfriend you want to introduce me to?"

He chuckled. "I wish. But no new relationships for the first year. Although my sponsor tells me if I can keep a plant alive for six months, he'll think about letting me get a fish." He raised his eyebrows. "Come on, why not come with me? It's an open meeting. Anybody can come. Be my support. What else are you going to do, sit around watching bad television?"

And so she had agreed.

The meeting was in the common room of an apartment building in Regent Park, a welfare housing community downtown. The floors were checkerboard pink and grey linoleum, and the walls, too, were grey. Windows looked out over the building's parking lot and a tiny, battered-looking park in which some teenagers stood about in small groups. Trestle tables had been put together to form a square around which sat about twenty people, male and female, white, black, Hispanic, mostly in their thirties or forties, with a couple of older men and two girls who looked to be in their twenties. Everyone had coffee in front of them, or bottles of water.

The leader of the meeting, a bearded man wearing a T-shirt with the words *I'm wearing this T-shirt ironically* read something called "How It Works," which listed the twelve steps. They went around the room saying their names and identifying themselves as addicts or alcoholics, or both.

"I'm Dave, and I'm an alcoholic and drug addict," the leader said.

"Hi, Dave," they all responded.

When they came to Colleen she looked at Liam, who smiled encouragingly.

She flushed as everyone stared at her. She thought they appeared a little hungry, as though she had a chocolate chip cookie glued to her forehead. "I'm Colleen. I guess I'm here to support my cousin."

"Hi, Colleen," the group said.

Introductions over, they read a passage from a little black book about the awful load the addict carries around with him and how the addict lives in constant fear of being found out. "When you come into AA, and get honest with yourself and with other people, that terrible load of lying falls off your shoulders."

People nodded. Clearly, Colleen thought, they'd drunk the Kool-Aid. Still, if it helped Liam, it couldn't be a bad thing. They seemed normal enough, if a bit . . . hardened—that woman sitting across from Colleen with the missing teeth, the coarse skin and green-painted fingernails; the men with their nicotine-stained fingers and tattoos. One of the twenty-something girls had a tattoo— some sort of writing—on her neck, for heaven's sake. Only the two older men, both of whom looked like retired farmers or stevedores—their hands heavy claws, their skin weather-beaten—showed no visible ink. One woman, at the far end of the tables, looked different from the rest. In her fifties, perhaps, and she wore a green cardigan and tan slacks. Her hair was pulled back into a soft bun. She looked to be the sort of person Colleen could see herself having lunch with, although she supposed a glass of wine would be out of the question.

One after another, they spoke of the challenges of staying away from drugs or drink. The woman with the green nails said her daughter had been arrested the night before for assault. "It was really hard not to go get drunk over that," she said, and people make sympathetic sounds. "I didn't, though. I called my sponsor. I'm here," the woman said with grim determination.

Someone else talked about wanting to quit his job, but knew he'd have to just accept it, no matter how much of an asshole his boss was. One of the girls said she was celebrating twenty-seven days sober. Everyone applauded. Liam talked about how grateful he was to have his family back in his life again, like his cousin, Colleen, who was letting him crash with her until he could move into his new place with sober roommates at the end of the month.

"And what about you?" Dave, the leader asked. He was looking at Colleen.

"Me?"

"Yeah, you," said Dave. He chuckled. "How you doing?"

"I'm fine."

They were all looking at her. "Obviously, there's a lot of alcoholism in my family. My father . . . Liam, others, I guess. So, I'm very aware, you know, I'm very careful. I watch my drinking, you know?"

"Oh, we know," said one of the men, and with that everyone burst into laughter.

She didn't see what was so funny. She glared at Liam. Had he brought her here to make fun of her? Who *were* these people but a bunch of drunks, anyway?

He patted her knee and smiled. "It's okay," he said.

"Keep coming back," the woman in the green cardigan said.

She didn't listen to much that was said after that. She had the feeling there was a set-up here. Is this how they recruited? Well, it wouldn't work on her. She supposed they couldn't help it; they must look around and think *everyone* was a drunk. Like all converts, they just had to *proselytize.*

After the meeting closed—with a prayer, all of them standing in a circle holding hands—the woman in the green cardigan walked up to Colleen, her hand extended.

"My name's Ginger," she said. "It's so nice to meet you. Liam talks about you a lot. He's doing really well, isn't he."

"We're all proud of him."

"Why don't I give you my number?" She held out a piece of paper. "Just in case you ever want to talk."

"Thanks," Colleen said, since it was the only polite thing to do.

Liam said his goodbyes and the group began to break up. Liam and Colleen, with a couple of others, left the room and headed down the corridor to the front doors. Two young men slouched against the wall there, their clothes baggy, their eyes bright.

"What you want?" one said. He was fat, with a bald head. "We got what you want? A little taste, baby, a little french fry." He licked his lips.

"Crunch and munch, come on, now. You know you want it." This one had a line of teardrops tattooed down his cheek, under his left eye.

They whispered them over, gesturing with their fingers, leering.

"Are you kidding me?" said Colleen. "You wait in the hallway? Outside an AA meeting? What are you people, vultures?"

"Be cool, Colleen," whispered Liam. "Just keep walking."

The guy with the teardrop tattoo stepped into her path. "You got a fucking problem?"

Her heart pounded but she couldn't stop herself. She was incandescent. "You should be *ashamed* of yourselves. They're not even out the door yet! What's the *matter* with you?" She sounded like a schoolteacher, when she wanted to sound like an avenging angel.

"You fucking with my business, bitch?" the fat one asked, in an ominously quiet voice.

Liam pulled at her elbow. "No troubles. We're leaving. She's not from around here, you know?"

"No kidding," said the fat boy. He made a little kissing noise as Liam urged her toward the glass doors. "I'll be waiting for you, mama."

When Colleen looked back, the two girls were coming down the hall with Dave. Dave laughed and said something to the men, and although they laughed back, he kept his hands on the girls' arms.

Colleen's breathing was ragged. "Do you go through that every time?"

Liam shrugged. "Temptation's always around. That's never gonna change. It's not about them. It's about me. There's a bar on every corner, a dealer down every street."

"If you say so. But that's insane."

Liam chuckled. "Not half as insane as doing what I used to do."

He sounded so strong, and so clear. She admired him, and told him so.

Liam stayed with Colleen for another week, and then he went off to his new apartment with his new clean-and-sober friends. She never found out exactly what went wrong, or when the wheels came off his resolve. Six months later he was back on the pipe, on the pills, on the booze, on whatever he found lying around. He disappeared into the streets. Three years later he collapsed in an alley. The police found him, and after a night in hospital his parents let him come back home. He lived in their basement, trying every day to get clean again. He stopped using, but when Colleen saw him she struggled not to burst into tears. Several of his teeth were missing and those that remained were cracked. His face was covered in sores. Brown lesions disfigured his long skinny legs. He crawled back to those meetings, but somehow he couldn't grab hold again. He said he'd do it his way and didn't need a sponsor, didn't need to "work the steps" as they called it.

One morning he said he was going for a walk. He took a rope from his parents' garage and hanged himself from a tree behind the Anglican church, the same church in which he'd sung in the choir as a child. If he'd lived to the end of that day, he would have had thirty days clean and sober, but it was just too late.

The Urban Angel

Colleen awoke with a start. She wiped drool off her cheek. It was dark. What time was it? 6:30. The reflected light from the city beyond her windows, such as it was, looked like greyish dishwater. She swung her legs to the side of the sofa and groaned. Oh, her head and her stomach and that taste in her mouth. She ran her hands through her hair, which was flat on one side and damp with sweat. The whole dreadful day lashed back at her, leaving welts of disgust. Fuck.

Someone knocked at the door.

"Colleen? You in there?" *Knock, knock, knock.*

Jake. She had spoken to him earlier. Yes, she remembered that.

She must look like hell on a stick. "Yeah, yeah. Hang on. Give me a minute." She lurched to the bathroom. In the mirror her face was blotchy and puffy, her eyes red. She ran the water ice cold and doused her face. She squeezed a glob of toothpaste onto her finger and rubbed it around her teeth. Powder. Lipstick. She brushed her hair and fluffed it.

It would do.

Jake leaned against the door jamb when she opened it, his head down but eyes on her. "Hey." He straightened and kissed her cheek with the corner of his mouth. "I been knocking. You all right?"

He was fresh from the office, topcoat open, black suit and white shirt, silver tie. His hair, which he had worn in an Afro back in the day, was shaved down to a mere shadow on his perfectly round head. He smelled of that scent particular to Jake, not cologne, just the scent of his skin, a little like cinnamon and cloves.

"Fine. I was asleep. Like you said, I needed a nap."

"Uh-huh." He walked past her and looked around the apartment. "Been a while since I been here. Nothing's changed."

"What were you expecting?" She closed the door.

He shrugged.

"You want something?"

"What you offering?" He cocked an eyebrow.

"Drink? Coffee? I don't know." She wasn't in the mood for his banter. She never could play the game for as long as he could. It always hurt her feelings in the end.

"Got a beer?" He took his coat off and tossed it on the leather chair by the window and then sat in the far corner of the sofa with his arms draped over the back and his legs spread.

"No beer. Wine. Vodka." She didn't want one herself. She wanted water, and lots of it, and some crackers.

"Glass of wine, then. You got red?"

"White."

"Whatever."

She went into the kitchen and drank two tumblers full of water and ate five saltines before pouring him a glass of wine. She poured herself a half-glass, just to be sociable. When she went back to the living room Jake was texting something.

"I hate those things," she said.

His thumbs, which looked entirely too big for the tiny keypad, twitched over the keys for a few more minutes and then he put the device in an inside jacket pocket.

"So," he said. "What's up?"

He reached over and grabbed her by the back of her neck, shaking her gently, but still, it made the room dive and pitch. She squirmed away.

"Don't."

"Having a rough day, huh?"

"Yeah."

"Decided what you want to do?" He picked up his wine. "Cheers."

"I just lost my job this morning, for Christ's sake."

"So, you did get fired."

"No. Yes. I don't know. Kind of." She had a sip of wine. Just a sip.

"Anything you can do to make it right?"

"I don't want to make it right. I don't have anything to make right. I didn't do anything wrong. Why would you even say something like that?"

"Listen, Colleen, I've lost a job or two in my time. It's not the end of the world. And, you know, maybe I deserved to get fired. I was hitting it pretty hard there for a while."

"What's your point?"

"Don't look at me like that. I'm not judging you, I'm just saying. You always liked working at the university."

"I'm not going back there. I've worked there too goddamn long as it is. I'm in a rut. I need something new, something challenging."

"Like what? Shit. Hang on." Jake pulled his phone out of his pocket, flipped it open and looked at the readout, but then closed it and replaced it in his pocket.

"You need to get that?"

"It's nothing. Right, so, what do you want to do?"

"Is there anything at Jenkins & McEwan?"

"My office?" He pulled his chin back and looked like he might laugh. "You're kidding, right? C'mon, Colleen. You and me can't work at the same place. Shit."

"I'm not saying I'd work for you. I wouldn't work for you, but in some other department maybe. The salary'd be a hell of a lot higher than I'm making now." She drank a little more wine.

"I don't think there's anything. Okay, okay, look, I'll ask, all right. But don't get your hopes up. You know what the guys in the business are like. They want their assistants to be, shit, you know . . ."

"What? I have experience."

He shrugged, holding his hands up in surrender. "Yeah, okay, I'll ask. I will. I can't promise, though. But listen, babe, that's not what I came over to talk to you about."

She was still muzzy and unfocused from her nap. She should never nap late in the afternoon like that. Waking up in the dark always disoriented her, made her feel as if she were viewing everything through a wall of water. The back of her head felt as though someone had driven a couple of screws into the base of her skull. She knew he probably wanted to talk about last night, but surely he could see this wasn't the time for it, not with everything she'd been through.

"What could you want to talk about that's more important?"

"You know I care about you, right?"

"I care about you too."

"Good. So you believe me when I say I want you to be okay and have a good life and all that. Because I do, really, I do. I don't know what's going on with you, or . . . I don't know . . . maybe I do. Like I said before, there was a time I was doing some stuff maybe I shouldn't have been doing, right? You know what I'm saying. I was getting high all the time and shit."

"You don't do coke anymore, though, right?"

"Nah, coke-free zone. I'm good." He sat forward on the couch, took a drink of his wine and rolled the glass between his palms. "Look, I'll just come out with it. Last night, when you called, you sounded pretty tanked."

"It was just a bad night. I might have had a glass or two, just watching television, and—"

"It was more than a glass or two and, babe, you call me like that, what? Twice a week, more maybe?"

"No, I don't." Something icy swirled in her belly. She had no idea what he was talking about, but something slipped in under her mind's door, some terrible draft of possibility. "I don't call you that much."

"Yeah, you do. And I haven't minded 'cause, look, I know it's not easy being alone and all that. No, let me finish. But the last couple of times you called, all this shit about killing yourself . . ."

Couple of times? She couldn't remember when she'd called him before last night. What on earth had she said to him? "You're exaggerating. What's with all the fucking drama, Jake?"

"You said you were going to throw yourself off the balcony. We were on the phone for three hours. I was going to call the police."

"What? Oh come *on!*" Colleen studied his face to see if he was, as he called it, yanking her chain. "You are joking, right?" The band of pain around her head throbbed. She couldn't think straight.

"You don't remember any of it, do you."

His eyes held something very much like contempt. That was worse than anything. If he was angry, they could yell and scratch and throw things. If he was sad, she could console him. But contempt was so close to disgust. She knew of no way to wipe that stain off. Jumping off the balcony didn't sound like such a bad idea after all.

"Jake, okay, maybe I had a bit too much to drink, and okay, to be honest, I'm not sure I remember the whole conversation. I don't know what you're getting so high and mighty about. It's not like I haven't listened to your bullshit for more hours than I can remember, over more years than either of us like to admit. You remember when I bailed you out that time you ran your car into a mailbox and were so drunk the cops had to have you sit on the floor in the station because you kept falling off the fucking chair?"

"That was fifteen years ago," he said quietly.

"You still drink."

"Not like you do."

"Fuck you." She stood up, although she didn't know where she was going. Or maybe she did. Perversely, she wanted a drink now, *really* wanted one, and it was her house and she'd goddamn well have a drink if she wanted to.

Jake reached over and grabbed her wrist. "Sit down, Colleen. Just for a minute."

He pulled her down and she sat, glaring at him. "Say what you want to, then."

"What you do is your business. How much you drink or don't drink is your business, and I'm nobody to tell you what to do. But things have changed, you know, and I can't have you calling me all the time, not now."

"I don't call you all the time." But that was only part of the story, wasn't it. She could tell that by looking at him. "You want to tell me what's changed."

"That's why I'm here." He took a deep breath. "You remember Taquanda."

"The receptionist at your office?"

"Yeah, I introduced you back in July at Le Select Bistro."

Colleen and Lori had gone out to celebrate Lori's birthday. Jake and this *Taquanda* had been at a window

205

table. She was late twenties, maybe, hair in dreadlocks down her back. Beautiful. The girl was beautiful. The girl was a child. She probably didn't know who Jimi Hendrix was; she probably didn't know who The Beatles were.

Her phone buzzed on the coffee table. It danced across the wood.

"You gonna get that?" Jake asked.

She picked it up. *Spring Lake Place.* "Fuck. It's my mother. She took a fall today."

"She all right?"

"Yeah, I'm sure she is."

The phone buzzed again.

"You should answer it."

She didn't want to. But what if this was *the* call. Jake would be here. He'd help her. "Hello?"

"Ms. Kerrigan?"

"Yes."

"This is Spring Lake Place. I'm calling about your mother."

"Is she okay?"

"We called you earlier today, and were hoping to hear back from you."

"Is she okay?"

"It was quite a bad fall. Worse than we initially thought. You know she refuses to use a walker and we can't watch her all the time."

Colleen hugged herself. "What's happening?"

"The hospital says she may have hit her head in the fall, either that or she's had another transient ischemic attack. She's not conscious at the moment. They're suggesting you should go there. There's a geriatrician assigned to the case. Her name is Dr. Joyce Chan. Do you have a pen? I'll give you the hospital's number."

And here it is, she thought. This is it. My mother. A cake her mother had baked her for her seventh birthday popped into her head. It was in the shape of a lion, with chocolate icing on the mane and black licorice for the legs, gumdrops for paws . . . it had taken her mother two whole days to make it.

Jake watched her, his brow furrowed, as she took down the information.

"We will, of course, be monitoring the situation," said the woman. "We really hope everything's okay."

Who the hell are *we*? Colleen wondered as she ended the call.

"My mother's fallen. She's not conscious."

Jake took her hand. "I'm really sorry."

She looked at him. She felt cold and as though she were watching a great roiling storm coming at her, all green and black clouds and distant thunder. It wasn't here yet, but it was approaching fast. This was far more upsetting than she had thought it would be. She thought she'd feel only relief when Deirdre finally died, if that was what was happening now, but Colleen didn't feel that. She wanted to weep for the tiny life her mother had, a life in which she was never happy and gave scant happiness to others.

"Oh my God," she said.

"You going down there?"

Colleen picked up her wine and drained the glass. "I think she's dying this time. Will you come with me? You will, right?"

Jake reached over and took the wineglass out of her hand. He put it on the coffee table, but kept holding her hand. She longed to lean into him, to have him put his arms around her and hold her tight. Maybe this would bring them together again; that wasn't such a mad thought, was it? That would serve everybody right, especially her mother, who had called Jake trash on more than one occasion. (Hell, she'd called him the *N* word once.) Of course he saw other women, but now he was in his mid-fifties, he'd be ready at last to settle down, and who knew him better, who loved him more than she did?

"She's had a good life," Jake said, patting her hand.

"She's had a fucking miserable life, and you know it. She never could get out of her own way." She squeezed his hand. "I guess we should go. Thank God you're here."

"Babe, I can't go with you."

"You can't go with me."

"I'm trying to tell you, about me and Taquanda."

Colleen looked down at their hands entwined, flesh against flesh. His skin was the colour of lightly creamed coffee. Hers was oatmealish. She had a large liver spot on the back of her right hand, and her veins were ropy. She pulled her hands from his and shoved them between her knees.

"I don't want to hear about you and Taquanda."

"She's not comfortable with you and me being so . . . you know."

"Since when do you let some girl tell you what to do?"

"I'm getting married, Colleen."

And there it was, plopping out of his mouth like a toad, a fat, fleshy, slimy toad, the kind of un-ensorcelled toad that never turned into a handsome prince.

"Get out," she said.

Jake sucked his teeth. "She's a last chance for me and I have to take it. I wanted to show you respect by coming and telling you myself. It's not like we're together,

Colleen." He spread his palms. "Come on, we haven't been together in a very long time."

Where was *her* last chance? After all the years he'd called her, kept her tied to him, falling back into her bed whenever he felt like it. He used to sit in his car across the street for hours, staring up at her window; he had admitted that. This cord had always bound them, frayed at times, nibbled at by other people here and there, but it had always held.

She stared at him. There was something else. Just there, in that guilty sheen on his upper lip. His eyes flicked away from hers and then back and then away again. She understood, in one slash of truth.

"She's pregnant."

Jake cocked his head. He smiled in a hangdog way.

"I said get out. Get out now."

"You could be happy for me."

"Happy for you? I could slap you. It would feel good to hurt you." She hadn't meant to say that. She realized she was on her feet.

Jake stood up as well. "You are some piece of work," he said. "I know you've got trouble, but half of it's your own fault and ain't nobody can help you but you."

Tears scalded the back of her eyes. "You do this now, with my mother fucking dying? After I lose my job? You choose today? You selfish shit."

Jake picked up his coat and shrugged into it. "You know what? There wasn't ever going to be a good time to tell you"—he walked to the door and opened it— "because every day is some new tragedy with you. Every day is some new drama. Get your shit together, Colleen, or you're going to end up like your mother."

A wordless, guttural sound escaped Colleen's mouth. She pushed Jake out the door and kicked it shut. It slammed so hard the air concussed and it seemed the walls shook. She leaned against the door and pressed her fists to her mouth. If she started screaming now, she'd never stop.

Lori, she'd call Lori. Lori would listen to her and come with her. Lori wouldn't let her face this alone. She called her friend's number, but it went through to voice mail. She hung up and called again. Again to voice mail. Her head whirled. Jake. Deirdre. Jake. Deirdre. Their faces flashed in front of her like a strobe light. Voice mail. Voice mail. Voice mail.

She was all alone and her mother was dying.

She dialled the number of a taxi company and gave them her address, telling them it was an emergency, and could they send someone as quickly as possible, please, she'd be waiting in the lobby. She went into the kitchen and poured herself a fair-size glass of vodka. She drank it right down. It hit her belly like a grenade, sending shrapnel straight to her brain. She didn't have time to find another salad dressing bottle, and that probably wasn't a good idea anyway, but still, she regretted having to leave the vodka on the counter. She had no idea how she was going to face what was coming at her next.

You See What They Are

Colleen worked in the English Department when Jake lived with her. It was a different neighbourhood back then. Lots more little shops, family run and a little scruffy. On Yonge Street a few corner stores still eked out a living, and two of them were owned by Poles, who lived in the Roncesvalles area but kept shops here for unknown reasons and had something of a rivalry going. Jake and she liked the one owned by Mr. Żeleński, who had a little sign that read MÓWIMY PO POLSKU—We Speak Polish—in his window, although since there were very few Poles in the neighbourhood Colleen wondered why he bothered.

It was mid-summer, when the asphalt was soft underfoot and everything felt gritty and sticky. Jake and Colleen had lunch and a few beers at a little Chinese place they liked and on the way back to the apartment decided to stop into Mr. Żeleński's and pick up what she needed for dinner that night.

Mr. Żeleński sat behind the low counter reading *Wiadomości*, the Polish newspaper. He was a little wrinkle of a man, wearing a woollen vest over his white shirt, even on the hottest days. His fingers were stained yellow from the omnipresent cigarette that dangled from them. Thin and quick of both movement and mind, Mr. Żeleński was a devout socialist and kept a stack of books next to his mammoth, ancient beast of a cash register—silver, weighing in at over a hundred pounds, with old-fashioned push buttons and a bell that rang for every sale. The books were political in nature—well-thumbed editions of

Trotsky's *My Life, The Permanent Revolution* and *Political Profiles; Pedagogy of the Oppressed* by Paulo Freire; *The Ragged-Trousered Philanthropists* by Robert Tressell; Upton Sinclair's *The Jungle.* Mr. Żeleński enjoyed nothing more than a political argument, and Colleen was sure he kept the books there as a provocation. She liked him for it.

"Ah, beautiful people," he said as they stepped in, squinting through the haze of cigarette smoke. "How is my favourite couple?"

He moved from behind the counter and shook Jake's hand. He barely came up to Jake's shoulder, but almost everyone looked small next to Jake. He was boxing then and his muscles bulged and rippled under his Electric Ladyland T-shirt.

Mr. Żeleński had taken a shine to them the first time they walked in together. They had stopped in for milk (dangerously near its sell-by date, but Colleen hadn't the heart to put it back) and when they went to pay he came from behind his desk and said, to Jake's initial alarm, "A mixed couple, so nice! I like you very much. Come often. I, too, am a mixed couple. My wife, she is Catholic, yes, and me, I am a Jew." He reached up and slapped Jake's shoulder in a friendly way. "Her family hid me from the pig Germans, may they have stones and not children, in the barn. I slept inside a dead cow for a week. Ack, the smell. She fed me anyway. What could I do when the war was over except marry her, eh?" As he grinned his face crinkled like that of an apple doll. He pinched Colleen's cheek. "You think this one would do the same for you, my friend?" he asked Jake.

Jake smiled, looking as much perplexed as amused. "She better, man."

"Of course I would." Colleen punched Jake in the shoulder. He pretended to be wounded.

"Excellent." The old man clapped his hands. "Then we are all friends together."

And so they had begun dropping in on him at least once a week, to pick up some small thing or another— usually something with a long shelf life.

Today Colleen needed spices, some rosemary and thyme. Mr. Żeleński stayed at the front, talking to Jake about U.S. President Ronald Reagan. Colleen half listened to the conversation as she scanned the rows of small dusty spice bottles.

"This is a friendly fascist," he said. "He wants families in need of public help to first dispose of household goods in excess of a thousand dollars . . . If there is an authoritarian regime in the American future, Reagan is to blame. He is a capitalist vampire." He pronounced it *vam-PEER*, and Colleen smiled, imagining the dark Carpathian Mountains and Bela Lugosi. "America does not want a moral president. It wants a thug in the Oval Office, one that carries the big stick, yes?"

"I don't know. I have trouble trusting any white man—present company excepted, of course."

"You must read George Washington Woodbey, a black man. A socialist. A Baptist preacher who saw the light." Mr.Żeleński chuckled, a phlegmy sort of hiccuping noise.

Colleen came to the counter with rosemary, a can of kidney beans and a package of spaghetti. "I found some rosemary, but not the thyme. Do you have any?"

"Ah, I don't know, beautiful, just what is on the shelf. But you want, I will order some for you."

"No, it's okay, we'll pick it up someplace else."

Mr. Żeleński shrugged. They paid and left the store, promising to see him soon. "Come back when you have time for coffee and cake," he said, as he always did.

As they passed the other Polish store, Colleen said, "Maybe he's got some."

Inside, this shop was a little cleaner, a little more modern than Mr. Żeleński's, with a gleaming counter and a rack of candy bars and glossy magazines. They nodded at the owner, whose name they didn't know. He never made small talk, never even smiled, but he did nod back, his hands flat-palmed on the counter.

"Spices at the back?" she asked.

"Second aisle."

They went to the back of the store, Jake carrying the plastic bag with their purchases from Mr. Żeleński's store.

216

She found the tiny spice shelf and looked, but no thyme. Salt. Pepper. Celery salt. Paprika. That was it.

"Oh, never mind. I'll pick it up tomorrow. I can do without it."

They walked back to the front of the store. Colleen raised her hand and said, "Thanks," and they were just about to walk out.

"Hold it," the owner said.

They stopped. Another couple stood at the counter, older than Colleen and Jake. The man was buying cigarettes and a bottle of soda.

"Yes?" said Colleen.

"Come back here," the man said.

Colleen looked questioningly at Jake. His face had gone stony, in that way it did sometimes just before a confrontation. He pulled into himself. Went blank. He stared flatly at the store owner.

"You want me to come back, huh? And you wanna tell me why?"

"I want to look in the bag."

Jake's nostrils flared and he pressed his lips together. He held out the bag. "So look."

"Bring it here," said the man.

Jake stayed where he was.

"You think we stole something?" Indignation rose in Colleen. "Are you kidding me?"

"What you got in that bag, you didn't pay for." The man came around the counter and Colleen thought he'd take the bag, but he walked past them, stood between them and the door.

The hand that hung by Jake's side opened, flexed, and then closed into a fist.

"We bought those things at Mr. Żeleński's. You have no right to accuse us," she said.

The man and Jake locked eyes. "I don't accuse you. I accuse him."

"I did not steal anything from you." Jake's voice was dangerously low, dangerously level.

At a party earlier that year Jake's best friend, Dalek, a Slavic guy who matched him pound for pound, egged him to throw a punch, just so he could see how it felt. Half an hour and a good deal of weed and whisky later, Jake obliged. Dalek's head snapped back, his eyes rolled and he went down like an axed oak. He called the next day with a swollen jaw and no memory of the incident. The shop owner was at least five inches shorter and seventy-five pounds lighter, but he looked like a fighting rooster.

Colleen knew if she didn't do something, and quickly, things were going to get ugly. She almost wanted them to. It would serve the racist little shit right to get knocked out, but then Jake would end up in jail . . ."Oh, for God's sake.

Give me the bag." She snatched it from Jake. "We've got a receipt, you can see for yourself, and then you owe this man an apology."

Where was the goddamn receipt? She took everything out of the bag. Rosemary. Beans. Spaghetti. No receipt. "Jake, did you put the receipt in your pocket?"

His eyes flicked to her. He shook his head.

The man's lip curled. "You see what they are?" he said to the couple who still stood silently near the cash.

"We'll go and get Mr. Żeleński. He'll tell you."

"You go." The man pointed at Jake. "He stays."

"Don't be ridiculous; he's coming with me."

"Go get Żeleński," said Jake.

She didn't want to leave him there. She would have done anything not to leave him there, but there didn't seem to be any other way. She touched his arm, his back, his shoulder. "I'll be back. I'll be right back. I won't be a minute." She glared at the man. "Get out of my way."

She pushed past him and ran down the block.

"Mr. Żeleński! The other store—the Polish man, he's got Jake. He says he stole from him." The words came out in a breathless rush.

"What? What you say?"

She repeated it as he came to her. She realized how wide-eyed and mad she must look. She didn't care.

He put his hands on her shoulders. "I fix this! The *kafin kup!*"

He didn't bother to lock the door to his shop or even close it. Colleen would remember this later and love him for it. He marched up the street and into his rival's store.

"*Kurwa mać!*" he bellowed. "You skinny dog-mothered barbarian! You accuse my friends of theft?"

The other couple had disappeared. Jake had not moved from the spot where Colleen left him. He seemed made of wood. Only his eyes were alive. They glittered, but revealed nothing.

The man said something in Polish and waved his hands in the air. The two shopkeepers faced off and screamed at each other, their spittle meeting in the air between them.

"*Odpierdol* się*!*"

"*Kutwa!*"

"*Palant!*"

Mr. Żeleński said, "You think anyone would steal the dreck you carry? Maggots and weevils, that's all you're good for." He took Jake's arm and pulled him to the door. "You no come in here no more. You come to me only. This is no good place with no good man."

Colleen followed them, and the other shopkeeper yelled, "You are not welcome here! Any of you. You are not welcome in my store. You come again, I call police!"

All the way down the street Mr. Żeleński cursed his rival and the food he sold. It was old, it was rotten, it was tainted, infested with vermin, like the man's soul. Jake and Colleen said nothing. They came to Davisville, thanked the little man, who hugged Jake and called him his brother. Jake rolled his lower lip between his teeth and nodded, but said only a quiet thank you.

As Colleen and Jake walked along Davisville, Colleen heard herself talking about how unfair it was and what a racist bastard that man was and how they should put in a complaint with someone, or picket his shop or do *something*. She felt as though the man had dug some chasm between her and Jake and she didn't know how to cross it. She kept patting his back. If he wasn't going to talk then she wanted to sense, through her fingertips, how he was feeling and get some clue how to reach him, to tell him . . . what? What on earth could she tell him?

She reached to take his hand, but as she did he transferred the bag of groceries to that hand and kept right on walking, his eyes fixed on the sidewalk a few feet in front of him.

My Wee Girl

Colleen arrived at the hospital, chewing a handful of mints, and asked the receptionist which room her mother was in. A matronly woman directed her with a minimum of interest. They must see this sort of thing all the time, she thought—distraught relatives, broken hearts, all just part of a day in the cream and brown halls, under the watchful eye of the St. Michael statue, known as the "Urban Angel." She had not slurred her words at all. She felt adequately muffled, insulated against bruising. She would not think about Jake, not now. She would concentrate on this next thing before her, on the next impossible task this mythologically bad day asked of her.

A silver-bearded man with uneven teeth and a female doctor with glossy black hair and a diamond stud in her nose waited at the elevator bank. Colleen did not make eye contact. She did not want anyone speaking to her, because if someone started talking she knew she would talk back, and she wasn't quite sure what she might say, or if she'd be able to stop talking once she started.

When the elevator came and they stepped inside it smelled of disinfectant and a soiled bandage lay abandoned in the corner, against all health code rules, surely. Both the man and the doctor got out on the floor below the one Colleen wanted. When the doors opened up they revealed a garishly lit hallway, painted a bluish grey. Colleen walked to the nurses' station, that bulwark against human contact, and waited until a mousey little nurse wearing pink scrubs looked up from her computer screen.

"Can I help you?"

"I'm looking for room 1462—Deirdre Kerrigan. I'm her daughter."

The nurse looked puzzled and consulted the screen again. "Deirdre Kerrigan, you said? I don't see that name here, but I just got on shift. Hang on a minute."

The nurse stepped away to consult with another nurse. The second nurse, a tall, heron-like, beaky creature, glanced at Colleen and said something, consulting a chart. Colleen's heart pounded. Her mother was dead. She was too late. Somewhere down the hall a buzzer went off with a bleating complaint and the heron-like nurse sighed and rolled her eyes before sauntering off in the direction of the call. The mousey nurse came back, shaking her head.

"Who told you your mother was here?"

"The nursing home where she lives called me and said she was brought here after a fall and that she was in a coma. They told me downstairs she's in room 1462. What's going on? Has she . . .?"

"Well, she's not in a coma now and I doubt she ever was, or they'd have kept her here. She's in the other wing, the North Wing, apparently. Right through those doors, go past the elevators, down the hall, turn left and then another left and through the double doors. I don't have her file anymore, but they'll tell you more over there. She just got moved about an hour ago apparently, before I came on shift, so I don't have any more information." The phone rang. "Okay? Excuse me. Through those doors." The nurse pointed, wiggling her fingers.

Colleen tried to remember the directions, but her mind wasn't holding onto details. Through the doors, and past the elevator. She got that far and then the words unravelled. Her mother was out of a coma. Had never been in a coma? What did any of that mean? She made a left turn and then another, since there was no other option, and passed through a set of swinging doors. The hallway was full of people all of a sudden. Gurneys and wheelchairs and a woman walking around hooked up to an IV drip, her pasty legs naked, her ankles swollen and sore looking. Orderlies pushed carts of food trays filled with leftover scraps of gelatin, green beans and mashed potatoes. A female janitor wearing a hairnet and blue gloves swabbed the floor. Colleen edged around her cart, which was full of mops and brushes, paper towels and disinfectant spray.

"Excuse me," Colleen said. "Is this the way to the North Wing nurses' station?

"You almost there," said the woman in a thick Eastern-European accent. "You go round by left turn. Not far. You see, you see."

This hallway was cream-coloured with a wooden handrail. The lighting came not from overhead lights but from boxes of opaque plastic spaced every few feet above closed electrical boards, which housed, Colleen assumed, medical devices of some sort. It would be a cluttered space even without anyone in it. Monitoring equipment of various kinds, walkers and IVs stood near the doors. Hand sanitizing posts hung at intervals. At the end of the corridor Colleen saw a group standing around what she assumed was the nurses' station.

As she walked toward it she glanced into the rooms to see if her mother might be there. Old people in every bed, some with their mouths gaping open, others staring at flickering television lights, two with family members huddled round. No sign of Deirdre.

The people at the nurses' station, a family from the looks of it, asked if they could bring food in for their father.

The nurse, a middle-aged and considerably overweight woman, said, "He's diabetic, and there are the kidney issues, so we have to be very careful about his diet. No sugar, low protein, low salt and potassium."

A young man appeared from a room behind the nurses' station. "Can I help you?"

"I'm looking for my mother. No one seems to know where she is. I don't understand what's going on."

The young man, whose name-badge read MATT DUDEN, R.N., smiled in a reassuring sort of way and said, "Well, let's see if we can't find her and figure out what's what, okay? What's her name?"

"Deirdre Kerrigan."

He consulted a computer screen and said, "Oh, she's here. Took a nasty fall from the looks of it. Might have a mild concussion. Some confusion."

"She's always confused. Nothing new there." Colleen laughed. She hadn't meant to. "So, no coma?" That didn't come out right.

Nurse Duden looked at Colleen, a little puzzled.

"I mean, they told me she was unconscious, you know, earlier. From the nursing place, the nursing home."

"Well, there's no coma. I don't know why anyone would have said that. We just want to keep her overnight to make sure she's okay. She was in Emergency and had CAT scans and so forth. But she was up and around this afternoon, even went to a singalong."

My mother went to a singalong? Colleen thought. It boggled the mind.

"She's in room 1411. Just down there." He pointed.

There seemed nothing else to do but see her mother. It was too late to turn around and just head home.

"Listen, before you go, look, uh, why don't you just step over here."

Colleen followed him to the end of the nurses' station. He consulted the chart again and then folded his hands over it.

"I think you should make an appointment with the social worker. They had to move her here from the other ward. There was an incident."

"What kind of an incident?" Colleen felt woozy. She understood the words the man spoke, or at least she heard them and could have repeated them back if she were asked, but their meaning evaded her. The words floated around her head, but lacked gravitas.

"Well, your mother . . . we know she has a frontal lobe injury and that does impair impulse control. She tried to escape a couple of times. They found her down in the lobby the second time. But there was something else." He looked serious, a little embarrassed. "One of the orderlies apparently found her with her hands around the throat of the woman in the bed next to her."

Colleen's hands flew to her own throat. She could see the expression her mother must have worn at that moment quite clearly—the lips curling back, the teeth gnashing, the eyes wide. How often she'd seen that expression in her own childhood.

"Christ," she said. "Did she hurt her?"

"No, no, she wasn't hurt. Frightened, I suspect, but not hurt." Nurse Duden came around the desk and put his hand on her shoulder. "Are you okay?"

"I'm okay." Colleen tried to smile. "That's my mum. She has a history of mental illness."

"Is that so? Well, that's why she's on this wing now. Easy to get in, but you need a code to get out through those doors. Maybe the doctor will change her meds. It's pretty unsettling for them when they come here. Routine is awfully important at this point, you know, when they've had the sort of brain injury your mum has. At any rate, we've given her something to calm her down and she's in a room with another woman for now, but we're keeping an eye out. She ate her dinner. She's fine." He smiled. "We were just about to go get her ready for bed. But you can do that now you're here."

It was what you would expect from a daughter, wasn't it?

Without quite knowing how she got there, Colleen was standing at the door to her mother's room. Another woman, sleeping from the looks of it, lay in the bed nearest the door. There was a lot of equipment around this woman's bed. Her mother sat on the side of her bed and looked, from the back, like a small child. She faced the window, which faced out onto little more than another building across the street.

"Hello, Mum."

Her mother didn't seem to hear her, so Colleen walked in and stepped into her line of sight. Her mother turned and smiled. Her teeth were small and yellow and her lips were thin. The skin on her face hung from her high cheekbones and fell beneath her jaw in wattles.

"Oh, hello, dear."

228

"I hear you took a fall."

"They're idiots at that place. And here too. The dishwater . . . the jam jar . . . oh, I can't remember. I'm too tired. Why are you here?"

More than anything in the world Colleen wished she'd brought that bottle of vodka.

"It's time for bed. Where are your pyjamas?"

"I don't know. A woman comes in at three in the morning and steals everything."

Colleen saw a Whole Foods canvas shopping bag by the nightstand. In it were her mother's pyjamas, a toothbrush and toothpaste, some underwear.

"Here they are. Let's get you into them."

Colleen's mind went blank. She was not in this room. She was not anywhere. She was not the person doing these things. It was some other woman, a capable woman who did not mind doing this, a woman unaffected by it in the slightest way. A professional woman, competent and detached.

Colleen helped her mother stand.

"I'm dizzy."

"It's okay, it's just because you stood up. Hang onto me."

Deirdre looked at her daughter sideways for a moment, settled her mouth into a line of disapproval and turned away, although she kept a grip on Colleen's arm. Colleen hoped the mints she had chewed disguised the smell of alcohol on her breath. Her mother had such extensive experience ferreting out the offending smells on her father, Colleen doubted she was getting away with anything, but with luck Deirdre had forgotten the word *drunk*.

The woman who swore she'd kill herself if she ever lost her privacy stood beside the bed and let her pants and her underwear drop to the floor. Colleen had never, in her recollection, seen her mother naked. Not completely. During periods when Deirdre's depression or mania was acute, she frequently insisted on showing Colleen parts of her body—her stomach, her back, her hips—standing within inches of her daughter's face and pulling up her shirt or pulling down her pants so Colleen could assure her that no, it didn't look as though she had cancer, or ringworm, or shingles or whatever she was paranoid about at the moment. Sometimes Deirdre repeated this over and over until Colleen yelled at her to *stop it, please, stop it! You don't have cancer for God's sake.* Often Deirdre, striving for control, jammed the bathroom door so it would not lock or close properly so she could (and would) walk in on Colleen while she was on the toilet. It was as though her mother were trying to prove there was no escape, there was no place she could not invade. Colleen learned to check for such booby-traps and dismantle them.

Colleen began to pray. *Let me, oh Lord, forget everything but compassion. Let me, oh God, do, think, feel, only what is for her good and for my good and for your greater good. Dear God, be with us here, be with us now.* She knew it for what it was, lush-speak, a drunk's prayer, filled with noble sentiment, wallpapering over the holes in her morality. She clung to it nonetheless and hoped for Grace.

Deirdre's legs were alarming. Papery-brown and red-blotched skin hung from withered thighs, little more than rag-wrapped twigs. Colleen wanted to look away, but she couldn't for fear her mother would fall. Her blouse covered her sex, and Colleen nearly wept with gratitude at being spared that. Deirdre's underpants were not clean. Brown marks. She held the pyjama bottoms while Deirdre, her hand on Colleen's shoulder for balance, stepped into them. Deirdre slipped off her blouse. Her bra hung over her breasts, not supporting them. Colleen could not look at her breasts. She could not.

Snippets of Psalm rose up unbidden. *Lord, make me to know mine end, And the measure of my days, what it is; Let me know how frail I am. Behold, thou hast made my days handbreadths.* Surely, this would be Colleen herself one day, raddled and infantilized by the ravages of time. *O spare me, that I may recover strength, before I go hence, and be no more.*

The bra was so old the elastic was utterly worn out. Colleen unhooked the clasps and tried to see what size it was, for she would have to buy her mother a new one. The tag was faded and unreadable. Colleen slipped the pyjama top over her mother's head. It was sleeveless and pink and frilly and her poor tattered arms were a cruel joke in this girlish garment.

Nurses and aides walked the corridor, tending to other patients in other rooms. *Won't anyone please come here and help? Please, someone come and help.* No one did, of course. Colleen was her mother's family. She was the one.

"Come on," she said. "Let's get you into bed."

"I'm tired," Deirdre said.

The two women spent a few moments in an awkward dance as Colleen got Deirdre settled. She looked at Colleen blankly, ill at ease now there was no more busy-work to be done. Perhaps she was not quite sure who Colleen was, or where she was, or why Colleen was here, or why *she* was. Colleen asked if she wanted to turn the television on.

She nodded. "That would be okay."

Colleen turned it to one of the bloody, car-chase-and-gun-battle shows her mother liked. On the screen the body of a battered young woman lay on an autopsy table. The knife cuts and tubes went into her flesh with amplified squelching noises. The scene shifted to someone ambushing someone else. Fists and bone-crunching punches. Men ran through a warehouse and guns blazed.

"I don't think I like this," Deirdre said.

"But you've always liked this show. It's one of your favourites."

"I think that's changed," Deirdre said, her sparse brows drawn down. She looked puzzled.

"Well, then. Off it goes."

They sat quietly in the room's perpetual twilight. Colleen took Deirdre's hand and for a horrible moment she imagined her mother's skin might slip off like a glove, so loose was it on the bones. She felt another urge to cry. What was wrong with her these days? She was always crying. She looked at their hands and could not help but think of her own next to Jake's. Those liver spots, the puckered skin around her knuckles.

"You had a fall. You gave me a scare, you know."

"Yeah, I guess I did," Deirdre said.

"Do you remember doing a runner?" She made it sound as though it were a joke.

"Me?" Deirdre grinned like a mischievous, if ancient, elf.

"You bet. They found you in the lobby heading for the door and out onto the street."

"Really?"

"You were truckin'!"

She laughed as Colleen imitated her determined walk, neck forward, arms pumping, the mad-hen expression.

"I don't think I'll do that again. I know I need to be here." She pointed behind Colleen. "You know, I look out the window and this is the first day it looks right, not really right but a little more."

Colleen looked out the window. Lights glowed from the windows of the apartment building across the street. It was easy to imagine happy families. "What do you mean? How did it look before?"

Even the hall had grown quiet now. Deirdre struggled to find the words. "I don't know. Not real. And I think I saw my mother"—she made motions with her hands—"working on something."

"Ah, so you've been seeing Grandma."

"I guess so." She plucked and fidgeted with the sheet for a moment, and then looked up at Colleen. "Now what will happen? Where will I live?"

"You'll live where you've been living. You have that lovely room overlooking the lake."

"I know that. It's been so long since I was there."

The woman in the next bed began snoring. It sounded like the death rattle of a brontosaurus. Deirdre glared at the curtain separating the beds and whispered, "She's awful."

"She is," Colleen said. "Mum, do you remember you got very mad at another lady this afternoon?"

"I did?" Her eyes were wide.

"You did. The nurse found you with her. You had your hands on her."

"*I did?*"

"I'm afraid so." The noise from the next bed was so dreadful Colleen understood how someone might get strangled.

Her mother bit her bottom lip. "Did I hurt her? I didn't hurt her, did I?"

"No, but you might have. You can't do that, Mum. You can't lay hands on anyone else." Colleen didn't know why she was saying this. Deirdre wouldn't remember, but somehow Colleen needed to hear her say she didn't want to hurt anyone; that she didn't *mean* to hurt anyone. Because really, she couldn't help it, could she? She'd never been able to help it.

"I think I've been very angry the past few days, haven't I."

"I think you have been."

"Isn't it funny. Your mind does things. And you're not there."

"It must be frightening."

She shrugged as though she didn't understand the remark. She kept hold of Colleen's hand.

"It's going to be okay, Mum. All you have to do now is let people take care of you."

"That'll be nice."

It dawned on Colleen that all her life Deirdre had fought against whatever she perceived to be the worst thing that could happen. She battled her husband's drinking and philandering. It didn't matter that he stopped drinking twenty-five years before he died. She never felt she'd won that battle because she couldn't forget. After he sobered up she still blamed him for every worry and disappointment in her life, and then, he died and left her alone. It changed practically nothing. Up until the day she had her first mini-stroke, she complained about her husband every time she and Colleen spoke. She traced all her woes, past and present, to her dead husband's drinking and his cheating and his death.

But her anxieties weren't limited to her marriage. She battled against moving from her house into a condo. When she finally did she forgot how hard she'd fought against it, and loved her new home, so with that fear gone she became a hypochondriac. When Colleen went in to clean out the condo, to get it ready to sell, she found hundreds of clippings from newspapers and magazines: *Warning signs of cancer/stroke/heart attack! Eat grapefruit/cranberries/bran/kale /blueberries, etc., etc., to avoid cancer!* Every drawer was crammed with them. They were posted inside every cabinet, stacked high on every table and counter and footstool. Articles on diabetes, cholesterol, vascular disease, arthritis, back problems, constipation and urinary tract infections. She stockpiled vitamins and herbal remedies, some of them going back years. The shower was unusable because it was filled with bottles of green tea concentrate, liniments and salves (some dating from the 1960s) cranberry tablets, fish oil capsules, sleeping medications like melatonin and valerian, St. John's wort, and more bran and toilet paper than a constipated army could use. And this from a woman who never spent a day in hospital until the past spring, a woman whose only prescribed medication was a cortisone cream for arthritis in her right thumb.

The war's over, Colleen thought. Mum lost. There is nothing left to fight.

Colleen reached over and picked up a bottle of hand cream from the bedside table. She held her mother's hand and smoothed lotion onto her skin. She kept an impassive smile on her face, for she felt her mother's eyes on her, looking for clues. Her arm was textured like the brittle skin of onions, overlaid with cobwebs, blotched with deep purple. The veins on the back of her hand looked like bloody worms. Colleen massaged her mother's forearms and wrists—gently, gently, for the bones could tear right through if she wasn't careful. Something gritty stuck to her palms. Her mother's skin was pilling like an old sweater. Colleen raised her arm and the skin flapped like soiled cotton, both elbows encrusted with thick black scabs. Colleen was afraid if she touched them they would peel off.

"That's nice," Deirdre said, her eyes half shut, her face fallen in on itself.

My mother's skin is breaking down, thought Colleen. Ten days ago when she called Spring Lake Place, Deirdre told her she had been in bed and used her elbows to scoot up higher toward her pillow. As she did, the skin on the arms tore open. There had been a lot of blood on the sheets, she said.

Lord, make me to know mine end, And the measure of my days, what it is; Let me know how frail I am.

Colleen put the cap back on the lotion. She resisted the urge to rush to the bathroom and wash her hands. Without Deirdre noticing, she wiped them off on a tissue. She put the lotion in the top drawer of the metal cabinet next to the bed.

"Cover that over. They steal things in here."

Colleen covered the plastic bottle with a Kleenex. Her mother blinked and smiled. Her teeth were yellow and brown with bits of hospital food lodged near the gums. Her white and grey hair curled randomly around her ears and forehead, but was flat on the back of her head. It was sticky to the touch. Her once-fabulous high cheekbones jutted out like stones beneath her red-rimmed eyes. She smelled slightly yeasty, slightly sour.

There was a noise, a sort of snort, from the woman behind the curtain in the next bed, and then she resumed snoring.

Colleen's mother pressed her lips together in an expression of suppressed anger Colleen knew well. "I hope I won't have to stay with that one, that one there, the one—she's, it's like that with the grocers, no, not the cats, when you go, want . . ." She made fists of her hands and shook them by her head in frustration. "Oh shit," she said.

"It's okay, Mum. It's all right."

"They're putting something in my food, you know. I don't like that."

"They're not putting anything in your food."

"Oh yes they are!"

"They're giving you some pills."

"That's what I mean. I don't want them."

"You're malnourished, Mum, and you need to take the pills to help you absorb the vitamins in your food so you can heal and get strong." It was a lie, of course. The pills were to make her *compliant*, as the staff at Spring Lake Place termed it.

Deirdre never weighed more than a hundred pounds, but now she was less than ninety. In her condo Colleen had found the charred evidence of a burned plastic plate in the microwave. The fridge was half full of mouldering, liquefied vegetables, milk past its sell-by date, packets of almonds and apricots neatly wrapped but bought more than five years ago. The cupboards bulged with old cake mixes, enormous boxes of cereal, and thirty-five rolls of Saran

Wrap. In the rag-and-bone "sewing room" where at the last her mother had spent her time no longer sewing but sitting in front of the television, Colleen found the waxed paper lining bag from a cereal box filled with what might once have been grapes, and leaves of some sort.

"Oh, all right," Deirdre said. "I'll take the pills. For you."

The woman in the bed behind the curtain had stopped snoring quite so loudly. Deirdre squeezed her hand and said, "I'm tired."

"Do you want me to go and let you get some sleep?"

"That would be okay."

Colleen hugged her bird-twig mother, whose hair smelled greasy, her skin unwashed. The skin on her mother's ribs and shoulder blades slipped over the bones. Colleen's throat closed over. Her eyes burned.

"I love you," she said.

"I love you too," Deirdre said, and patted Colleen's back. "My wee girl."

Colleen was at the door when her mother called out. "Hey, don't think I don't know what you're up to." She pointed a finger at her, trying to rise up on her elbow. Colleen pictured the scabs tearing and winced. "You're nothing but a selfish bitch, a little . . . toast . . . you know, the rain barrel . . ." She made a sort of growling noise. "I never could have anything nice around you. Dressing like a

. . . horse . . . a slut, that's it. Sitting in bars. Don't bother coming back."

And there it was. How many times had she heard that in the past few months? And more than that. It had always been there. Her mother just said it out loud now. Good old frontal lobe. Good old impulse control.

"Good night, Mum. I'll check in with you tomorrow." Even as she said it, she doubted she would. Maybe she'd call, but she wouldn't see her. It occurred to Colleen that she never had to see her mother again if she didn't want to. Even now Colleen felt the festering infection of her mother's vitriol spreading along her spine, up into her brain, where it would stay for days, and then, just when she thought she was finally getting over it, *bam,* she'd speak to her mother and it would start all over again.

Deliver me from bloodguiltiness, O God, thou God of my salvation.

Where had that arisen from? What angel had whispered these lines into her ear? Depression wrapped around her like a wet cloak, but still, surely that had been a moment of grace there with her mother. *My own wee girl,* she had said. Surely that was her mother's soul speaking, not her bitter heart, her shadow-filled mind. It was a message, one that would release Colleen from the bloodguiltiness that grew like a fungus in the undergrowth of her apprehension, fearful as she was that her mother was right. She was a selfish slut.

In the taxi on the way home, entombed in the claustrophobic wretchedness that always followed an encounter with her mother, Colleen could taste the wine on her lips. It would be waiting for her, the French fairy. Or no, vodka, the Russian fairy, all fire and ice with a melancholy soul. She would read Dostoyevsky's *Memoirs from the House of the Dead* or *Diary of a Writer* while sipping what the Great Russian called the elixir of suffering, ever-present and unquenchable, everywhere and in everything.

She snorted. She always became overly dramatic when she was tired. She had been neglecting herself. Colleen vowed to live her life, from this point forward, as one reborn, resurrected, and all the wickedness of her life would be washed away. *As smoke is driven away, so drive them away: as wax melteth before the fire, so let the wicked perish at the presence of God.* She would lead an elegant life now, freed, cleansed, and purified by the fire.

Jake's going to be a father. The thought came back to her like an arrow through the chest. She chewed her knuckle. No. She did not want Jake. She'd been the one who left him, after all, and it had been the right decision then, so why did she care now? She did not *need* Jake. She should have cut ties a long time ago. It was just laziness and habit, nothing more. She looked out the taxi window. They passed a store selling glassware. The window sparkled and gleamed, as though filled with jewels.

Clever Sparkling Fakes

She hadn't seen Jake in a while. (She lived with Frank then, a nice enough guy who fancied himself a filmmaker, although he worked at a video store to pay the rent. It lasted less than a year, but at the time she was trying to make it work, and Frank didn't like Jake much.) They were in Le Select Bistro. The burgundy walls, the low lights, the pleasurable scents of garlic and fresh bread, and the soft voice of Edith Piaf combined to create a slightly erotic atmosphere of indulgence. All through dinner, which had consisted of Manhattans before, two bottles of wine with the delicious *cassoulet* they barely touched, and Grand Marnier after, Jake kept excusing himself and disappearing to the washroom. His nose was red and raw. He was thin. He talked a great deal. He suggested they run off together and start a life of crime. He drank more than she did, although she drank her more-than-fair-share, but even with whatever he was doing in the bathroom, she was more sober than he. She slid into the version of herself that sometimes appeared when she was just the right amount of "tipsy." Her movements were languid. She ran her finger lightly around the rim of her wineglass. She took tiny bites of her duck, the fork held just so. She brushed her hair behind her ear. Her laughter trilled, while he guffawed. Her voice was gentle and melodious, while his was loud, the language coarse. She was the beauty to his beast. She allowed him to take her hand, but pulled away in a ladylike fashion when the fingers of his other hand crawled up her thigh. She played the game that he so loved like an expert. He leaned back in his chair, his thumbs in his belt, and

243

leered at her in that way of his that made her feel as she had back in the first days of their romance—proud of who she was, and a little superior, she admitted that, a little like an uptown girl with a very bad downtown boy. She was lovelier in the light of his admiration of her.

And then he said, "You ever tell Frank I called you Moan-a?"

"Of course not."

His wolfish grin shifted to something smug and a little nasty. She knew that look well and her stomach tightened as the light around her darkened.

"And why's that? Maybe he doesn't make you moan the way I used to."

A woman at a nearby table glanced at them, a perfectly arched eyebrow raised in disapproval.

"He does just fine, thank you." Colleen kept her voice low, her smile impassive.

Jake reached over and pinched her stomach. "Getting you all fat and happy, is that it?"

At the nip of his fingers, before she could stop herself, she flinched and he laughed. As invariably happened when she allowed herself to be seduced by Jake's soft mouth and strong hands and beautiful—albeit mocking—hazel eyes, the snug little bubble of self-delight she'd basked in just a moment before burst open and let in a cold gust of shame. *Oh, that's right, this is how he is. This is why I left him. I remember now.*

She must not let him see he'd hurt her. This was always the set-point for the game he played—she the mouse; he the cat with the cruel claws. What was wrong with her that she never remembered? She tried to think up some clever retort, something that would put him on the defensive for a change, but it wasn't in her make-up; she simply didn't have the mind for wicked repartee, especially not when it came to hurting the feelings of someone she . . . well . . . *cared* for.

"I am happy," she said. "Happier than I've ever been."

There might have been the tiniest of droops in his self-satisfied expression, but perhaps that was nothing more than wishful thinking on her part.

They got the bill shortly after that, and at least Jake paid. As they left the restaurant he leaned, rather heavily, on her and said, "Come'n, I'll drive you home, Porkie." He laughed. "I'm just yanking your chain, don't be like that."

She disentangled herself from his embrace. She was on the down-slide of tipsy now, feeling as though something had been ruined, like a child whose birthday party has been spoiled, whose favourite doll has been broken. It was important not to let him see how he hurt her. She put her arm through his. The night was cold and their breath hung in misty wreaths before them. He took a little misstep and she realized, even half in the bag as she was, that he was truly plonked. He draped his arm over her shoulder again.

"Car's right over there." He pointed eastward along Queen Street.

"I'm not getting in a car with you," she said. "And you certainly shouldn't drive."

"I'm fine." He said. "Fine."

He took his arm off her shoulder and stood, wide-legged and balancing. Without the steadying effect of his big body Colleen found her own balance was none too great. She wavered slightly and adjusted her stance. Jake looked past her at a shop window. He walked toward it and stood staring at the contents. Bracelets, watches, necklaces, and rings dazzled. Colleen didn't suppose they were real, just clever sparkling fakes, or else surely the shop owner would have taken them out of the window for the night. From the ceiling hung threads and on these hung crystal prisms, four or five to a thread, which caught the display light and scattered it in multicoloured shining confetti even out onto the street. Glitters of blue, green and pink light spangled their boots and the sidewalk.

Jake put his finger up to the glass, pointing at the engagement-style rings. "I can't have one of those," he slurred. "Nope. Can't ever have one."

"Of course you can," Colleen said.

Jake simply kept staring into the glass, swaying on his feet and staring.

"I'm not getting in the car with you," Colleen said. "I'll get us both a taxi."

"Do what you want," said Jake. "I'm staying."

"What do you mean you're staying?"

"Just am. Get on home, little bird, get on home."

She didn't know what else to do. The cold air made her head spin and she realized she was quite a bit drunker than she'd thought. Not as bad as Jake, but still. He wasn't her responsibility. He'd have to take care of himself. She reached up and gave him a peck on the cheek.

"Get a cab," she said.

She walked to the curb and hailed a taxi. As it drove away she looked back. He stood there, still staring into the window. She wasn't quite sure, but later, when she ran the scene over in her mind, she wondered if he hadn't been crying. She called him the next day and asked if he was all right, but he just laughed and said, "Why wouldn't I be? Whatsa matter? Still can't tell when I'm yanking your chain?"

We'll Just Leave It at That, Shall We?

So, let him have his baby now, and his child bride. Good riddance. What had he ever done for her anyway, except break her heart and treat her like shit. She looked at the taxi driver's name. *Faisal Naseem.* He was a youngish man with a shaved head and prominent ears. He smiled in the photo. He looked kind.

"Where are you from?" she asked.

He glanced at her in the rear-view mirror. He was speaking, but the radio was playing something that sounded like Indian hip hop, and he spoke softly, so she couldn't understand him.

"I'm sorry, I didn't hear you."

His eyes flickered back to her and she realized he was talking on the phone, a little bud and wire coming out of his ear. He was speaking . . . what? Arabic?

"Sorry," she muttered.

"You say something?" he asked, although clearly he knew she had spoken.

"No, nothing at all."

He returned to his conversation. She wanted to tell him not to talk on the phone while he drove, and she would have done if she hadn't already tried to start a conversation with him. Now it would only sound as though she were being vindictive. She hunched in the back seat, watching the street outside her window. Two young women, obviously prostitutes, loitered at the corner of Jarvis and Carlton. One wore a tiny red skirt and thigh-high black boots, the other a rabbit-skin jacket and skin-tight jeans. They looked young, under eighteen surely. They looked cold. The taxi driver stared at them while the light turned green. He said something into the phone and then laughed.

"It's green," Colleen said, and he started forward without acknowledging her.   She found her own phone in her purse and opened it. You never know. A text message. From Lori, bless her, half an hour ago. *Saw u tried to call me. Hope ur ok. Will call tomorrow. L.* Colleen dialled her number. Voice mail. Fucking voice mail.

They passed a church and in the parking lot a group of men and women congregated, many of them smoking. Several looked twitchy and agitated. Others seemed to share a joke, and one of those, a grey-haired woman in a big puffy coat, leaned over to a particularly jittery young woman and put her arm around her, drawing her into the group. Colleen knew who they were. Alcoholics, waiting to go into one of their fellowship meetings. She saw them now and again at the entrances to church basements, looking both furtive and resolved. Sometimes it looked like a party she wouldn't mind joining, other times it looked like a penal colony. Tonight she felt the twinge of a yearning to be that young woman, to have someone put an arm around her. She could tell the driver to stop. She could get out. She could go into that meeting. She wondered if anyone would remember her.

Aside from the meeting she'd attended with Liam, which had been for *him* after all and not for her, Colleen had been to a meeting only once before, many years ago or so it seemed now, although it was only . . . well, yes, two years ago. After the Father Paul incident. She sat in the back of the chilly basement room, under the glare of fluorescent tubes, on a hard plastic chair, and listened to a rumpled, tattooed bear of a man talk about driving so drunk he had to stick his head out the window to keep himself from passing out. Sadly, it was a particularly cold winter night and he froze his eyeball and lost his sight in that eye. Colleen was speechless. How drunk did you have to be not to notice your eyeball was freezing? She had never been *that* drunk. He said when he was young it was so easy to get him drunk it was a shame to keep him sober. Everyone laughed at that and she thought they were mad. They laughed, too, when he said he'd once fallen into the grave of a friend who'd died in a drunken car wreck. Hitting the bottle hard in his grief, he arrived at the funeral plastered. At the gravesite he stumbled and fell right in on top of the casket and lay there on his back looking up at the sky, thinking maybe he was the one who'd died after all. It took three men to drag him out.

A thin woman with broken blood vessels all over her face spoke about burning down her house with her two children inside. She wasn't sure how she would live with the guilt. Colleen didn't see how she could either. Another woman talked about how she hid bottles all over the house and then, in the dead of night, wearing only her nightgown, went up and down the street putting the empties in her neighbours' recycling bins, since she was still a good environmentalist. How all those drunks laughed.

Colleen was glad they had a place to go if it helped, but she wasn't anything like them.

No, that wasn't for her.

The taxi raced up Mount Pleasant and soon they were at her building. The fare was $16.88. She gave the drive $17 and listened to him curse her in Arabic as she got out and walked away.

From the apartment three doors down from Colleen's came laughter and music—bass-heavy and electronic sounding. A man lived there, coffee-skinned and quite handsome in a pudgy, doe-eyed sort of way. His lashes were so long Colleen suspected he used mascara. She saw him in the elevator in the morning sometimes, and always in the company of a different man.

All these lives going on behind doors, in rooms so close to hers, and yet so different, self-contained and isolated one from the other. She thought of the poem by Edward Booth Loughran, called "Isolation."

Man lives alone; star-like, each soul

In its own orbit circles ever;

Myriads may by or round it roll—

The way may meet, but mingle never.

She was a middle-aged woman, alone, more alone than she had ever been before. She understood Lori could no longer be depended upon. Lori was locked in her own life now. A text message was the modern version of the butler who stood guard over the Victorian doorway. *Madam is indisposed. Madam is not home at present.* What could one infer except *Madam* does not want to be bothered with *one*. Jake done. Dead to her. And she to him most likely. He was a narcissist who simply didn't understand why she wouldn't go away now that he was done with her. Another inconvenience. She was an inconvenience to her once-friends. She used to have an address book full of names and numbers. No more.

Colleen put the key in the lock to her door and the sound of metal against metal grated loudly in her ears. It might be a prison door. A jail cell. She once dreamed that she was locked in a cell for life. A cot. A wooden chair. A desk in front of a window that looked out over rolling fields and forest beyond. A shelf of books. In the dream she had been utterly content. She had been at peace. There was no door in the cell. No one could get at her. That was the way she felt: that she was safe at last and able to sit and read and think without anyone disturbing her. She could have that in real life, couldn't she? She could make for herself a simple nun's cell; live the life of the contemplative, with Thomas Merton and the Benedictine Order as her guides.

Colleen walked in and closed the door behind her. The silence she had felt in the afternoon, silence like a bell jar, slipped over her and she found it hard to breathe.

She wanted a drink, but wanting it flushed her with shame. She had sobered up enough while seeing her mother for a glimpse of objectivity to slip in under the fairy-built fortifications. She had spent the day running from one catastrophe to another and bouncing like a little silver pinball to the bottle in between. Lose job. Drink. Feel lonely. Drink. Bumble job interview. Drink. Jake. Drink. Mum. Drink.

Drink was the only constant.

She wanted alcohol so badly now that her teeth hurt, her fingers ached to hold it, her mouth shrivelled up in anticipation of the revivifying potion.

Call Helen. The idea appeared like a St. Bernard with a flagon of brandy round its shaggy neck. Yes, her neighbour, Helen. It wasn't late, just coming up to nine o'clock. Helen was a night owl. She would be up and, as always, longing for company and someone to deliver supplies. That was one of the downsides of the panic attacks and agoraphobia Helen suffered—although it saved her from having to deal with the heartless masses, it meant she couldn't pop out to the shops for a loaf of bread or a bottle of wine.

Colleen didn't bother to take off her coat before calling.

"Yes? Who is this?" It was Helen's way of answering the phone, for she was always on the defensive against robo-calls, survey takers or scam artists.

"It's Colleen, Helen. How are you?"

"My arthritis has been terrible. I couldn't even open a jar of raspberry jam this morning. You should see my thumb; it's swollen like an apricot. I'm watching that *Idol* program with the singing kids. What are you doing?"

"I was wondering if I could come over. It's been just an awful day and I could use a friendly ear."

"I don't think I've got anything to drink in the house."

"I could bring a bottle of wine."

"Do you have any bread? Can't even make a sandwich."

"Yes, probably."

"Come on over, then."

Colleen found a frozen loaf of sourdough in the freezer, only slightly iced over. She picked up one of the two remaining bottles. The one she had left behind in the door was already half gone. She realized she'd have to go to the liquor store again tomorrow. Or she could use the home delivery service from The Beer Store. She hadn't done that in a while. She could get a case of wine then . . . What was she thinking? She wouldn't buy any more. When this was gone, that was it.

She promised.

Helen lived in a basement apartment in one of the houses along Davisville. Colleen walked up the ill-lit shared driveway to the door at the side of the house and rang the bell. After several minutes the curtain over the glass moved aside and Helen looked out at her and then craned her neck, peering up and down the driveway, before letting Colleen in.

"Come on in, sweetie. You look like something the dog's been dragging round the yard."

Stairs led down to the apartment and Colleen followed Helen's broad back. Helen walked with a wide-legged rocking motion. She held onto both the wall and the railing for support. She wore a velveteen track suit with the word *Juicy* written across her buttocks in gold letters. At the base of the stairs she turned and looked at Colleen.

"Oh, good, you got the bread, I see."

Colleen handed it to her, along with the bottle of wine. Helen walked across the tile floor, on which a white and blue carpet delineated a seating area containing a grey overstuffed sofa and chair, a wooden and glass coffee table and a large television on a wooden stand. A British man was telling a crying young girl that her singing sounded like a cat having its tail run through a cheese grater. Colleen spotted two centipedes—one by the television stand and another by the pot containing a plastic palm tree.

Photos of sunsets and sunrises graced the walls. Pot lights on the ceiling and a single floor lamp gave off a cold, hard light and made the salmon colour on the walls look sickly. The small but fully equipped kitchen stood at the end of the room. Beyond that was a hallway leading to the toilet and bedroom. The sole window was at the front of the living area, shoulder high. In the daylight the only thing visible were some bayberry bushes. To herself, Colleen called Helen the Mole Woman.

"So, what's up with you?" Helen uncorked the wine. "Another terrible awful day from the sounds of it. You do have a lot of those, don't you."

"Where do I start?" Coleen took her coat off and tossed it over the railing leading up to the door. She chuckled, trying to make her voice sound light. "The nursing home called to tell me my mother was in a coma—no, no, it's okay, some mix-up, she had a fall but—"

"A stake through the heart couldn't kill her, right?" Helen snorted, and waddled back to Colleen.

Colleen took the glass and sat in the fluffy chair. Helen flopped down on the couch and put her slippered feet up on the coffee table. She pointed the remote control at the television and turned down the sound.

Colleen said, "I'm not so sure that's true anymore. She's bound to wear out sometime. I just got back from the hospital."

"How grim."

Helen's hair was the same colour as the upholstery on the sofa, and her skin was almost the same shade as the walls. Colleen had the feeling Helen had been down here so long that she was *becoming* her apartment. She imagined coming to see her one day and finding nothing more than an extra, equally overstuffed armchair.

"It was, and weird. She was actually sort of nice for a few minutes."

"Good drugs." Helen raised her glass. "Here's to your mother, may she die in peace."

The first time Colleen met Helen, at the grocery store nearly a dozen years ago, when the woman still ventured outside regularly, Colleen was taken aback by her blunt humour, but as time passed she found it refreshing. Helen was quite likely to say the very thing you were thinking but did not dare give voice to.

Colleen looked at the wine in her glass. It twinkled golden. It was impossible to resist, even if she wanted to. Her shrivelled tongue sang the praises of angels when the wine floated across her taste buds.

"To Mum," she said.

"When are you finally going to get it through your head your mother can't hurt you anymore? You're not seven any longer, Colleen. She only has whatever power you give her. What did she do this time that was so bad?"

"It's not just my mother. So many things happened today. In the morning I lost my job, in the afternoon I figured out Lori isn't really my friend anymore, and then later, I found out Jake's getting married and is about to be a daddy." She tried to smile, raised her glass again and said, "L'chaim."

"Maybe you should sleep in tomorrow."

"I was just thinking the same thing."

"Jesus, what did you do to piss off God?"

"I have no idea." Colleen sniffed. It smelled pretty ripe in the apartment. Kind of stinky, actually.

"I'll start backward," Helen said. "Who's Jake marrying?"

Helen knew all about Jake, of course, and had told Colleen a million times to stop thinking about him and move on. He was, Helen said, nothing but a fallback position, a just-in-case-nothing-else-worked-out card up her sleeve, and that was a cheat to both of them. He hadn't worked out the first time—had *cheated* on her for God's sake—and people don't change, Helen insisted. Men doubly so.

"His receptionist."

Helen threw her head back and laughed. "Oh, perfect. And I suppose she's twelve."

"Maybe thirteen."

Helen laughed again. "Well, let's hope that's the last you'll see of him, although I know his type. He'll get bored of bottles and diapers in a few months and he'll be scrounging around out there somewhere. You're better off—at last, at last!" There was something bright and sharp in Helen's eyes.

"I know you're right. Wasn't it Ambrose Bierce who called love 'a temporary insanity curable by marriage'?'" said Colleen. She paused. "So why does it still hurt?"

"That man's rejected you in one way or another so many times. You've kept each other on the string all these years. You're both nuts. Well, he's finally cut the string. You have to make sure it stays cut."

"I slammed the door in his face." She smiled, just a little.

"Good for you. About time. There should be more door slamming in this world."

That smell. The apartment smelled odder even than usual. Mouldy, perhaps, the damp—but with something thicker, sweeter beneath. Colleen's nostrils flared. Was it Helen? Her hair didn't look clean, and there were stains of some sort on her clothing.

"So, your mother's not dying, at least not today."

"Doesn't look like it."

Helen drank some wine and sighed. "She can't hold on much longer. The old bitch is an antiquity."

"True." Something pierced Colleen's heart. How strange that although she felt she had every right to complain about her mother, she reared up when anyone else did. Her mother might be an ogre, but she was Colleen's ogre. "It's a pretty sad life she's had. The only thing worse than being around her is *being* her."

"Fuck that. We all have sad lives," said Helen.

How tart Helen sounded tonight. Still, what she said was true. Here she was, alone, middle-aged, jobless, nearly friendless (did Helen even really count?), selfish (yes, add that), half sauced all day, in a centipede-infested basement apartment that smelled of old lady—what *was* that smell?—drinking cheap wine on a Monday night. One day soon she might *be* Helen; she might morph into Helen as Kafka's Gregor morphed into a cockroach. She shuddered and drank a large gulp of wine. It tasted like copper pennies on her tongue. *Oh no, not that.* It happened more and more frequently these days. She'd get to a certain point in her drinking when she should be flying on gossamer wings, only to find the potion had turned rancid and bitter somehow, and no matter how much she drank, she couldn't get lift-off. Not tonight, she prayed, good fairy, don't turn on me tonight.

"It doesn't have to be that way, does it? We're not just all locked into suffering, are we? No matter what the French say."

Helen chuckled. "Ah, *oui, les* French, who believe all life is tragic and if you don't understand that, you're an idiot. I respect them for it. I think I have a French soul."

"I've decided mine may be Russian." Pretty little Russian fairy, wearing that fetching wolf-fur hat, waiting for her back in her apartment. "They believe in suffering as well. Tolstoy and all that." This was the best sort of conversation to have with Helen—something philosophical. God, that smell again. Colleen held the wineglass under her nose, pretending to inhale the bouquet.

"You'd never make a Russian."

"Why not?"

"All that queuing for bread. You have no patience."

This was also true, but Colleen didn't like Helen saying it. She scanned the room. The cheap carpet, cheap furniture. Those hideous porcelain ducks forever flying along the wall leading to the bedroom. All those photos of sunsets and sunrises Helen would never see because she never left the basement.

"Perhaps you have too much patience," she said.

"I think you're right. I put up with entirely too much. You're lucky," said Helen. "You don't have to worry about money at least. I'm existing on scraps. Thank God for Old Age Security or I'd be out on the street."

'What do you mean I don't have to worry about money?"

"You've got your mother's money."

"That's for her care."

"Don't play noble with me. She owes you, Colleen, and you know it. She's in the nursing home and that's mostly paid for by the province. You only have to pay, what, a couple of hundred a month?"

"Nearly a thousand." Colleen kept a finger under her nose. How could Helen not notice that smell? Maybe something had rotted. Surely that was it. Colleen came over once a week and took Helen's garbage out to the street for her. She couldn't remember if she'd been by last week, or if it was the week before. She'd have to take it out tonight. This was unbearable.

"You sold her condo, so you've got a few hundred thousand in the bank," Helen was saying, "and she's not going to live much longer. You've got more than enough to live on yourself until your pension kicks in."

Pension. That wasn't for years and years yet. How old did Helen think she was?

"Don't look at me like that; it'll be upon you before you know it. A girl can live on it, if you don't squander your inheritance and if you don't drink it all up in the first year."

"Very funny," said Colleen. Her glass was empty. She got up and poured herself another. Why not, it was her bottle, after all. But this visit wasn't going as planned. She glanced at Helen, who was watching the television—a shampoo commercial—even though the sound was off.

Helen had shown her a photo album once, all these pictures of Helen as a young woman—slender and like something out of a Pre-Raphaelite painting. Helen on horseback. Helen with several handsome young men, one in a U.S. Marine uniform. Helen in the garden. Helen and some girlfriends in London, Paris and Rome. The photos stopped abruptly when Helen was in her late thirties. There had been some tragedy of which Helen refused to speak. And now . . . this. A basement apartment. A cat. Her only contact with the outside world through delivery people and Colleen, and a niece named Janet who came by once in a blue moon.

Colleen carried the bottle back and set it on the coffee table. "You want some more?"

"Half glass."

Colleen filled Helen's glass. "Helen, I don't mean to be rude, but—" And then a terrible thought. "Where's Minoche?"

"Now you ask. I'm surprised."

"When was the last time you saw her?"

"Why?"

Colleen put her glass down. "You don't know? Well, was it today, yesterday, the day before? I'm sorry, but something smells pretty awful in here."

Helen's features screwed up tight, the way they did when Colleen suggested she try walking outside for just a minute, just down to the edge of the driveway, just halfway down the driveway. "I didn't ask you to come over," she said.

"I'm not criticizing you."

"Yes, you are. You think I'm dirty. You think I'm a crazy old lady who never bathes and eats cat food and one day you'll come in here and find my swollen body lying on the bathroom floor."

Helen stood, picked up the wine bottle and tromped to the kitchen area. She wore slippers with no backs and the sight of her cracked, thickly callused yellow feet was stomach turning.

"What are you talking about? I didn't say anything like that. But you can't tell me you don't smell that, whatever the hell it is?"

"I don't smell anything unusual." Helen poured herself another half glass of wine and knocked it back in one gulp before slamming the cork back in the bottle with the heel of her hand. She put it in the refrigerator.

Fuck her, thought Colleen. That's my bottle of wine. She thinks I'm leaving it here, she's crazy.

"I'm going to use the bathroom."

Colleen walked down the hall and, just as she feared, the smell got worse the nearer she got to the bedroom. She had never been in Helen's bedroom and didn't want to go there now. She wanted to go home. This was what always happened: she felt locked in the apartment, alone while all the rest of the world was at a party to which she wasn't invited, but when she did go out, conversations twisted round like snakes eating their own tails and she got panicky and wanted to be alone again. Is that how the agoraphobia started for Helen?

The wine wasn't working. She felt lightheaded, but there had been none of the chattiness, none of the lubricated conversation she so craved. Instead she felt thick-tongued, and her head hurt, right at the base of her skull, and the pain radiated up over her head to behind her right eye. Maybe whatever was causing that smell was toxic.

In the bathroom the kitty-litter box stood between the toilet and the bathtub. It was full of feces, and clumped with dried urine, the fumes positively wavering in the air above it, acrid and sharp. That might have contributed to what Colleen smelled in the living room, but it wasn't *the* smell; in fact it masked it somewhat. Colleen peed and washed her hands, letting the cold water run over her wrists. Her head pounded, and she patted water onto her temples and the back of her neck.

When she came out of the bathroom she turned right and headed for the bedroom despite her apprehension; whatever the smell was, it emanated from there. The bedroom was tiny and painted yellow. A double bed with a white and grey coverlet was pushed into the corner and pink curtains hung from a small window high on the wall. Another curtain, this one a yellow shower curtain, hung in front of a closet. The smell was thickest here. There was no doubt: whatever it was, was in here. Minoche wasn't anywhere to be seen—unless she was under the bed. Colleen bent down and looked, her heart in her throat. A fair amount of dust and one sock, but no cat.

"What do you think you're doing?"

Helen stood in the doorway, holding onto the jamb with both hands. She was shaking and pale with fury.

"I was looking for Minoche. That's all, Helen, I wasn't snooping. I just wanted to see Minoche."

"Well you can't, okay, you can't, nobody can see her anymore—you're not the only person with problems, you know." And with that Helen sank to the floor and began blubbering. "You're not the only one in the world with a broken heart and no one at all to care about her. That cat loves me. She loves me."

Colleen knelt down next to her. "It's okay, it's okay." She patted her friend's shoulder. "Where is she? Where did she go?"

Helen pulled a wad of Kleenex from her sleeve. She rubbed her eyes and blew her nose. She pointed to the closet.

"Can I look?" asked Colleen.

Helen nodded and went on crying. Colleen was, as always in a moment of crisis, calm and sure of her competence. Even as a child Colleen knew that no matter what happened, it was best not to become too emotional when someone else was breaking down. (The pull to join them was often great, however, because it would be a kind of relief to be the one other people had to deal with instead of the one having to do the dealing.) And so now, with Helen dissolving into puddles and what was clearly something revolting behind curtain number one, Colleen steeled herself and strode to the closet. *Remember the Alamo. On Donner and Blitzen. Into the Valley of Death . . .* It was possible she was drunker than she thought.

When she pulled aside the shower curtain Colleen found Minoche's red velvet bed on the floor by a pile of shoes, and on the bed was a cat-shaped form in a blue pillowcase. Rust-coloured seepage stained the cloth. The smell was pungent and eye-watering.

"Okay, okay," said Colleen. She went back to Helen. "Let's get you up, come on." Helen was heavy and it was hard to pull her to her feet, but they managed to move her so she sat on the bed.

"I'm so sorry, Helen."

Through a slurry of snot and tears Helen said, "I just woke up in the morning and there she was, dead. Poor little kitten. Poor little Minoche. I should have taken her to the vet."

"You weren't to know." Colleen was not entirely sure Helen would have taken her to the vet even if she had known. No matter how sick poor Minoche had been, it was unlikely Helen would have made it out the door. "You could have called me, though, if there was a problem. I would have taken her."

"What are you talking about? I *did* call you."

"No—"

"Of course I did. I called you last week." Helen stood up and pushed past Colleen. She went to the closet and squatted next to the corpse. "I tried for two hours to get through to you, but the phone was always busy, and when I did finally get you, you were too drunk. I could tell. Spouting some crap about how you were going to go off to Tunisia and walk the desert alone in search of your soul like Melville did. You weren't any good to me then." She turned, dabbed at her nose and glared at Colleen. "And you aren't much good now."

Colleen did not remember the phone call. She did remember reading about Herman Melville and how he sought relief from his depression by long sojourns in the desert wilderness outside Jerusalem. It had sounded attractive when she read it; it still did.

"If it wasn't for you," Helen said, "Minoche would still be alive." She burst into tears again.

"Well, wait a minute," said Colleen, but then she stopped. It would be easy to say it wasn't her fault—she wasn't the one who couldn't leave this *oubliette,* who would rather let her beloved cat die than step into the open air—but she couldn't. Helen was a wretch and Colleen understood wretchedness. She understood the impossibility of stepping over the wreckage of your own life to get to something better. "Minoche can't stay here, Helen. You know that, right? So, would you let me take care of her?"

"You'll just throw her in the garbage."

"No, I won't. I promise. I'll wrap her up in some plastic and I'll take her to the twenty-four-hour vet up on the Danforth. They'll take her and see she's properly . . . They'll take care of her. You can't keep her here."

Helen sank into the considerable bulk of herself as if a balloon inside had collapsed. "I know. I know. My landlord's been complaining. Threatening to come down with the Health Department. Accused me of hoarding." She let out a juddering sigh. "Promise me you won't just throw her away. Promise me."

"I promise."

Helen buried her head in her hands. "Do what you have to."

"Come back out to the living room and let me handle it, then, okay?"

Helen stood and walked down the hall with Colleen following, breathing through her open mouth. She could taste the decay on her tongue. She took the bottle out of the fridge, uncorked it and poured herself a full glass. She drank half of it. There wasn't much left and after considering what she had to do, she finished it off.

While Helen sat on the couch, crying again, Colleen found a garbage bag and went back to the bedroom. It was a horrible task. She gagged several times, swallowing repeatedly to keep from being sick. When the cat's liquefying body was safely in the plastic bag, Colleen washed her hands under water so hot they remained red for minutes afterward.

Minoche had been about eight years old. The cat, Colleen realized, had spent its entire life in this basement. Chasing centipedes and spiders had been its greatest joy. Colleen wondered if it might not have committed suicide. Insects would take over the place now.

By the time she came back to the living room carrying the bag as gently as she could, cradling it and not letting it hang at the end of her arm like so much trash, Helen had pulled a coverlet up to her chin and was curled in the corner of the couch. The television sound was back on. A doctor holding a cane in one hand and a clipboard in the other told a patient, "I like you better now that you're dying." Helen looked away from the screen and when she saw the bag she moaned. There was such pain in the sound that Colleen felt a stab in her chest. It was just a cat, just a fluffy grey cat with a bad habit of trying to climb up your leg, but when you had so little, such a loss was great.

"Do you want me to stay with you for a while longer?"

"No. I don't. Just take her and go, will you?"

Colleen set the bag down on the floor while she put her coat on. Helen didn't move to help her, or even look at her. "I'll take good care of her, Helen, and I'll check on you tomorrow."

She was halfway up the stairs when Helen called out to her. "You should have been there when I needed you, when Minoche needed you."

The words were scalding, and although Colleen did not deny the truth in them, nor her own self-loathing, something in her rebelled. Was Helen responsible for nothing? "I've said I was sorry."

"Go home, Colleen. Thanks for taking care of her body. We'll leave it at that."

It was tempting to leave the cat's body on the stairs. Then what would the old recluse do? As Colleen walked toward the street she wondered what the hell she should do with the carcass. She wasn't about to take a bus to the subway and then make the long journey over to the Danforth, and she wasn't going to pay for a cab either. When she'd walked far enough from Helen's low window that if the woman stood on a stool to look after her she wouldn't be able to see her, Colleen shifted her burden and let the bag dangle. Now what? The night was cold as iced steel and the stars were bright, distant and utterly disinterested. No one had their garbage cans out, which left only one solution.

Colleen didn't want to go through the lobby of her building dragging a dead cat, nor did she want to walk all

271

the way around to the back. It was cold. She was cold. Her nose dripped. The situation was absurd. As she neared the building entrance a car pulled up alongside her and stopped at the front doors. It was a sports car, bright yellow, low to the ground. Nobody living in this building could afford a car like that, surely. She walked past, determinedly not looking at it. A girl giggled and told the driver she'd be back down in a minute. Colleen opened the door to the building and the girl followed her in.

"Hey. Wow, it got cold, huh?" said the girl. She was dark haired, with a lot of eye makeup and very red lipstick smeared around her mouth. It was on her teeth, as though she'd taken a bloody bite out of something. Perhaps she had.

"That will happen in Canada this time of year," said Colleen.

The girl chuckled as though what Colleen had said was funny, and then she looked down at the bag Colleen carried and wrinkled her pert little nose ever so slightly. The smile on her face faltered.

Oh, charming, thought Colleen. Now I'm the old lady who smells. She was just at that point when she could see behind the masks people wore, could see down to what they really thought and felt and understood the judgments they passed—and it was always so ugly, so wounding.

She kept her stride long, and pretty darn even, all things considered, and made her way to the back of the building. Laughter, inappropriate and slightly worrying, bubbled up her throat. Oh dear. Oh dear. That wasn't a great sign. Next she'd be laughing and crying all at once and if that was going to happen she really needed to be in her own room where no one could see her and think they should call the cops. She would not look good in a straitjacket. Almost no one did.

The rear door was heavy and the wind was against her, so she shouldered into it. It slammed back in a gust, and as it did it caught the garbage bag in the jamb. Something, possibly a leg bone, snapped and the bag tore slightly. The smell, which she really hadn't noticed before in spite of the red-mouthed girl's insulting nose crinkle, now burst up with the power of a stink bomb. Colleen would not look at whatever poked through the plastic. She heaved herself against the door and it gave way so that she stumbled into the parking lot. Holding the bag as far away from her body as possible, she jogged to the three rusty rubbish bins standing in a row by the service entrance. It wasn't hard to toss the mushy bundle over the side of the container. It hit the metal with a sickening thud and rustled to the bottom.

And then it was done. Minoche was no more. She wondered if she should say some words. The only thing that came to mind was "the song of mehitabel," Don Maquis's poem about a free-spirited alley cat in her ninth life: "*wotthehell wotthehell / there's a dance in the old dame yet / toujours gai toujours gai.*" There was no denying Minoche was an alley cat now.

Oh dear, there was that laughter threatening again.

What was wrong with her? She was not a callous person. She had loved the little fluff-ball, so imperious with her green eyes and aloof flick of the tail. She had been such a pretty cat and poor Helen's only friend. Gone for want of a phone call, perhaps. Dead for want of someone to take her to the vet.

Oh dear, there were the tears.

Colleen hurried back inside. In the lobby—thank you for emptiness—into the elevator—still no one, bless you, elevator—along the blissfully vacant hall to her door. Click, you lovely lock, get ready little Russian fairy, here comes Colleen.

The door closed behind her and once again the unoccupied apartment, which just a moment before had seemed such an appealing sanctuary, took on a sinister aspect. The bone-grey light from the city outside flowed through the windows. Such an aggressive, soulless light. It made the table, the shelves, the television, the sofa, all look malevolent, as though they might come to life at any moment and hunch across the floor toward her. Ridiculous, she told herself, and flicked on the lights. That was better, but she couldn't get over the feeling something might come slouching along the hallway from the bedroom. Some hand might grip the corner of the wall. Colleen's chest tightened.

Get a hold of yourself. Why was she suddenly so frightened of the place that had been her home all these years? She reached for the vodka bottle on the kitchen counter without taking off her coat and—to hell with it— lifted it to her lips and drank. One gulp and then several

274

more. Hello, little Tatyana, Fairy Queen. *Dance me a pretty Cossack dance. Dance away my fear.* She would be like Dostoyevsky—a realist who did not fear the results of her study.

The apartment was impossibly, accusingly quiet. She removed her coat and dropped it on the floor next to her purse. Who cared? She poured a glass of straight Russian courage—why bother with the cheap illusion of a mix? She went to the living room and popped Tom Waits into the CD player. Tom sang about orphaned things left out in the rain, things no one wanted. She sang along to the music. Was there a sadder song on the face of the planet? The despair tango. She drank and swayed and turned out the lights. The place didn't look so frightening anymore. Tom sang on about all the broken and rusted things he'd never throw away. And then the long lonely train whistle. She sat on the couch. Ah yes, here came the tears, the pretty tears, sparkling like diamonds on her lashes.

Tom Wait's gravel-velvet voice floated over her. Such sweet sorrow. Someone knew her, someone sang her soul. She was born in the wrong time. She should have been a young woman in the 1930s, working in a diner, maybe, pouring coffee for the customers, engaged in repartee. Her eyes would be haunted with some past heartbreak of which she never spoke. She would answer the invitation to the blues. In fact, maybe she'd start leading that life now. She'd just take off, leave her crazy mother in the semi-capable hands of the nursing staff. She'd cash in her inheritance and buy a silver trailer, one of those round ones— Airstream—that's what they were called. She'd drive it out to cowboy country and get a job in a bar. Why not? Or a desert restaurant. She'd be the one all the regulars told their stories to and she'd write those stories down and just like Annie Proulx out there in Newfoundland or Montana or wherever she was these days, she'd tell the truth about the lives of everyday folk and she'd be a great success. A great success at last.

But first, she would send Jake an e-mail. Tell him exactly, and finally, what she thought of him.

In the bedroom, glass nicely full and sitting there so prettily next to her laptop, she stared at the computer screen. How to begin? Somewhere from the region of the living room came Waits' voice, singing about a girl sending someone blue valentines from Philadelphia. Oh, that was a message from the gods, surely.

Dear Jake,

This will be the last you'll hear from me. But I couldn't go without reminding you of a certain afternoon. I'm listening to Tom Waits right now. Do you remember? That's what we were listening to: we were listening to Tom Waits singing a song about a man haunted by the only woman he'd ever loved, whom he treated so badly she left him and never came back.

You were high. You were always high then. You only told me you loved me when you were high. You sat on my old brown plaid couch and I sat on the floor in front of you

276

and you tangled your fingers in my hair. I ran my nails along your thighs and felt your muscles jump.

It was snowing outside. I remember that. Snowing so hard the late-afternoon light coming in through the window looked bright even though it was almost dark.

I'd never loved anyone the way I loved you and it didn't matter to me that we fought as much as we did. I couldn't get enough of you. I didn't know what you were thinking just then. I used to think I understood you, but now I'm not so sure. The man I thought I knew wouldn't have done what you did today. Wouldn't have been doing what you've been doing all these years. I see that now. Maybe I just made you up. But that afternoon, what you did took me by surprise. You lifted me up and held me on your lap with my face buried in your shoulder so I couldn't see your eyes. I tried to pull back but you wouldn't let me.

"If I ever fuck up, I mean really fuck up," you said, "you do what it says in the song. Send me a blue valentine from wherever you are."

We sat like that for a long time, till long after the song had finished.

"Promise me," you whispered.

"I promise," I said.

But I never did. Why should I be the one to keep a promise? Then again, maybe I'm keeping it now. Consider this your blue valentine, you cold-hearted, manipulative shit.

It wasn't bad. It was almost poetic. Maybe she had what it took to be a writer after all. She imagined Jake reading it. She imagined his great regret. She imagined he'd see how much he lost when he lost her. She imagined him tossing in his bed at night, calling out her name when he made love to that ridiculous Taquanda. She pressed send. And there it was, gone.

She hummed along to the music as she danced a little dance on the way back to the living room. Waits was singing now about his bad liver and broken heart. She sang along. She knew all the words, every stinging soul-etching word. She'd been singing along with Waits since the mid-eighties, back when she could drink anyone she knew under the table and then, what? What had happened? When had it happened? All those people she knew once upon a time were somewhere else now, married with kids, driving BMWs and Audis and working as stockbrokers or insurance executives or lawyers. She still had her writing. She should be writing this very minute. She would get her journal and begin immediately. Inspiration twirled along the notes of Wait's poetic dissolution . . .

She stood up, a bit too quickly, and yelped when she cracked her shin against the coffee table. She grabbed her leg, lost her balance and ended up on the carpet with vodka spilled down her chest. For a moment she simply sat there, shocked by the fall. For the second time that day she was covered in spilled booze. It was unbearable. She drained what was left in her glass. Her vision swam. She'd gone too far. Had had too much. She needed food. It took her a few minutes to get to her feet and she used the wall as a support as she made her way back to the kitchen. Crackers and butter. Cheese. A piece of bread and butter. She hadn't known she was so hungry. She considered making scrambled eggs, but even in her vodka fog she understood using a gas stove at this precise moment might not be prudent.

Oh, little Russian fairy, don't you turn against me now. The Russian fairy was one of the more perfidious. It could snap from fire-honey comfort to sweet restful sorrow to Rasputin rage to Gulag horror in a matter of minutes. She should have remembered that when she bought the bottle. Why did she never remember these things when she was sober? It was as though the mystical knowledge acquired when drinking was only accessible again when drinking.

She half stumbled down the treacherous hall and into the bedroom. She stripped off her clothes and left them pooled on the floor. It was important to move with deliberation. She pulled sweatpants and her favourite manky black sweater from the bottom of the closet. She wrestled her way into them. She was chilly. She put heavy socks on her feet. She would write, she would.

At her desk the lines on the paper slithered and slipped. But, to begin was everything. She wrote that down. *To begin, to begin, and I am here beginning and you and me and we are all here together. I see you, Moon. Don't think I'm blind. It's not true. True is that I've come home by way of you. By your full-blown light here in the muslin night, filled with concertos and kindness least expected. There will be a battle . . .*

What utter bullshit, she thought.

Colleen threw herself on the bed and sobbed. The bed spun and her stomach lurched and she slid halfway to the floor to stop it. She knelt by the bed and found herself praying. She prayed for something to happen, anything to make the pain stop, and death would be fine, right now, if she could just slip away in her sleep and have it all be over.

She stood up and headed for the bathroom. Perhaps there was something in there with which she could kill herself.

Pardon me?

Colleen stopped at the threshold. Had she really just thought that? She had. A hole gaped where thought should be, black as the dark side of the moon. She sat on the side of the bath. On the shelf above the toilet stood the pretty perfume bottles: Dior, Trésor, Chloé, Oscar de la Renta, Angel, Perry Ellis 360, Intuition, Ysatis, Opium, L'Air du Temps, this last with the pair of tiny doves on top. Sweet little bottles, magical potions of promise.

What a fucking joke. How many times had she sat right where she was now, staring at those toy bottles, believing their cheap plastic promises? Lies. Why had she never seen that before? Like her job, like her friends, like her family, like her dreams of one day being a writer, it was all tawdry, cheesy, imitation life.

The sound that came out of her mouth was of something ripping inside, something that could never be stitched up again. Colleen launched herself toward the shelf and smashed her fist down on it. The bottles flew every which way, crashing to the floor, in the bath, the sink. The star on the Angel bottle cracked and a point fell off. The Trésor bottle broke, as did the Intuition. The others lay scattered on the floor. The air reeked of stale perfume, the mix of odours so astringent and sweet at the same time that it smelled like decay.

Some of the glass bits were nice and sharp. A hot bath, a lovely glass of Chablis and a glass shard, followed by an eternal restful sleep. What more could a girl ask for? She pictured herself in the bath, her hair streaming out in the water, the water itself the colour of a garnet, her skin the palest ivory.

A part of her retreated to the far corner of the small tiled room and considered. It appeared madam was earnestly contemplating taking the great leap, the final fall, the last bus, the long walk off a short plank. That was a sobering thought, although not nearly sobering enough.

Here was the truth of her situation at last. Here was the moment in which she arrived at the closing act of her life. Her mother appeared before her—she who had threatened so many times to kill herself and never did. Colleen bet she regretted that now. Helen's face, twisted in grief, popped into her mind. What was it that stopped *her* from killing herself? Colleen would probably end up exactly where Helen was in a few years, although her delivery bills from the Dial-a-Bottle would be considerably higher. The question was not why did people kill themselves; it was why didn't *more* people kill themselves? Life was, after all, so incredibly futile. The trick was to choose the right moment. Wait too long and the decision might be taken out of your hands, as it had been for her mother—whom all the world seemed intent on keeping alive as long as possible, regardless of how miserable everyone was.

She sat down again on the side of the bath. The question was: was this the right time? Colleen was alone, and would likely remain so. (How interesting it was to have such a rational conversation with one's self about this. There was no emotion involved at all. Such a relief.) She was jobless. She was, let's face it, friendless—she was not a success as a friend, or anything else. Well, that wasn't quite true. She was a great success as a drunk.

In this detached, analytical state of mind, she wondered just when it was she had first known she was a drunk. She might not have admitted it to others, but her own alcoholism was no surprise to her. She was an alcoholic, and one who, just at this moment, wanted a drink very badly, since the black hole in the centre of her mind was growing larger with every passing minute. It was enveloping her whole head and creeping slowly down toward her heart and gut. Soon she would be nothing *but* that great hole.

The hall was empty. The living room was empty; the kitchen, empty; and the world beyond her window full of ghosts. How empty she was too. Where had all the vodka gone? Less than a third of a bottle left. It was nearly ten-thirty now and she should be sleeping; all the world, it seemed, was sleeping. So she would have just this, a nightcap, while Tom Waits sang.

Oh, the long walk down the hall. How vast it seemed, how treacherous with angles. It was an epic quest, from bathroom to kitchen. But at last, the holy grail lay on the counter within reach, shimmering and clear-eyed. As she drank, however, the vodka was like a snakebite on her tongue. No fairy appeared. On the counter the knives in the rack gleamed temptingly. She took the glass, smudgy with her greasy fingerprints, and sat on the middle of the couch.

She thought of the myth of Sisyphus, the deceitful and avaricious king condemned for all eternity to push a great boulder up a hill, only to have it roll back down again. Meaningless. Futile. She thought, through the misty vapour of alcohol swirling through her mind, that she might be a sort of Sisyphus, with each day being the boulder she must conquer, only to inevitably fail and be forced to begin again. Why not let the rock simply roll back over her and crush her like a beetle? Then it would be over, this terrible ordeal of life.

It wasn't as though anyone would care, or even grieve her. Lori would probably cry, but those tears would quickly dry. Besides, the thought of other people's grief might be enough to stop one killing oneself, but it wasn't enough to make one go on living.

She could jump from the balcony. But that seemed so messy and even that was uncertain. What if she simply crushed her spine or mangled herself? Then where would she be? Strapped to machines. Forced to watch reality television in some hospital day-room, unable to wipe the drool from her own chin, let alone change the channel. No. That wouldn't do.

The vodka tasted worse with each mouthful. It felt as though her tongue were being gnawed. Wormwood and acid. It occurred to her that she could stop drinking. That was an option. Or was it? How many mornings had been like this morning, which she only vaguely remembered? She woke up. She felt like death. She loathed herself. She vowed never again. And then a few hours later that little voice popped up. *Oh, come on, have one, just one, anyone can have one, and you of all people are justified in having a drink because, good Lord, look at how awful your life is.*

But her life was so awful because she drank so much.

She swallowed another mouthful.

And she couldn't seem to stop. And perhaps she needn't. She could just sit in this empty room. She could call up good old Dial-a-Bottle and have them deliver a crate of vodka and scotch and maybe some Grand Marnier. She wondered how long it would take to drink herself to death.

Her grandmother had, after all. Or close enough.

You and I Are a Lot Alike

Colleen was eight and she and her parents were in Florida visiting Deirdre's parents. Nanny and Gramps had moved there when they retired, choosing the Florida heat over the frigid Manitoba winters. They lived in a tiny two-room cottage in a strip of attached cottages in a section of St. Petersburg not far from the beach. When Colleen and her family came to visit, Colleen and her mother shared the bedroom with Nanny, while Gramps and Colleen's father slept on a cot and the pullout couch in the living room—kitchen.

Colleen was fascinated by all things Floridian—the little lizards who sunned themselves on the windowsills, the names of the nearby motels (Sandy Toes, Dis'll Do, The Rusty Anchor), the fleshy flowers and hanging moss. Her grandparents had mysterious items in their home—Gramps brushed his teeth with a powder that came in a pale blue can, and the screen of the television, which stood on a metal stand in the living room, was covered with a coloured piece of plastic—blue at the top, green in the middle and brown at the bottom. It was supposed to add colour to the black and white images, but Colleen thought it made the faces look very strange indeed.

Every day the family went down to the swimming club her grandparents belonged to. It had a big pool and a snack bar and her parents and grandparents sat under cabanas, their skin all shiny with oil, except for her father, who burned easily. He wore a shirt and covered his skinny legs with a towel. They took long walks on the beach, even past the fence that marked the end of the private beach and the start of the public one, where the black children played. Colleen wanted to talk to them, and maybe make a friend, but was told she wasn't allowed to, although no reason was given. She fed the seagulls instead.

Nanny's real name was Edith, but everyone called her Gypsy because of her dark hair and eyes. She smoked menthol cigarettes in a long ivory holder studded with rhinestones. Her hair was tinted with a blue rinse and her skin was brown as a nut. She laughed a good deal and liked to have what she called "elevenses"—a beer or a gin and tonic at eleven in the morning. She said everyone in Ireland, where she and Gramps came from, had a little something at eleven in the pub. Colleen's father always joined her, but Gramps and Colleen's mother never did.

Nanny's best friend lived in the cottage to the right of theirs. Her name was Winnie and she used to be a card dealer in Las Vegas. Colleen thought this very sophisticated and glamorous. Winnie had never been married, which Colleen found astonishing. She had one blue eye and one green eye and they never seemed to be looking in the same direction. She taught Colleen how to shuffle cards like a real Vegas dealer, in what she called a *riffle*. Colleen was clumsy at first, but Winnie just sat there patiently sipping her Southern Comfort. She let Colleen try a little and it tasted like spoiled peaches, but felt very nice and warm in her tummy.

"Don't let your mum know I gave you that, okay?" Winnie said, touching her nose. "It'll be just between us."

Colleen understood. Nanny had said the same thing to her on a number of occasions.

Winnie and Nanny often went out together in the afternoon, and often where they went was a "nice place," as Nanny called it, named the River Queen. One day, when Colleen had to stay out of the sun because she'd been so badly burned the day before that there were blisters on her nose and shoulders, she asked if she could go with them.

"No, precious, it's not a place for children."

Gramps, who was reading the *St. Petersburg Times* at the small kitchen table, grunted. "It's not a place for any decent person."

Gramps was what Colleen's mother called "a Victorian throwback." He was born in the impossibly long ago, in 1896, when Queen Victoria was still on the throne in England and when people did things like dress for dinner and keep their upper lips stiff. (Colleen had attempted this once, but only managed a horrible grimace she couldn't possibly maintain.) Gramps wore a shirt and tie at the dinner table, even in Florida at the Formica and chrome table where he now sat, even when it was so hot and steamy the newspaper curled and Colleen's hair stuck to her head like seaweed. His moustache was always tidily combed and his spectacles gleamed. He knew how to do wonderful things, like make chewing gum from the sap of trees and fashion tiny canoes from birch bark. He exercised religiously every morning—deep knee bends and running in place and push-ups, fifty of them. Nanny never participated, but she watched, sipping her black coffee and nibbling her toast with "just a scraping of butter" on it to settle her stomach, which she frequently said was bilious early in the day. Nanny had lots of stomach trouble, and Colleen knew that when her mother was a little girl Nanny had been in and out of hospital for mysterious reasons having to do with her biliousness.

"Don't be absurd, Henry," said Nanny now. "Those young men are artists."

Gramps snapped his paper shut and went out onto the porch, where Colleen's mother and father sat on lawn chairs, watching the pelican that had built a nest on the top of a nearby telephone pole. "You know my feelings on this, Gyp," he said as he left.

Nanny watched him go and then went to the cupboard and pulled a bottle of Worcestershire sauce from the back. She poured some into her coffee. "Don't tell on Nanny now, will you, precious?"

Colleen was less interested in her grandmother's strange beverage preferences than she was in the artists at the River Queen.

"What kind of a place is it?" she asked. "What kind of artists? Do they paint?"

Nanny laughed. "They are beautiful young men who dress up as women. You wouldn't believe how lovely they are." She looked wistful. "So perfect in their gowns, their hair just so. Their makeup flawless. One of them, his name is David, although he likes to be called Glenda, did my makeup one afternoon, but your grandfather didn't like it. He's such a stuffy old thing."

This sounded wonderful—grown-ups who played dress-up and did each other's makeup. It seemed a magical world. "Can I come with you, please? I want to see them." What she really wanted, of course, was to dress in the beautiful gowns and have her own hair just so.

Nanny came over and put her long, red-nailed fingers under Colleen's chin, tilting the child's head toward her. She smelled of coffee, cigarettes, lavender talcum powder and something else, something a bit like the floor polish her mother used. "One day maybe, when you're older," said Nanny. "I think you'd like it there. You and I are a lot alike. You're my special girl, aren't you."

Not special enough to take along, however.

That afternoon Nanny and Winnie went to the River Queen without Colleen, and they didn't come back until after supper. Nanny had fallen down in the street. Her nose was bloody, her eye was black. Her mother banished Colleen to the bedroom where she couldn't help but hear the snarling words through the wall. Gramps called Nanny a disgrace and said she'd ruined his retirement, ruined his life, and he was so ashamed of her he was going to cancel their membership to the beach club, since surely everyone had seen her stumbling through the streets. Nanny cried and said she was sorry over and over again. Her mother spoke to Nanny disrespectfully, calling her a liar and someone who broke promises. If Colleen had ever spoken to her mother like that, she would have been beaten within an inch of her life. Hearing her mother's vicious tone was both electrifying, since apparently it *was* possible to argue with one's mother after all, and terrifying; it appeared there was no one her mum couldn't attack. Only Colleen's father had nothing to say.

Colleen pulled the covers up over her head. She didn't understand why Gramps and her mother were so mad at Nanny. She'd had a fall. Why were they all so ashamed of her for that? Anyone could fall. Colleen herself had done it hundreds of times, from her bike, from her roller skates, from swings and trees. She always had scabs and Band-Aids on her knees. Were they ashamed of her the way they were of Nanny? Maybe they just weren't saying so because she was so young and they hoped she'd grow out of it, like being afraid of the dark (which she still was but didn't tell anyone, since it made her mother angry to be pulled away from her television programs to see to her). Colleen resolved to do better, and if she fell again, she wouldn't tell anyone.

And then her mother spit out the words "Stinking drunk!"—the very words she'd used on more than one occasion to describe Colleen's father. Colleen had some understanding of the term. She knew her father drank too much alcohol and when he did he spent time with women he worked with and squandered the money that was supposed to go to something called the mortgage. And now Nanny was spending time with Winnie instead of Gramps, and going to the place where men dressed up as ladies. It didn't seem such a bad thing, to be able to get away from this crazy family, to go where people liked you and had fun.

But the fun always ended badly, as it did for Nanny a few years later. The doctors said it was a stroke, but Colleen's mother said she might as well have put a gun in her mouth. Colleen had loved Nanny. Love was such a failure. It saved no one.

Sailing Away

No, drinking oneself to death took too long, Colleen thought as she stared dully into the night sky beyond the window glass. It might well take years, sitting on this very couch, grimly downing bottle after bottle. Colleen looked at her hands, no longer the long-fingered delicate things they once were, now more like hag's hands. Years more of this? Years of watching her liver swell, her eyes go yellow, feeling her esophagus ulcerate, her stomach bleed? Years more of the wine trots and the shaking, anxiety-ridden nights, the shame-filled white-light mornings? She didn't think she could bear it. She wanted the pain to stop *now*, not six months from now, not six years from now.

She tried to remember the last time she had been happy. Blank. She tried to remember *any* time when she'd been happy. Scenes presented themselves for consideration: the first date with Jake when she'd invited him to her house and cooked sole almandine, which they ate by the light of a solitary candle on that very table there. It had been a nervous-in-a-good-way night and he'd kissed her before he left, but that memory was now encrusted with all that came after. It was tainted by heartbreak. Impossible to think of part of Jake-time without thinking of all of it. *Taquanda.* So, not that. None of that. What about the Christmas when she was thirteen and her parents gave her a guitar? Her mother, in that spooky-smart way of hers, had hidden clues to where the gift might be all over the house, starting with a note in the over-decorated tree. Each note was written backwards, so Colleen had to hold it up to a mirror to read it, and each was in rhyme. There were at least a dozen notes, leading her on a merry chase, until she finally found the guitar in her father's clothes closet. Colleen smiled. How surprised she'd been, and how elated. Her mother had gone to a lot of trouble for her. Mother. Best not to think of Mother . . . She strained to think of other happy moments. That time in Nova Scotia, the falling snow. Yes. There. Brief, but undeniable. And walking in the Mount Pleasant Cemetery one autumn afternoon when the leaves were a garland of garnet and ruby overhead and the sky was rough and ragged with pewter clouds. A feeling of peace there, and *rightness.* Pixie. Best of all friends. In the fields with the dog. As a little girl, to see the big old horse who ate apples from her hand. Stolen hours in Hart House Library, on rainy days when no one else was there and she spent her lunch hour nestled in the deep stone sill of the leaded glass casement windows, reading C.S. Lewis or Chesterton or Loren Eiseley. A time or two in bed, just before falling asleep, when she thought that if she slipped away, if she died right then, it wouldn't hurt at all and she wouldn't mind a bit. Colleen snorted. What a curious image to include among a list of possible joys. It occurred to her that the only times she'd been truly happy, or at least the only times that weren't tarnished by the stain of future unhappiness, were when she'd been alone, or in the company of non-humans.

Pixie had lived to the ripe old age of sixteen, but then she'd become incontinent and Deirdre had her put down. Just dropped her off at the vet and left her there one day when Colleen was at school. "You *left* her there? Colleen had shrieked through her tears. How could you *do* that?" Her mother looked at her as though she were speaking a foreign language. She said the dog was better off.

The idea of Pixie dying in the company of strangers still haunted Colleen. If she did get a dog, she'd never do that. Never. She thought of Minoche. Cats, they said, were easier to care for than dogs, but she hadn't been very good at that, had she. Minoche might still be alive but for her selfishness, but for her drinking.

In truth, not only had there been few happy moments, but also Colleen hadn't done much to make those around her happy.

On the end table was a stack of books. She picked up a collection of Australian poems and turned to one marked by a yellow sticky-note. It was by Edward Booth Loughran, the poem she'd thought about earlier in the day.

> *And temptings dark, and struggles deep*
> *There are, each soul alone must bear,*
> *Through midnight hours unblest with sleep,*
> *Through burning noontides of despair.*

That pretty much summed it up. For her. For all the souls alone.

Those pretty knives. A nice hot bubble bath. A ruby bath.

Tom Waits, bless him. The last note faded away. She could put it on repeat and slip under the waves of her claret bath just as easily as that. Like that time her mother cracked her one across the face when she'd come home plastered. She was so drunk now, she wouldn't even feel the knife slice. It would be heaven just to make it all go away. So peaceful. All problems resolved and nothing left to do.

She remembered Robert. Was this how he'd felt?

Nothing Left to Worry About

Robert had worked at the university in the Department of Medical Research Office, where he helped prepare research grant proposals. Colleen had met him at a university Christmas party and they hit it off immediately, in the way two people do when they both feel out of place and achieve that instant level of intimacy one can establish over a double scotch. Blond and handsome in a Germanic sort of way—fleshy with soft lips and rosy cheeks and solid thighs—he'd go to fat as he aged, she knew, but at thirty there was something sensual and cherubic about him. The sort of young man one could imagine in lederhosen without laughing out loud.

They spent the evening swapping gossip about how the research fellows in the Department of Medicine stored their lunches and bottles of booze in the vast refrigerated rooms where the rabies vaccines and various bacteriological cultures were left to grow in their Petri dishes; which professor was most likely to be forced out because he was sleeping with his students, *again;* and indeed, who was most likely to pair up at the end of that very party. They laughed a great deal, and by the time they realized almost everyone else had left and the bartender and wait staff were looking at them pointedly, they had recognized each other as kindred spirits.

Thus began a friendship defined by frequent lunches on Baldwin Street, mostly at John's Italian Caffe, where the wine was served in little jam-jar-style glasses. At first the conversations were all gossipy and fun, all about movies and books and Robert's fabulous and utterly eccentric friends, but as the months passed, clearly all was not well in Robert's world. Darryl, his boyfriend, had a wandering eye, it seemed, and the lunches regularly turned maudlin, with Robert in tears.

By July Darryl had left him for an art dealer with a gallery in Yorkville, and Robert was one big soggy tissue. He ate too much and was putting on the pounds. He couldn't sleep. He walked the streets at night, finding himself time and again in front of the gallery Darryl's new boyfriend owned.

For some reason, Colleen and Robert's friendship was confined to lunches; but these lunchtime therapy sessions seemed so important to him. Colleen held his hand and told him that of course he was grieving, that the loss of love was not unlike grieving after a death, but that there were thousands of men who'd be thrilled to have Robert in their lives.

"I don't want thousands of men. I want Darryl," Robert wailed. "He's the one who always wanted more. I've always wanted less. And even that seems like too much to ask for."

As the weeks passed, it was as if Robert were in a room with no door, just feeling his way around the same walls, day after day. And then, in August, he brightened ; he laughed again, even told wicked little jokes about his co-workers ("he's so dumb he thinks the English Channel is a British television station"), and the subject of Darryl's betrayal no longer came up. Robert was going to be just fine after all, Colleen was sure. And what a relief it was to have him back, since even Colleen's patience had begun to wear thin.

He said he was planning a dinner party for everyone who'd been so kind to him in the face of his recent "troubles," as he put it.

"Come Friday," he said. "I'm in the mood to cook— stroganoff, I think."

"Oh, honey, I can't on Friday," she said. She and Lori had plans for a girls' night out.

Robert merely shrugged. "No worries, darling. Next time, then, yes?"

"We'll have lunch on Monday and you can tell me all about it."

That Monday, in the morning, she called his phone, but he didn't pick up. It went straight to voice mail. When he hadn't called back by noon she walked over to his office to pick him up. He wasn't there, and his desk was completely cleaned off, a bland expanse of oak veneer. Puzzled, she asked the departmental secretary where he was.

"You'd better ask Dr. Klinehoff," she said, and she wouldn't meet Colleen's eyes. "There he is."

Colleen turned and saw tidy little Dr. Klinehoff, the departmental Chair, just coming in the door with a bunch of papers under his arm.

"Dr. Klinehoff? Excuse me, I was looking for Robert."

He stopped and regarded her over the top of his pince-nez. "And who are you?"

"Colleen Kerrigan, I work over in St. Mike's. I'm a friend of Robert's. We're supposed to have lunch. Is he sick?"

Dr. Klinehoff took her by the elbow and moved her into his office. "I'm sorry to have to tell you this, but . . . Robert died."

She felt as though someone had slammed a crowbar right in the middle of her chest. She couldn't breathe.

The story came out over the next few days. The dinner party had been a going-away party. A little gift had been given to each of the six people who came—a thank you, he'd said, for seeing him through his hour of darkness. An antique copy of *Peter Pan* for one, a hand-blown glass vase for another, a watercolour painting, a ring . . . his own things, chosen especially. Robert said he was like Bilbo Baggins, having an un-birthday party.

He had made up his mind, it appeared, in the weeks preceding the dinner when Colleen thought he was getting better. The change of attitude Colleen sensed, the calm and return of good humour, had been the result of his having made the final decision. There was nothing left to worry about. The pain he felt would soon come to an end. He tied up all his financial affairs, selling his car and some of his furniture to wipe out a debt he shared with Darryl, so that his ex-lover, who apparently had no head for money, wouldn't be left holding the bag. He rented a room in a motel by the lake and it was there, on Sunday, that he hanged himself.

On Wednesday a little package arrived in the mail for Colleen. It was a tiny gold Celtic cross on a chain. *Because you believed in me*, the note read. *Love, Robert.*

Timing Was Everything

How awful that had been. She let her head flop onto the back of the couch as tears trickled from the corners of her eyes. The terrible finality of it all. When it happened she told herself that if he'd lived, after a few years he would have been with someone else, happy again and caring little for the callous Darryl. Suicide was, as they said, a permanent solution for a temporary problem.

She went to the funeral. It was a sad little affair, with Robert's mother and two sisters, a smattering of cousins and a few people from the university. A depressingly low number of his friends attended, and Darryl was not among them. Nor was Robert's father, who Colleen learned had disowned his son after he informed his parents he was gay. No, at the time, she hadn't understood why he couldn't have held on just a little while. Now, she understood perfectly.

And how quickly life had gone on after Robert's death. It was as if he had been little more than a hand in a bucket of water. Once the hand was pulled out, there was no evidence of its having been there. She never even wore the cross. She couldn't bring herself to. It lay in the bottom of her jewellery box.

It would be the same for her, if she did what she was contemplating. A few tears shed, but just a few; many who would say they saw it coming. And a lot of *tsk-tsk*ing. Now that she thought about it, she realized she knew quite a number of people who had committed suicide—a boy named Gary in her high school who locked himself in the garage with the car engine running; the sister of a friend who injected herself with an overdose of insulin and left a note so bitter and filled with rage it took one's breath away; a girl from high school who upon graduation went out to Vancouver and stepped in front of a bus after checking herself out of a mental hospital; B.B. Gabor, the musician Jake had been friends with and who'd been over for dinner a number of times. He'd hanged himself. Aunt Flo, Deirdre's aunt, had jumped from the cliffs back in Ireland, and some cousin Colleen never met put rocks in her pocket—very Virginia Woolf—and went into the sea. And Liam, of course. When you went looking for them, suicides were everywhere.

And, thought Colleen, let's not forget Mum, who had threatened to kill herself so many times that one afternoon about six months before she'd had those fateful strokes, when Colleen called her and was met with another conversation that began, "I'm going to kill myself. I'll do it this time. What's the point? It's not like you give a damn," finally said, "You know, Mum, if you really want to kill yourself, you'll have to be careful about it. You don't want to do it only halfway and end up drooling and incontinent. Pills will work, if you have enough, but you need to take anti-nausea medication first, so you don't just spew them all up, and you should drink quite a lot of alcohol. Do you still keep the bottle of medicinal scotch? Because that will certainly work. But the thing you must remember is that, just before you nod off, you should tie a plastic bag around your head. That's the important bit. The sure thing. If the pills and the booze fail, you'll suffocate." Her mother hung up on her and for a few days Colleen told herself, every time the pangs of culpability flooded her, that her mother was the one who should feel guilt, for she'd hung the Damoclean sword of her suicide over Colleen ever since she was a little girl.

In fact, Deirdre never mentioned suicide again. For a while Colleen thought she just might do it, but if she meant to, Deirdre had left it too late. Timing was the trick, of course; timing was everything. Colleen doubted now that her mother could even remember wanting to.

If Colleen was gone, Deirdre would be utterly alone in the world—tiny as a broken, wizened child beneath the thin hospital blanket. The government would step in, assign a trustee. This pierced her, but dully. She thought of Pixie at the veterinarian's, without anyone she knew to hold her in the final moments. Was it not at least equally horrible to contemplate leaving her own mother to a similar fate? It was, but even as she knew this, and thought it a decent enough reason not to kill herself, it simply didn't feel like a strong enough reason to stay alive. Her mother might even understand.

Alas, Colleen had no pills.

If she was going to do it, it would have to be the knife. This was a thought, cold and clear and barren as the Namibian Desert at midnight, which called for a drink. Her legs were unsteady as she plowed back to the kitchen. A little more, just a slippery lick should do the trick.

By the time she made it back to the living room, Colleen wanted to talk to someone. What time was it? How difficult it had become to focus on her watch. She picked up her phone from the coffee table. It was nearly midnight. Jake never went to bed until at least midnight. She should call him and apologize for the way she'd behaved this afternoon. She shouldn't have slammed the door in his face. Helen was right; he wouldn't last with this girl. He'd come back to her the way he always did. She fumbled for a few minutes, trying to find his number in her list, but yes, there it was. The call went directly to voice mail.

"Yeah, it's me. You know what to do."

Beep.

"It's me. I wanted to say to you that I was not my best. Did I tell you I got fired? Yeah. My own fucking fault. Fucked up, you know?" This wasn't what she wanted to say at all. "Never mind that. Forget that. Shit. Call me, okay? Just call me."

She sat looking at the phone and then realized she hadn't disconnected, so she did. She kept looking at the phone. Waiting for him to call back. He'd call back. But maybe he wouldn't. It was too late to call Lori. Ah, right, she knew what to do.

She hit another number.

"Spring Lake Place."

"Put me through to my mother's nurse."

"Uh, sure, okay, who would that be?"

"You know who it is. Unless you fired her. Probably should have."

There was muffled talk, as though the woman on the other end had her hand over the phone. A new voice came on, a man's voice.

"Can I help you? Who is this?"

Hadn't she said who it was? "This is Colleen Kerrigan. Deirdre Kerrigan's daughter." Oh, she had mangled that last bit, very slurry. Deirdre had come out as *Dedruh*. Shit.

"It's late to be calling your mother, Ms. Kerrigan. They go to bed at eight-thirty on that floor, you know."

"She's not even there, you idiot."

"I beg your pardon?"

"Why I'm calling. Somebody called and told me she was dying, and she's not fucking dying. A stake through the heart couldn't kill her."

He didn't laugh. Didn't he find that funny? It *was* funny.

"I think perhaps you might want to call back in the morning, when you've had some sleep."

"You people should be careful calling a person like that."

"I'm happy to have someone check on your mother if you'd like, but it really is quite late."

Typical. They were morons. "She's in hospital. Fell again." Oops. Words had become quite impossibly complicated creatures. Perhaps calling hadn't been the best idea. *Flegain* surely wasn't a word.

"I beg your pardon?" Oh, the ice a man could put in his voice.

"Never mind." She hung up.

It wouldn't matter. Either she'd be dead tomorrow or she'd just deny it. She'd done it before.

The silence. It was so loud. It was the freight train of silence, the Krakatoa, the Hiroshima of silence. Emptiness wasn't empty at all; it was a thick block of solid no-sound, no-presence. An empty room was filled with all the things that weren't in it.

A person could drown in silence.

One last thing and then, if that didn't work, Option B. It seemed quite simple all of a sudden. She understood Robert's calm, the peace of those last days. It was such a relief. Let the world run on without her, let the water in the bucket close over her absence, let the last note ring and fade, let the shadows lengthen to darkness. Fade out. Done.

Glass in one hand. Phone in pocket. Into the kitchen. Top off the Russian fairy. Yes, there she was, performing a frantic Cossack dance between the sugar canister and the knife block. Colleen slipped the butcher knife out of its slot and as she did it seemed to sing with a high whine. Pretty knife, such a talented blade. Beverage, phone and knife, what else did a girl need? All contingencies covered.

And now, to navigate the great long hall of angles and wobbles. It would be too ironic if she were to trip and fall onto her knife now. There is a certain decorum one must follow, a certain ceremony, at times like this. But the walls stayed put, more or less, as did the floor. It was amazing what one could accomplish with a little resolve and the balancing power of one's elbows.

In the bedroom she sat at the desk and opened her laptop. As it booted up she looked out the window. That vast green (now black) space to the south—the Mount Pleasant Cemetery. Oh, perfect. The peace, the gentle surrender of flesh and bone to earth—it moved her and calmed her, but really, does anyone really go for long walks in the graveyard without wondering if maybe they shouldn't just lie down and stay? Inevitable. Why bother with all the messy in-between bits?

The computer lit up in a friendly way. She keyed "Alcoholics Anonymous Toronto" into the search window. She kept misspelling it. But finally managed. The homepage. Such a lot of information. Look at that, a meeting close to the liquor store at Yonge and Eglinton. How convenient. And there, at the top of the page, *Have Questions? Need Help?* And after that a phone number. The knife lay quietly, for the moment, beside the computer. Well yes, she suspected she just might be able to use the tiniest bit of help. She took a drink. She punched the number into her phone.

"Alcoholics Anonymous, how can I help you?" said a man.

Since Colleen didn't have the faintest idea how he could help her, she said nothing.

"Hello?" said the man.

"Hello," she said.

"My name's Neil, and who's this, then?"

He was entirely too fucking cheerful. "Barbara," she said.

"Well, Barbara, how can I help you tonight?"

She took another sip. "I have no idea."

"Ah. Well, is it possible you've been drinking a little?"

"Not calling you 'cause I'm interested in tap dancing lessons." Tap dancing lessons. That had seemed such a simple phrase when it was still in her head, but on the way out it had been a treacherous piece of tongue-twistery.

"Ha!" Neil laughed, which startled Colleen. If he was laughing at her slurry-ness, she'd hang right up. He had a funny, honking kind of laugh. "It's good to have a sense of humour," he went on. "The devil does so hate a good laugh."

Lovely, now there would be talk of God and the devil. "I don't believe in the devil," she said.

"Then you haven't met my mother-in-law," said Neil, and again, the big laugh.

"Are you there all week?" asked Colleen.

"What? Oh, good one. Yeah, don't forget to tip your waitress!" He was quiet for a moment and then said, "Can I assume your drinking isn't making you happy?"

"Lots of things make me unhappy. I lost my job today."

"I'm really sorry. What happened?"

"Working at the university. I worked there forever. Years and years, and now they tell me I have a problem and that I'm a lousy employee. It's not fair."

"At the university, huh? We got quite a few members from the university. All kinds in AA, you know? Drinking have anything to do with you losing your job?"

Barbara was anonymous, so why not just say it? "I think so. Maybe. A little."

"I lost a lot of jobs because of my drinking. Good thing, too, since I drove long-distance hauls. Nothing like a drunk in the cab of an eighteen-wheeler to screw up the traffic flow. What happened to you?"

"I don't know. I don't want to talk about it." She rested her forehead in her hand. This was worthless. She was tired. So tired. If she was going to do what she was going to do she'd better just get on with it.

"Feeling pretty bad, right?"

"Yup."

"Do you want to quit drinking?"

"I want to stop feeling like shit." She was crying. Salty drops hit the laptop's keyboard. "I want the fucking pain to stop. I can't take the fucking pain. It's all so fucking hopeless. I killed my friend's cat." Why was she saying all this? Her lips where thick around the words, like she'd been to the dentist and was all frozen. "I'm frozen," she said.

"I hear you. But you can stop the pain. I promise. How much have you had to drink tonight?"

"I have no idea."

"That much, huh?" When she said nothing he went on. "Are you feeling sick?"

"Don't feel much of anything. That's the point, isn't it?"

"Yeah, it is. We drunks drink for oblivion."

Drunks? Fuck you, she thought, but there seemed no point in saying it. "Oblivion," she muttered. "That's where I'm headed."

"I'm sorry, what was that?"

"Nothing."

"Think you can just go to sleep tonight, and then tomorrow, can you get to a meeting?"

"Been to meetings. Not for me." My God, but she was tired. What had she been thinking this guy would do? It wasn't like the movies where worried strangers showed up at your door and held your hand while you cried out all your troubles. Nobody was coming.

"Tell you what, why don't we make a plan, okay? Tomorrow morning I'll have a friend of mine call you, a really nice woman, and you can arrange to go to a meeting with her. There are a couple of meetings around noon, or earlier if you like. Think you'll be up early? I used to wake up about 4 a.m. every single morning, just feeling like crap, you know? You awake that early you could get to a 7:30 a.m. meeting. Or a noon meeting. She'd go with you. You'll like her. She works at the university too."

These last words hit Colleen's brain like water on a hot skillet. Suddenly her mind was popping and fizzing. She didn't want anyone at the university knowing she'd called AA. What if it was someone she knew?

"How about it?" Neil asked.

"I have to go."

"I wish you wouldn't—"

Colleen hung up. She hit her temples with the heels of her hands. Stupid. Stupid. Stupid. What had she been thinking? She checked her messages. Nothing. No one. *Nada.* The silence crept up behind her, making the hair on her neck stand on end. It stalked her. It was coming for her. An inch or so of vodka remained in her glass. She knocked it back and picked up the knife. She would run the bath, she would sink in, sink under, and say goodbye to all her friends on shore. *Friends.* That was a joke.

She stood up, but the floor danced beneath her feet. She dropped the knife by the bed. No matter. She'd get it in a minute. She was so cold. She must make sure the water in the bath was very hot. The path to the bathroom was a funhouse obstacle course of slip-sliding floors, glittering bits of glass and moving walls. At last she reached the tub and turned on the hot water. She considered bath salts. Why not? Why not pamper herself on her last night? She reached for the plastic jar of lavender salts and poured in a great deal. The scent was cloying and reminded her of old ladies. That wouldn't do. She let the water run out and started again. She had some sandalwood oil in her bedroom. She would get that.

It took some minutes to make it back to the bedroom, and the last few yards she managed on all fours. The sandalwood oil, in such a pretty little bevelled bottle with a gold lid, was all the way over on the dresser. It was exhausting, this business. She needed a moment. She pulled herself onto the bed and looked at her wrists. They were so fragile-looking, with the green and blue veins like ribbons just under the thin white sheath of skin. Almost anything could tear through that skin. She ran her fingers over one wrist and then the other. It tickled a little. The sound of the running water came from the bathroom. It would be steaming up the mirror, making the edges of everything soft and warm. She looked at her wrists again. Poor little things. Poor wee delicate things. Like baby skin.

She drew the covers round her. She sobbed. In a few minutes she would get up and do this thing. And then it would all be over and she'd wake up somewhere else entirely, or else she wouldn't wake up at all and both possibilities were just fine with her.

Good night, world.

They Don't Call It "Spirits" for Nothing

Colleen felt as though she were scrabbling out of a grave. The earthen sides slipped away beneath her fingers and feet. She kept sliding back down to the black pit. She was sure she was awake, but then she realized she was still asleep and great red-fire danger crouched at the end of her bed. She had to wake up. She tried to move her little finger, to cry out, and it took a terrible effort; her chest felt weighed down by grave dirt. She would suffocate. She would be crushed . . . Then she woke with a heart-pounding start, swatting at her head, filled with the image of bats swooping down on her. No bats. Just dark dreams. She was damp with sweat and her breath was foul even to her. What time was it? Something other than her breath smelled like death itself. Her eyes were caked shut, and something horrible stuck to her cheek and mouth. She pried her eyes open, pulling lashes out as she did, knowing she must look, but not wanting to see. A pool of yellowish slime lay near her pillow. Jesus, she'd vomited in her sleep, and . . . more than that. She reached between her legs. Her pants were wet. She'd thrown up and wet herself. A flush of shame seared her nerve-exposed flesh. And what was that fucking noise, like a dentist's drill in her head? On the desk her phone buzzed. It might as well have been in Antarctica. She tried to sit up and as she did an invisible axe planted itself between her eyes. She wiped away the matter from around her mouth. She had to get to the bathroom. *Now.*

As her legs swung over the bed and her stomach cramped, her foot hit something. A butcher knife. The big one from the kitchen. She staggered to the bathroom, her mind racing. Why was there a knife in the bedroom? Had there been an intruder? She envisioned an attacker standing over her bed with the knife in his hand as she sprawled before him, dead drunk. Had someone done something to her? The water in the bath was running. What the fuck? Bile filled her mouth and she clutched her belly as she bent over the toilet. Little came out. What did was a yellow-greenish colour, flecked with blood. My God, she was dying. Her face streamed with tears and her nose ran. She gagged and retched and retched until she thought she'd eject an organ. Her stomach, perhaps, or her spleen.

Slowly the sickness subsided. She flushed the toilet, sank to the floor and pressed her face to the cool tiles. Something sharp dug into her cheek. Glass, there was glass on the floor. She ran her hand along the tiles. The perfume bottles. What had happened to the perfume bottles? She realized she'd cut her foot, and blood now seeped from the wound, leaving a red blossom on the sole of her sock. She got to her knees and crawled to the bath. Water ran down the open drain. She turned off the tap.

What the hell had happened last night? Had she meant to take a bath and forgot? Thank God she'd left the plug open or the whole apartment would have flooded. Yes, she vaguely remembered wanting a bath, pouring salts in. Sure enough, the plastic dish of salts was empty.

She peeled her sock off. It was just a little cut. Given the state of her, it was hardly worth noticing. She used the sock to sweep up the rest of the glass. All the pretty bottles, all her treasures, shattered and smashed. She found the tiny L'Air du Temps bottle. There was a chip out of the base, but the doves were intact. It made her want to cry, seeing those doves. The Chloé bottle was also unbroken, but the perfume had leaked out. Feeling a trickle of something, she put her hand to her cheek. Blood. Just a little. She got to her feet and went to put the bottles back on the shelf, but the shelf was gone. There it was, broken off its plugs, behind the door. She put the bottles on the back of the toilet tank. Had there been a fight?

Without looking in the mirror—certainly not that horror—she turned on the taps and ran water over her face. She cleared off the mucus and bile. She peeled off her filthy clothes. *Do not look too closely, just kick them into the corner.* Shower. She needed scalding water, and fast. She'd have to call the office, tell them—oh, right, there was nothing to tell them. She was the one who'd been told.

She stood in the bath and let the shower, the water hot as she could bear, sluice over her. She was covered in bruises. Her hip hurt. Her stomach was lined with sandpaper. Her mouth was lined with dead-horse glue. Images flickered through her mind. A sense of urgency, of vital information withheld, nipped at her.

It was important to remember what had happened. Colleen trembled and kept a hand on the tile wall to ensure she didn't fall. She remembered the scene in David Moore's office. The woman from Human Resources. She remembered telling them to fuck off. (That was clever, wasn't it, a bell she could not now unring?) Buying booze. Oh, shit, the bathroom stall incident. The moment of the falling bottle playing over and over again in her mind, like some old movie reel on a loop, in which the bottle kept falling and shattering, falling and shattering. She had seen Helen after that. She remembered going to Helen's. Her mother. Jake. Who was about to be a father, apparently, with no more use for her. So many snippets, but even more holes.

Jesus. If time existed so that everything didn't happen at once, and space existed so it all didn't happen to *you,* well, something had certainly fucked up somewhere.

She had to sit down, or lie down. She had to get something in her stomach. She carefully stepped out of the shower and grabbed a towel. It smelled of mildew and she threw it on the floor with her pile of clothes. She grabbed her old green bathrobe from the hook behind the door and inched into it, trembling like a beaten cur. She made her way down the hall. The light from outside was the sort of indistinct grey that could mean it was any time at all. It looked wet, the sky rough with low clouds. The clock on the stove said11:30. Daytime, then. The bottle of vodka lay on its side in the sink and the lid was off. She righted it. An inch of liquor remained. That wasn't possible, it must have spilled. The fumes hit her nose and she gagged, her stomach convulsing. She considered taking a swig. It would settle her. At the thought, sour liquid squirted into her mouth. She spit in the sink. *Please God, no more. Please,*

please, please. She ran the water and hung her head. Nothing more. *Thank you. Thank you.* She was feverish and chilled at the same time.

The water was cold now and she filled a glass to the brim. Even in the hangover fog she knew she mustn't give in to the desire to gulp. She must be moderate. Sips. Small sips. Her tongue, which was a desiccated lump, began to plump under the water's revivifying effects. She took the water and a handful of crackers and made her way to the living room. Never had the couch seemed so far. She curled up and pulled the throw over her. She nibbled and sipped. She wanted to die.

A flash from the night before. The knife. Her wrists. She cried out. The intruder had been her. *She* had been the murderer at the end of the bed. In a moment of terrible clarity, she pictured a kind of demon, a malevolent spirit she had called to her by drinking so much. She imagined she'd sent a beacon out into the cosmos and this hideous, silence-souled creature had slithered down it, all the way to her door. It would always know where she lived, now. There was no hiding from it.

They don't call it "spirits" for nothing.

It tiptoed up her spine on cat's paws. It peeked out from the corners of the room. It lay beneath her pillow, waiting for her to fall asleep so it could reach up with its skeletal fingers and tightened its grip around her throat. It whispered in her ear.

It was the King of the Twisted Fairies.

It was a deft hand with knives.

Even as she vowed she would not drink today, a small clear voice in the back of her mind sniggered. *Wait an hour,* the voice said. *There's a dance in the old girl yet.*

Colleen stuffed the corner of the throw in her mouth. She shook and tried hard not to scream. Her bowels cramped and the ice-pick pain curled her into a ball and she knew she'd have to run for it. Then the mad, hands-out-in-front lurching stumble down the hall to the toilet. The fire in her gut. The hot, shameful splash. The stench. It was as though she were rotting from the inside.

Minutes later she rose and huddled in the shower, cleaning herself again. She got out, dried off, and sprayed the room with air freshener. The cloying scent made her gag. She felt hollow, feverish and shaky. She wanted to go back to bed.

In the bedroom she realized she'd have to strip the filthy sheets. She picked up the butcher knife, gingerly, with only the ends of her fingertips, and laid it on the desk. It seemed to twinkle malevolently. She didn't want to look at it. She managed to get the sheets off the bed, her muscles aching with the effort, her joints throbbing. The mattress protector had to go, too, since it was damp, but the urine hadn't soaked through to the mattress proper. Be grateful for small mercies. The duvet, too, seemed stained only in one patch. She could live with that for now; she craved warmth more than cleanliness. She threw the mess of sheets and mattress protector into the bathroom where her clothes lay in an accusing pile. Later. She'd face washing everything later. For now, all she wanted to do was get more water and more crackers and crawl into the bed and sleep and sleep and not wake up until it was all over.

There were some bottles of club soda in the kitchen, unrefrigerated. She found one and, hugging it to her chest, walked like a person just getting her sea legs back to the bedroom where the bed and duvet waited for her. It was to have been her refuge, this room. Her writing nest. The stupid picture of Dylan Thomas's writing shed, her ridiculous journal, the cold-eyed computer, even the Bible, so mute and black-covered and phony with those gilded edges. They mocked her. She grabbed her cell phone from the desk as she half-fell onto the bed. The message light blinked. She flipped it open and saw she had two messages. She lay on her back with the phone clutched to her breast. She was not at all sure she wanted to see who the messages were from. It was quite possible she'd made phone calls last night. It was quite possible the nursing home had been trying to get hold of her. It was quite possible she'd done some damage and would be expected to clean it up this morning. She couldn't face it. Still, she had to know. She scrolled through the call history.

The nursing home. No surprise, only the rancid acid of humiliation. And a number she didn't recognize, or did she? It had the same three digits as the university. Some bureaucrat wanting her to fill out forms, probably. To hell with it. She tossed the phone onto the bed beside her, reached for the computer and flipped it open. She hadn't shut it off the night before and when the screen came alive it did so to her e-mail program. Junk mail in the inbox. A note from Lori: *Hey, kiddo, just checking on you. Hope you're okay. I'll call later.*

At the top of the sent list was an e-mail to Jake. She had no recollection of writing it. She did not want to see what she'd written to him, but couldn't stop herself.

Dear Jake,

This will the last yor hear from me. IBut I couldn't go wiorthout reminding you of a afternoon. I'm listening to Tom Waits right now. Do you remember? That's what we andI listening to: Tom Saits a song about a man haunted by the only womoon heever fucking lijved, treated herlike shit andleft, sound famiar? . . .

Colleen slammed the computer shut. Tom Waits? "Blue Valentine"? Oh, delightful, she'd ended up in that emotional cul de sac again, had she? Jake would read it. He'd know he had made the right decision. She was contemptible.

She wrapped the duvet around herself. It was obvious she owed a number of people apologies; possibly she owed *everyone* apologies. It was wisest to assume there wasn't anyone she hadn't offended in one way or another. The tricky part was going to be figuring out what for.

Should she check the mystery phone message? Perhaps with luck it would be the imagined intruder from the night before. Perhaps with luck he'd agree to come back and finish the job. She'd even pay him.

For several minutes she sat at the edge of the bed, staring out the window over her desk. From that angle she saw nothing but sky, that putty-coloured smudge of indistinct clouds, the horizon invisible. There might be nothing out there at all save a muffled vapour pressing again the window. She could hear nothing, not even a car horn from the street so far below, not a bird cry, not the hum of the elevator gears, not voices in the hall. It was a silence so complete it was thick with all the things it was missing. It was hard to breathe through such a silence.

"*You know my folly, O God; my guilt is not hidden from you.*" She had said the words aloud and they sat in the air before her, nearly visible. Psalm 69. Where had that come from? "*They that sit in the gate talk of me; and I am the song of the drunkards.*" An apt description, she felt. She *was* the song of the drunkards.

Colleen rolled into a ball on the bed. She reached out and picked up the Bible on the nightstand. Old training kicked in. She turned to Psalm 69 and, through cracked lips, began to read.

"*Save me, O God; For the waters are come in unto my soul.*
I sink in deep mire, where there is no standing: I am come into deep waters, where the floods overflow me.

I am weary with my crying; my throat is dried: Mine eyes fail while I wait for my God."

She stopped reading. If there was a God, surely—and quite wisely—He or She had written off Colleen long ago. She was on her own. The orphan, the outcast, the leper.

The phone buzzed and vibrated from somewhere in the vicinity of her left foot. It startled her and she fumbled for a few seconds to find it in the duvet folds. She flipped it open. That unknown number again. The university, but not her department. What the fuck, she might as well get it over with.

"Yes," she said, one hand over her eyes.

"May I speak to Colleen Kerrigan, please?" said a woman's voice.

"This is she."

"Oh, good. Colleen, I'm so glad to reach you at last. This is Pat, Pat Minot, from the HR Department at the university. I have tried calling several times but there was no answer. I was beginning to get a little worried, to be honest."

The woman made a sort of noise in her throat, perhaps her attempt at a chuckle. To Colleen's ears it sounded as though she were gargling thumbtacks.

"What can I do for you, Ms. Minot?"

"Call me Pat, please. I did leave a message. Did you get that?"

"I don't know. I didn't check."

"Oh, I see, well, probably just as well. These things are often better done face to face—well, not face to face, but you know what I mean. Although, I would like to see you."

Colleen's mind simply could not take in what she was saying. Whatever the woman wanted, Colleen didn't have it.

"Are you still there?" asked Pat Minot.

"Yup. It appears I don't have anywhere to go this morning."

"No, of course not. I'm doing this poorly, I think. But I am worried about you, especially after yesterday. That didn't go at all the way I hoped it would."

"Sorry to disappoint you." It would be best not to tell the woman to fuck off a second time. Still, it was so tempting. Colleen heard her draw a great breath and then exhale.

"You haven't disappointed me, Colleen, but I suspect you may have disappointed yourself. I know that was something I did on a daily basis when I was an active alcoholic."

Colleen took her hand away from her eyes. Despite the crushing headache, the itch and bone-ache and nausea; despite the sensation her skin had been grated off exposing all the nerve endings, this new information flapped its way into her foggy brain. Colleen was more alert than she had

324

been a few seconds before. *The woman who had fired her for being a drunk was a drunk herself.* My, my. Emily Post simply didn't cover this sort of thing.

"Are you there?"

"Yes."

"I haven't made this kind of call too many times before, Colleen, maybe two or three times, but frankly you reminded me so much of myself yesterday that I wanted to talk to you right then and there, and I would have, but you didn't seem entirely open to anything I might have said. Is that true?"

"I was pretty upset."

"Of course you were. Anyone would be. I've been in your position, you know."

"You have."

"Oh, yes. I was given exactly the same ultimatum you were given, and I took it no better. For what it's worth, I didn't take anything you said personally, and I don't think Dr. Moore did either."

"I said some awful things."

Pat chuckled. It didn't sound like gargled thumbtacks now, but was rather a nice sound, deep and genuine. "Not the first time someone's told me to fuck off, and you are entirely within your rights to tell me to fuck off again if you'd like. Would you like to?"

"Not right now. I'm not feeling quite up to it."

"Glad to hear it—I mean, not that you're under the weather; although to be honest, I suspected you might be. I bet you're hungover as hell. Yes? Well, never mind. When my boss told me to sober up or get lost I spend a week trying to crawl through the bottom of a tequila bottle. That was my poison of choice. Well that and a certain white powder."

Cocaine? Who *was* this woman? Colleen was momentarily speechless. She tried to picture the woman she'd met the day before—the grey tweed suit with gold buttons, that quasi-military air, the head of purplish red hair, the large rings on her large hands. It was impossible to picture her bending over a makeup mirror cutting coke with a credit card. On the other hand, some people might find it difficult to picture Colleen waking up in bed covered in vomit and urine. Some people.

Pat was still talking. "Crashed my car. Cheated on my husband. Ended up in hospital with a broken collarbone, three cracked ribs and a buggered-up knee. There was a policeman standing at the foot of my bed. I felt like everyone was against me and I didn't have a hope in the world."

King of the Twisted Fairies. Knife thrower. Colleen found herself crying. It hurt to cry. Her hair hurt. Her fingernails hurt.

"Are you okay?" asked Pat softly.

"More or less. Mostly less," Colleen managed to get out.

"Does any of this sound familiar?"

"I think I might have felt like that. I may have tried to do something . . . stupid." She hadn't meant to say this, but it dashed out as though someone had slipped her a truth serum. Her teeth chattered now. It was that sort of crying. "I'm pretty scared."

"I'm sure you are, dear. I'm sure you are. That policeman I said was at the foot of my bed? You know what he said to me? He said he had once been in the same position I found myself in. He told me he'd tried to kill himself, but that he didn't and got better and I could too. So, now, I'm saying the same thing to you. Here's a remarkable piece of good news: from this moment on, you don't ever have to feel this way again. Will you let me help you?"

"Can I have my job back?"

"Before you can do anything else, you have to get sober."

"I don't want to go to any rehab."

"Well, let's take this thing one step at a time, shall we? For right now, I just want to make sure you're safe."

"I'm not going to try and kill myself." She was almost positive of that.

"Good to know, but I'm concerned about withdrawal. I'm not sure you realize this, but detoxing from alcohol can be life-threatening. If you're getting off heroin you'll feel as though you'll want to die, but you won't. If you've been drinking enough, however, you might actually go into convulsions and die. So we have to be a little careful here."

"I wasn't drinking that much."

Pat laughed again, and this time it was an unmistakable hoot. "Oh, dear, I'm quite sure you were. I know I was, and I also know I lied to everyone about how much I drank. That's what we do, we alcoholics."

The room spun and just for an instant Colleen saw herself as if from a distance, huddled under the soiled duvet, ashen, pasty, trembling, snot flowing, sick as a poisoned dog. What a pathetic bag of bones, what a waste of skin, what a piece of human wreckage. And yet, and yet . . . the voice on the other end of the line seemed to believe there was something in her worth saving.

What if that were true? *What would life be like if that were true?*
"Colleen? . . . Colleen?"

"Yes. Okay, fine. I've made a really awful mess of things." Toes at the edge of the cliff, breathe deep and push off into empty air. She wanted to speak but her mouth was dry, her tongue thick and heavy. She could almost hear the shrill squeaking of desperate fairies. It felt cruel to leave them when they'd been so faithful to her. Faithful. Like in a marriage. Until death did them part. That was the truth of it. Something was going to have to die, wasn't it? She had never wanted to say anything less than she did the words now pressing against her lips. And yet. And yet.

"I'm an alcoholic," she said.

She closed her eyes, expecting to plummet into some sort of bottomless emotional well . . . but . . . she didn't. She was still here. She stood. She imagined the words, like little shining balls, flitting out into space, leaving glowing trails behind them.

She felt slightly light-headed.

"Congratulations, my dear. That's a big step. I'm very proud of you."

The tone of the woman's voice was so gentle, so kind and comforting. It was enough to break Colleen in two.

"Now, I tell you what . . ." She was all best-foot-forward and heartiness again. "I think it would be best if I took the rest of the day off and came over to your place, yes? We can spend the afternoon together and have a little chat. We'll figure out exactly what sort of shape you're in, and then we'll go off to a meeting a little later. How does that sound?"

"An AA meeting?"

"Well, not a meeting of the garden society." She laughed.

"Thank God for that." Colleen looked around the room. She saw it for what it was, the nest of a sick middle-aged woman. Dirty. Disorganized. Overwhelming. "The place, me, it's all a horrible mess."

"I should be there within the hour. Do you think you can stay away from the booze until then?"

"You're beginning to sound a bit like Mary Poppins."

"I'll take that as a compliment. Hang on, okay. I'll be there as soon as I can."

Colleen felt like a cartoon character, suddenly off the cliff edge, legs pedalling away a mile a minute, waiting for the death-fall. Pat Minot had better be quick.

"Okay, then."

They hung up. Colleen gripped the phone as though it were a grenade and she was holding the pin in place. She imagined herself in the back of a church basement, surrounded by the human flotsam such places attracted. She did not want to go. She simply wouldn't answer the bell when Pat rang it. She didn't have to answer the door.

No, she didn't, but if she didn't, what then? What would she do?

If she didn't answer the door she would spend several hours being sick, and then she would have a drink, and another, and another, and she would make some phone calls and she would, by the end of the night, be dancing with the King of the Twisted Fairies again. The knife still lay within arm's reach, right there on the desk in that bit of watery light.

Colleen closed her eyes. She saw a great rock coming toward her, rolling down the hill, about to crush her; she could push and push against it for all eternity and she'd never win.

Let it come. Let it come. She was done.

She opened her eyes again. Such an empty, messy room. Such an empty, messy apartment. Such an empty, messy life. First things first. She picked up the knife and walked to the kitchen. She put the knife back where it belonged, in its slot in the wooden block. It had no power. It was just a thing. She would have a cup of coffee. She would make enough for Pat.

She opened the fridge to get the milk. There, in the door, on top of the one remaining half-empty bottle of Chablis, sat the pretty little French fairy, beret at a jaunty angle, waving her baguette at Colleen. Apparently it would take more than a simple admission of her disease to banish the faithful little beings. *They don't call it "spirits" for nothing.* Colleen ignored her, grabbed the milk and slammed the fridge shut. She'd ask Pat to help her get rid of the booze. Maybe the spirits knew where she lived, but that didn't mean Colleen had to make them welcome.

She chewed her knuckle. She was terrified, but she wasn't going to drink over it. She would stay busy until Pat arrived.

She fussed with coffee beans and hot water, with cups and spoons and milk and sugar, and behind her the silence in the apartment grew heavier, as though it were freezing lake water, bucking and heaving as it thickened against the shore, pushing itself upward and outward. It would entomb Colleen as well, and crush her like the hull of a flimsy boat.

Soon the smell of coffee warmed the kitchen, and Colleen poured herself a cup and added three spoons of honey. She sipped it, letting the sweetness into her body slowly for fear of gastric revolt. She carried the cup to the bathroom and set it down to splash water on her face. She considered putting on a little makeup, just some lipstick, but decided (although she was not ready to look in the mirror yet) she would face whatever came next clean-faced, without a disguise of any sort.

As she walked back to the living room, she thought something flitted past, some ragged-winged thing, frantic and foolish. She would not go chasing fairies. Not now. She stood at the window, looking out onto the parking lot and the silo and the cemetery green with promise. It occurred to her just how much of her life she had spent in an empty room, waiting for something to happen. She was good at it. She would just stand here now, just stand and wait and drink this coffee.

When the buzzer went, it was as loud as a fire alarm. Her heart pounded. To answer the door or not to answer the door? She had made up her mind that she would, and yet now, a great part of her did not want to. A part of her wanted to hide behind the couch and wait until whatever was outside the door went away. She thought of the coming night and how she'd want a drink, how she'd crave it like a dying plant craves rain. She thought of her birthday and Christmas and parties and vacations and endless weekends with nothing to do without the festival of the fairies . . .

The buzzer sounded again. Like a wall full of angry wasps.

Colleen couldn't seem to move her feet. She pictured Pat Minot downstairs in the lobby, her ringed fingers against the buzzer, her potato-y face under the red hair registering concern first, and then her mouth pursing with anger, setting in a little pout of disapproval. Finally, she would shake her head sadly. She would turn and leave and Colleen would be left alone. Alone with the frantic fairies.

Another buzz. This one less insistent, it seemed to Colleen's ears, fading a little, burning out. Parties? Christmas? Vacations? When was the last time she had been invited to a party? She'd never gone on a vacation. Christmas? Really? But what if she wasn't funny anymore? It occurred to her that perhaps she hadn't been funny for a while. She couldn't remember anyone laughing, not lately.

As though she could see through walls, all the way down to the chilly white lobby, she saw Pat Minot drop her finger from the buzzer, turn and . . . A rasp escaped Colleen's throat and suddenly her feet were free again and she lunged to the intercom by the door.

"Hello, hello? Yes?"

"Colleen? It's Pat. I was afraid you weren't there."

"I'm here. Come up. Apartment 805. Please." She pressed the button to open the door downstairs and heard the electronic whine and click below.

"On my way," said Pat.

Colleen opened the door and moved halfway into the hall. As she did a rush of air swept outward from the apartment. It was just the physics of open doors and airflow, she knew that, but it felt like something more. As if something swooped past her and swept down the hall. She heard the elevator hum, and realized she was holding her breath.

The elevator doors whooshed open and a second later Pat Minot's face, as wide-open and hopeful and solid a face as ever there was, peeked round the corner. "There you are," she said, smiling.

"Here I am," said Colleen, smiling back as best she could. Her lips quivered as tears approached, but that was all right, she decided.

As Pat walked the last few yards to her door, Colleen glanced back into her apartment. An empty room. Just an empty room. Just a room in need of a good cleaning. Why, Colleen thought, I might fill that room up with anything I please, with anything at all.

Acknowledgments

Thanks to my agents David Forrer at Inkwell.

Thanks to David Kent, a dear friend and a hell of a champion.

Enormous thanks to Maria DiBattista and Michael Rowe for reading early versions and helping me see the path through the trees.

Thanks to Sister Rita Woehkle for the continuing epiphanies.

Thanks to all the other people who walk the sober road with me. One day at a time.

The epigraph is taken from "Good Morning, Midnight" by Jean Rhys. Originally published 1938. First published as a Norton Paperback 1986; reissued 2000.

The quote from St. John of the Divine's "Dark Night of the Soul" was taken from a 1959 public domain translation by Image Books (third edition).

The lines from Edward Booth Loughran's poem "Isolation" are from the 1906 edition of *An Anthology of Australian Verse* edited by Bertram Stevens and published in London by Macmillan & Co. Limited.

The lines from "*the song of mehitabel*" are from the 1973 version of "archy and mehitabel" by Don Marquis, published by Anchor Books, Doubleday & Company, Inc., New York (first published 1916).

All Bible passages are based on the American Standard Version, public domain.

A portion of this novel first appeared as the essay "Breaking Down" in *Winter Tales II: Women on the Art of Aging*, edited by R.A Rycraft and Leslie What, Serving House Books, 2012.

Made in the USA
San Bernardino, CA
20 February 2018